THE HOUSE SITTER

KERI BEEVIS

First published in Great Britain in 2025 by Boldwood Books Ltd.

Copyright © Keri Beevis, 2025

Cover Design by Aaron Munday

Cover Images: Shutterstock

The moral right of Keri Beevis to be identified as the author of this work has been asserted in accordance with the Copyright, Designs and Patents Act 1988.

All rights reserved. No part of this book may be reproduced in any form or by any electronic or mechanical means, including information storage and retrieval systems, without written permission from the author, except for the use of brief quotations in a book review. This book is a work of fiction and, except in the case of historical fact, any resemblance to actual persons, living or dead, is purely coincidental.

Every effort has been made to obtain the necessary permissions with reference to copyright material, both illustrative and quoted. We apologise for any omissions in this respect and will be pleased to make the appropriate acknowledgements in any future edition.

A CIP catalogue record for this book is available from the British Library.

Paperback ISBN 978-1-83533-591-8

Large Print ISBN 978-1-83533-590-1

Hardback ISBN 978-1-83533-589-5

Ebook ISBN 978-1-83533-592-5

Kindle ISBN 978-1-83533-593-2

Audio CD ISBN 978-1-83533-584-0

MP3 CD ISBN 978-1-83533-585-7

Digital audio download ISBN 978-1-83533-587-1

This book is printed on certified sustainable paper. Boldwood Books is dedicated to putting sustainability at the heart of our business. For more information please visit https://www.boldwoodbooks.com/about-us/sustainability/

Boldwood Books Ltd, 23 Bowerdean Street, London, SW6 3TN

www.boldwoodbooks.com

For my sister-in-law, Nicki.
Always smiling, never complaining, and one of the bravest people I know.
(Though she can be a muppet at times!)

PROLOGUE
SIX YEARS AGO

Right about now, the woman in the barn is supposed to be getting married. She is wearing her wedding dress, but her beautifully styled hair is coming loose from its bun, her carefully applied make-up covered in dirt, and instead of walking down the aisle, she is on her hands and knees crying and begging for her life.

Her mum and dad, her husband-to-be, her bridesmaids, are all waiting for her back at Rosewood Manor, the pretty but exclusive venue in the Lake District with a ridiculously long waiting list, and today – Saturday the eighth of June – is the date she has been planning for the last two years. The sunny, cloudless blue sky she had hoped for should be making her smile. Instead, the heat has been irritating her all morning, the sticky warmth enveloping her, her bridal gown almost suffocating. It's why she had made excuses, telling her mother and bridesmaids she needed a moment to herself.

That was when clarity had hit and she had realised she couldn't go through with the ceremony. At least not until she had spoken to him first.

That's the worst bit. She came here willingly, so eager to see him. She was giddy with nerves and desperate to escape, but now she understands it was all a set-up.

What a fool she has been.

She is supposed to be the star of the show today and the rest of the wedding party will be looking for her. They have probably tried to call her, but her phone is back at the venue, in the pearl clutch bag she had bought to go with her dress.

Although this abandoned barn is just five minutes' drive from the village of Hawkshead, it is discreet, set back from the road and approached by foot. No one will have heard her screams.

Her pretty white wedding dress, the one with the delicate lace bodice and the price tag that had made her father visibly wince when he saw his credit card bill, is now torn and dirty. The first blow from the shovel had caught the back of her skull, sending her crashing face first to the filthy floor, and for a few moments she had lost consciousness. The second strike had come as she managed to roll over, staring up at her attacker in a blur of confusion, pain and nausea. She is certain it has broken her nose.

As her head throbs and the metallic taste of blood drips into her mouth, she looks up through tear-stained eyes and pleads for mercy.

Rage stares back at her and she understands it won't be forthcoming.

Her final thought as the shovel raises, ready to strike again, is that today was supposed to be the start of her new life. Instead, it's going to be the end of it.

1

PRESENT DAY – SATURDAY 2 AUGUST

When Nina Fairchild was first asked to look after her brother Dexter's cat while he was away, the plan was to pop in once a day, make a fuss of Hannibal, and take care of his food and litter. But then three days before Dexter was due to leave, her boyfriend, Michael, had proposed, and the shock of seeing him down on one knee, the sparkling ring staring up at her from the box in his hand, had changed everything.

For starters, Nina realised that she wasn't in love with him.

She cared about Michael and there had definitely been a spark in the early part of their relationship, but attraction had settled into friendship and then into a routine. She had moved in with him after just three months, which, in retrospect, was probably too soon, and if she was honest, she knew back then that their relationship was never meant to be long term. But three months had turned into six years and although they had stagnated, it had become easier to stay.

There was nothing like the cold, hard shock of a ring to sober her up.

Nina had believed Michael was on the same page as her.

They had reached a point where sex felt like a chore and conversation had become mundane. And she was certain that the quirky little things he had once found attractive about her now annoyed him, as they did her about him, but it would seem not. They weren't vibing at all.

She never had the chance to answer him when he'd popped the question, as apparently her face said it all. The fight that followed was spectacular and had perhaps been brewing for a long time, with both of them finally revealing how they felt. Michael had admitted that he hoped his proposal would breathe new life into their relationship, while Nina had finally plucked up the courage to call time on it.

Fire had burned and then simmered, fading away to a passiveness that she couldn't deal with. Michael had used the word 'fine' a lot and kept reiterating that they would be okay living together until they sorted things out.

Truthfully, they both knew she would have to be the one to leave. It had been his house first and although she had been contributing to bills over the time she had lived there, he earned a higher wage and could afford to buy her out. Meanwhile, Nina, who worked as a freelance editor, had no idea if she would be able to scrape enough together to afford a one-bed flat.

Initially, she had thought she might have to move back in with her parents – a humiliating prospect given she had just turned thirty-five – but then Dexter had suggested she house-sit for him and his partner, Mark, while they were away.

'It will help us out,' he had said, pointing out that being a Ragdoll breed, Hannibal, with his striking blue eyes and lilac mitted grey and cream coat, loved having company, before adding, 'Plus, it will give you a bit of breathing space and you won't have to go stay with Mum and Dad.'

Nina hadn't taken much persuading.

So far, Dexter and Mark were the only two she had told about the break-up, and Dexter knew she wasn't relishing breaking the news to their mother, who adored Michael and kept dropping hints about grandchildren.

Dexter and Mark were going to be away for all of August, using the bulk of their summer holiday – they were both teachers – to fly over to Hong Kong where Dexter was going to meet Mark's family for the first time. While they were gone, she would have time to try to find somewhere else to live. Telling Michael it was best they had some space, she had packed a suitcase and left the house they shared, moving herself into the plush apartment at River Heights on the first Saturday in August, hugging her brother tightly before he and Mark left for the drive to the airport.

The complex was one of the newer builds in the city and only about seven years old, sitting on the banks of the River Wensum on the opposite side of the water to the law courts. It opened back into a V shape and comprised two identical blocks of apartments, generously spaced apart with their balconies overlooking pretty courtyard gardens. And, to top it all off, in the basement of the opposite building to Dexter was a swimming pool and gym for the exclusive use of the residents.

It was definitely a different style of living to what Nina was used to. The house she had shared with Michael was an older-style, traditional property in the quiet village of Rackheath, which was about six miles out of Norwich. Here in the city, in Dexter's sleek apartment with its huge waterfall shower, impressive walk-in wardrobes and smart appliances throughout, was like being in a different world.

And thank God for the air-con. After a couple of wash-out summers, Britain was in the grip of a heatwave. The temperature had barely dipped below thirty degrees for the past week and it was expected to get hotter.

Right now, walking back from the city centre, she was dreaming of that air-con. It was gone 6 p.m., but the heat of the sun still burned through her T-shirt, drenching her in sweat.

After Dexter and Mark had left, she had unpacked, familiarising herself with the apartment – although she had visited her brother on plenty of occasions, she wanted to know how everything worked – then she headed on foot into the city centre.

She had only meant to pick up a few supplies she needed, but had been tempted by the stalls on Norwich market, reasoning it was an affordable place to stock up on fish, fruit and veg. Now the handles of the carrier bags were digging into her fingers as she lugged everything back across the bridge that led to the apartment complex.

Glancing up, she spotted a man walking towards her and her attention immediately piqued. His gait was confident and he was classically handsome, dressed in beige chinos and a white linen shirt. He looked a little older than her, maybe early forties, and reminded her a little of an old-school movie star.

Did he live in one of the apartment blocks?

As he neared, she noticed he had threads of grey streaking through his carefully styled dark hair. And, oh dear God, he was looking at her now and he had the palest of eyes. Blue, she thought, though they were almost silvery, so perhaps grey.

Suddenly, she was regretting the old clothes she hadn't bothered to change out of and wishing she wasn't such a hot, sweaty mess. Pasting a quick smile on her face, she nodded at him, feeling more than a little self-conscious.

'Hey,' he muttered in response as they passed.

Not a 'hey, let's stop and talk', just an acknowledgement, but his deep voice and confidence was enough to quicken her heartbeat and leave her feeling a little flustered.

Nina carried on walking, not daring to look back until she reached the entrance to Dexter's building. By which time he was gone.

Inside the fifth-floor apartment, she cranked the air-con as high as it would go, thoughts of the man gone as she packed away the groceries and considered her evening plans.

Usually the first Saturday of the month meant drinks and dinner with her three closest friends, Rachel, Charlotte and Tori. Something Nina normally looked forward to, though this time she had cried off sick.

Their meals out were never the cheapest and until she had gone through her finances, working out exactly how much money she had and what she would need to get her own place, she wasn't sure an expensive dinner was something she could justify paying for.

Luckily, Michael had been fairly amicable when it came to picking up her share of the mortgage. She just hoped he would be as generous when it came to sitting down and discussing what he was prepared to offer in terms of a buying-out settlement.

She also hadn't told her friends about the split yet, needing a few more days to process everything. It was too new and messy, and she wanted to get things straight in her head before making it public.

Tonight, she would take time for herself, she decided. It was her first night in the apartment and she would cook herself a nice meal, enjoy a glass of wine and maybe watch a movie, indulging in the fact she could eat and watch what she wanted, without having to consider Michael.

Their tastes had never been that compatible, Nina preferring spicier food to him, and Michael was only ever interested in watching arthouse movies and oh so serious dramas, while she loved horror films and laugh-out-loud comedies.

She would get to control the remote and not have to listen to his annoying sniff. A habit that hadn't bothered her in the early days of their relationship, but over the last year had set her teeth on edge whenever he did it.

Deciding she would try a Moroccan spicy fish recipe she had seen, she pulled out her phone to google the recipe and make sure she had all the ingredients, immediately distracted when she saw she had six missed calls and a WhatsApp message.

The calls were all from her mother and a little ball of anxiety knotted in Nina's stomach, despite knowing that Aurora Fairchild erred towards the dramatic.

Was everything okay?

She was about to return the call when the sound of a key turning in the lock had her looking up.

Who the hell was letting themselves into Dexter's apartment?

The door swung open before she could react and her eyes widened as her mother stepped inside.

Aurora was impeccably dressed as always, her presence eating up the room, even though she stood six inches shorter than Nina at just five foot tall, and she didn't look distressed at all.

Still, Nina couldn't help worry. Was her dad okay?

'Mum. What are you doing here?'

Aurora's dark eyes locked on her daughter and she muttered in Spanish, before marching across the room.

'More like, what are you doing here?' she reproached. 'Michael tells me you've moved out. That he proposed to you and you decided to end things between you. Care to tell me why I didn't find this out from my own daughter?'

Oh. So that was why she was here.

Nina had been wracked with guilt over dumping Michael, but right now she wanted to kill him. How dare he go to her mum? Did he think Aurora would be able to persuade her to go back?

This wasn't how she had envisioned the rest of her Saturday going and a knot of stress was already tightening itself between her shoulder blades. She still hadn't cooled down from her walk back from the city and she was sticky and uncomfortable despite the air-con.

'Why don't I put the kettle on and we'll talk?' she suggested diplomatically, offering her mum a smile, which wasn't returned.

'You have some explaining to do, young lady.'

Despite being a fully grown adult capable of making all of her own life decisions, and having a fiery temper herself, Nina went straight back to feeling like a teenager.

'I was going to tell you...' she began.

'Going to tell me when? Next week, next year, wait until I'm in my grave? Honestly, *mi hija*, have you gone mad? What are you playing at?'

'Michael and I—'

'Yes, I know. Michael told me everything. Is this some kind of mid-life crisis, Nina? He's a good man. He deserves better than the way you treat him.'

Mid-life crisis? 'I'm thirty-five, Mum. And it's not any kind of crisis. I don't love him.'

'And you decide that now, after all these years? After moving in with him?' Aurora paused for breath, holding her hand up when Nina went to speak. She wasn't finished. 'It was the ring, wasn't it? You panicked, but it will be okay. You and Michael are meant to be together. Once we start shopping for wedding dresses and find you the perfect venue, you will be fine.'

'Mum, no, stop. *I don't love him.*' This time, Nina enunciated the words. She could feel the beginning of a headache and although she was trying her best to keep hold of her temper, the edges of it were fraying. 'Staying with Michael isn't what he deserves. And it's not what I deserve either.'

Aurora looked affronted and she still had plenty to say, veering between English and Spanish, something she tended to do when annoyed, and Nina listened with one ear as she finished making the tea. She knew her mother – sharing that same temper as well as her dark hair and olive skin tone – and sometimes it was better to let her run out of steam, even if it wasn't good for the stress levels.

* * *

It was gone 7.30 p.m. when Aurora finally got up to leave; a full hour and a half of being talked at and told she was making a mistake, and even though her mother had eventually calmed, seeming to at least accept she couldn't fix the relationship, Nina was shattered.

'Your room is there for you to move back into. If you're certain you're not ready to go back home.'

Nina didn't correct the 'not ready' comment, keen to stop dwelling on the topic.

'I'm housesitting for Dexter, Mum. Thanks, though.'

'He knows about this, I take it?'

When Nina nodded, Aurora tsked and muttered under her breath. Not because Dexter hadn't said anything; her gripe seemed to be that Nina had chosen only to tell her brother.

This was only the first battle over Michael, she understood

that. There would be more to come, but at least so far she had stood her ground. As an olive branch for not telling her parents about the break-up, she agreed to go over for a BBQ the following afternoon.

Finally, kissing her mum goodbye and closing the door, she drew in a steadying breath and took a moment to enjoy the peace and quiet of the apartment.

Hannibal wandered out from behind the sofa and looked up hopefully at Nina. He probably just wanted his dinner, though in that moment it appeared he was checking the coast was clear.

Nina fed him and checked his litter tray, then, remembering the fish recipe, picked up her phone again.

The unread WhatsApp message was still there and, glancing at it, she saw it was from Michael. As she read it, she wished she had seen it earlier.

> Hey N. Quick heads-up. Your mum is on her way over. She called in to see you and was very surprised to learn you're living at your brother's place!!

The double exclamation mark was Michael's passive-aggressive way of telling Nina he was annoyed that she hadn't told her parents about their break-up, and she kicked herself, regretting telling him she would be staying at Dexter's.

Angry that he had told her mum everything, Nina didn't bother to reply. Instead, she pulled off her sweaty clothes and tossed them in the washing machine, then took herself off for a cool shower, needing to douse her temper.

It did the trick and, feeling clean and refreshed, she headed back into the shadowy living room. The sun was already setting through the balcony doors; her evening slipping away from her, and she hadn't even started to prepare dinner yet.

Determined she was going to enjoy the rest of her Saturday night, she activated the apartment's smart hub, turning on low lights that bathed the kitchen and living room in an ambient glow and selecting a chilled playlist. The rich sounds of Lana Del Rey filled the room, filtering through the expensive wall speakers, as Nina checked the recipe again, hunting through Dexter's cupboards for utensils and the rest of the ingredients she needed.

There were a couple of things she would have to improvise on, but she had enough to make the dish. Turning on the hob and letting oil heat in a pan, she sang along with Lana while chopping lemon and red peppers.

Moments later, everything went dead.

2

It took Nina a moment to realise the power was out.

Initially, she swore at the lights, trying to get them to reactivate so she could see what she was doing. It was a second or two later that she noted the room was in silence. The washing machine stopped mid-cycle and Lana was no longer keeping her company.

And damn it. The hob was off too.

She tried to turn it back on, even though she knew deep down it was futile, swearing under her breath.

Through the closed balcony doors, she could see lights twinkling in the distance. Other buildings still seemed to have electricity, so was this power cut isolated to Dexter and Mark's apartment or was the whole complex affected?

In another five minutes or so she would lose all light in the apartment, and conscious she needed to find out what was going on, she referred to the folder of information her brother had left her, grateful she had the contact details for the maintenance room and didn't have to wander downstairs in the dark.

She phoned the number, glad when her call was answered after a couple of rings.

'River Heights. Dylan speaking.'

Nina would have recognised his voice even if she didn't know his name, remembering how their paths had crossed this morning when Dylan had helped her upstairs with her luggage after seeing her struggling to carry everything as she headed from her car through the courtyard garden.

'Hi, it's Nina Fairchild in 5A. All of the power has gone in the apartment and I can't get it back on. Could you come and have a look please?'

'Sorry, Nina. It's out for everyone on the complex. But we're on it and trying to get it fixed, I promise. If you can just bear with us.'

He sounded a little harassed and she felt bad. He was probably fielding calls from other residents too.

'Yes, of course.' It was frustrating, but not his fault. 'Do you know what's caused it?'

'Not at the moment, but we're working on getting it back up and running as soon as possible.'

There wasn't much more she could ask, and she didn't want to keep him from fixing the problem. 'Okay, thank you,' she told him, ending the call.

Although her belly was rumbling, light was currently top of her priority list and she hunted through Dexter's cupboards and drawers for matches. He had plenty of candles scattered around the living room, so he must have a way to light them.

It took her ten minutes to locate the matches using the torch on her mobile phone, by which time it was pitch black outside, and after lighting a dozen candles, careful to place them all high enough that Hannibal wouldn't knock them over, the room looked like she was about to hold a séance.

Turning her attention back to her stomach, she considered what to do about dinner. Although she was reluctant to spend the money, she needed to eat and didn't fancy salad or a sandwich. Resigned that she wasn't going to be able to have the fish tonight, she caved and ordered a pizza.

By the time it arrived, she was hot and bothered again. Lack of power meant no air-conditioning and with the heat of the candles, the apartment was stifling. Opening the balcony doors made little difference, thanks to the humidity still clinging to the air.

The delivery driver wasn't happy either, grumbling about having to negotiate the stairs using his phone light, and Nina was guilted into giving him a generous tip that she couldn't afford.

She closed the door, the aroma of the food making her mouth water, deciding to take her dinner outside. Despite the damp heat, there was a light breeze making it slightly more tolerable and at least here on the balcony, the traffic noise offered a reminder that the rest of the city was operating as normal.

Sat back in one of the patio chairs, her bare feet rested on another, Nina tied her long hair back into a knot to try to cool her neck, before tucking into her pizza, comforted by the connection with the rest of the world that still had light.

She could see buildings twinkling across the river and the reassuring glow of street lamps below, though across the courtyard gardens the second apartment block on the complex was also shrouded in darkness.

Turning to her phone, she started to scroll through her social media pages, conscious her battery was on 16 per cent charge. She didn't want to run it down to zero in case she needed to contact anyone.

Dexter and Mark would be in the air now, on their way to Hong Kong. She wouldn't be able to speak to her brother until he landed. Not that he would be able to do anything to help when he was halfway around the world.

From far off, sirens wailed, and Nina glanced up, seeing a flash of blue in the distance. It seemed to be heading in the direction of the apartments, but then it stopped. On Riverside Road, she thought, though she couldn't be sure.

Briefly, she returned to her phone, but then more sirens and flashing lights distracted her.

Curious, she peered over the balcony, wanting to know what was going on, but too far away to be able to see anything other than the lights.

That was when she remembered the pair of binoculars sat inside on the dining table.

They belonged to Mark and she recalled how she had smiled when seeing them, knowing he was a big nature lover.

It amused Nina and her parents, as Dexter didn't know anything about or have any interest in wildlife before meeting Mark, but since they had been together, he now readily agreed to go birdwatching on the North Norfolk coast and sometimes spent his weekends out on a boat on the county's waterways looking for otters and heron.

Heading inside, dismayed that it was like walking into a sauna, she grabbed the binoculars, then went back out onto the balcony. Peering through them, Nina could see the flashing lights, but her view of what was going on was obstructed by trees. The sirens had stopped, and realising it was probably just someone pulled over for speeding, she quickly lost interest.

In the homes across the river, she could see windows illuminated, but most of them were too far below her to have a clear view. In a couple of them, she saw movement, though not enough to ascertain who was inside or what they were doing.

None of her business anyway.

Bored, she nibbled at another pizza slice and sipped at her wine, glancing at the time on her phone and wishing the power would hurry up and come back on.

Idly, she raised the binoculars again, scanning them over the city. From her vantage point, she could see Norwich Castle in the distance, perched on its hill and overlooking the lights of the city centre. The bars and restaurants would no doubt be heaving on such a warm summer's night. The cathedral stood out, perhaps more so than the castle, its elegant spire illuminated, as were the grounds below, and she had a good view of the law courts too.

Dexter was so lucky having a home with this view.

Well, technically it wasn't actually his place. He rented it. The apartment belonged to his best friend, Zac, and Dexter was Zac's tenant. Initially, they had been living together, but then Zac had upped and left to go travelling, and now her lucky bloody brother had the whole apartment to himself with zero rent increase, even though Mark had moved in with him. The perks of being friends with someone who apparently had more money than sense.

Okay, that was a little unfair. Zac's parents had been killed in a car accident a few years back and, as their only child, he'd ended up inheriting everything.

Nina was sorry for what he had gone through, even if he was her childhood nemesis and had always tormented the hell out of her.

Following the path of the river brought her back to where the apartment complex was and as the binoculars flickered over the other block, a few of the windows that had a couple of minutes before been dark were now illuminated, revealing whole new worlds. And they weren't lit by candlelight. The light was brighter than that. Had the power returned?

A quick check of the light switch in the living room and the lack of humming from the air-con confirmed it was still out.

Electricity must have just returned in the other block. Hopefully, it was a good sign that she would have power back soon too.

For now, she watched more windows lighting up in the other block, envious of the residents who were able to once again enjoy their building's air-conditioning system.

No such luxury for Nina, whose hot body was damp against the plastic patio chair. Sweat moistened her armpits and trickled between her breasts.

The temptation not to pan back for a closer look was too great and raising the binoculars, ignoring the stab of intrusive guilt, she found herself looking into the apartment opposite, where the inhabitants appeared to be having a poker night. Plates of nibbles sat on the table between the group as they sipped at drinks, and the conversation seemed to be in full flow. Candles still burned in the centre of the table, even though there was no longer a need for them.

Moving along to the next lit window, the room appeared to be empty, but the glow from a table lamp showed her an apartment that was similar in layout and style to Dexter's, even down to the wide leather sofas and dark oak furniture.

Further down, a woman was on her balcony sat at a patio table, same as Nina, and was engrossed in her Kindle, and in the apartment next to her, a couple were moving around, looking like they had just arrived home. The woman, who was wearing a pretty summer dress, kicked off sandals before opening the balcony door and stepping outside.

As she spoke with her partner, Nina switched apartments again.

The neighbour next door was still reading and the poker game continued. In the apartment that reminded her of Dexter's, a man was now sat on the sofa and although Nina couldn't see the screen, she assumed from his stance he was watching TV.

There were two further lights on now.

In one of the apartments just below her, the soft glow of a floor lamp showed another empty apartment, but the owner must be home as the balcony door was wide open. And the penthouse apartment, one level above her with its floor-to-ceiling windows was lit up. A man with dark hair paced back and forth along the wide balcony, a phone to his ear.

It took Nina a second to realise she recognised him. He was the man from earlier; the attractive one she had passed on the bridge.

And he looked angry.

Intrigued, Nina watched, curious who he was talking to. Was it a fight with his wife or girlfriend, or perhaps it was a work call? His free hand was agitated and kept pushing back into his hair, dishevelling it.

She wondered what he did for a living. These apartments weren't cheap and the penthouse would be next-level expensive. He still wore the linen shirt and chinos, and although his attire was casual, there was something commanding and confident about him that told her he liked to be in charge and not have to take orders from anyone.

The call had ended now and he was staring in disgust at his phone.

Nina watched as he went back inside, then disappeared from sight. But then he was back again, and she could see he had made himself a drink. It looked like whisky from where she was sat. Or a similar liquor.

He downed the contents of his glass, then, leaning against the railing, he stared in Nina's direction.

She quickly dropped the binoculars.

The two buildings were far enough apart that she didn't think he could see her, especially in the dark, but on the off chance he could, she didn't want to get caught snooping.

With her naked eye, she could just about make out the silhouette of his figure and when he disappeared back inside, she dared raise the binoculars again.

Hoping he would reappear, she kept them focused on the penthouse apartment. Its balcony was far bigger than the one she was sitting on and from what she could see, it wrapped around at least two sides of the building. Instead of a patio table and chairs, it was decorated with stylish sofas and a coffee table, with wall lanterns adding mood lighting. And was that a water feature nestled between a couple of tall potted palms?

Yes, she was pretty sure it was.

Nosing through the open doors, all of the furniture she could see looked expensive, with lots of galvanised metal and reclaimed wood, while elegant artwork and mirrors, and delicate ornaments adorned the walls. It was like a show home, at least from this distance, and Nina doubted any children lived there.

Unless he was divorced and had lost custody. Perhaps that was who he had been talking to, arguing with his ex-wife.

She pictured him as a hard-working father with a high-flying, stressful job. Maybe he had put his career before his family, and his wife had ended things. So here he was with his new bachelor pad and custody of his daughter every other weekend. Yes, it was definitely a daughter, not a son, Nina decided, and he adored her. He had his show home apartment and could afford all the fine things in life, but what he really wanted was his family.

For a moment, she actually felt sorry for him, before realising the life she had just created for him was entirely fictional.

Briefly, she felt foolish, but then thought to hell with it. She was stuck sitting here in the dark, five storeys up, and with her phone battery running low, this was her only entertainment. She was hardly harming anyone if she made up a few stories in her head about the tenants in the neighbouring apartment block.

It didn't look like penthouse man was coming back out any time soon, she realised, and reluctantly she lowered the binoculars, returning to the other residents.

The lady who had been reading had gone inside, the lights to her apartment switched off, and the couple next door to her were now cuddled up on the sofa watching TV. Meanwhile, the poker group, who all looked to be a similar age to herself, were still going strong.

It was yet another reminder of what she had just given up.

She and Michael had often had friends over, either for dinner or a games night, but that wouldn't be happening any more, and it occurred to her for the first time that their split would be awkward for their friendship group. Although they both had friends outside of the relationship, the other key couple they socialised with was Tori, who Nina had known since high school, and Michael's cousin, Kyle. Would Tori be biased and try to persuade Nina she was making a mistake?

Was she making a mistake?

Until now, Nina had been so certain leaving Michael was the right thing to do, but sitting here alone in the dark with her thoughts, doubts crept in.

Michael was safe and kind, and although they weren't always compatible, he had made her feel comfortable. She did love him, but in a fond way that had grown out of familiarity. There was no longer any passion in their relationship.

But then, perhaps she was expecting too much, and the spark was meant to die down into friendship.

Could she go back?

Did she want to go back?

It would be easier.

Scary as it was taking this next step alone, Nina knew the answer was still a resounding no. She wanted the chance to carve her own path, even if it meant making sacrifices, and Michael deserved someone who truly loved him and wanted to be with him for all the right reasons.

Pushing him from her mind, she put the binoculars down on the table, then took her plate and wine glass inside, surprised by the drop in temperature as she stepped through the patio door.

It took her a second to register, but then she heard the low hum of the air-conditioning and realised the power must have come back on. Trying the light switch again, a warm glow lit up the room and Nina sighed in relief. She had started to worry she would be without power all night and wondered how the hell she would manage to sleep.

There were still several slices of pizza left and deciding she would have those for breakfast the following morning, she put the box in the fridge, then restarted the washing machine cycle.

It was only 10 p.m. and she was too restless to go to bed yet, so she poured another glass of wine, blew out the candles and switched on the TV.

At some point while watching an episode of *The Graham Norton Show* on catch-up, she fell asleep, Hannibal snoozing on her lap.

It was some time later that a piercing scream awoke her.

3

The blonde had caught Julian Wiseman's eye as he was sipping his second whisky. She was at a table with friends – some kind of celebration meal, judging by the gift bags and balloons on the table. She was the loudest, talking over everyone, but she also kept glancing in his direction, with her smoky eyes and red smirky lips, and he could tell she'd had a little too much to drink.

Just the way he liked them. Vulnerable, promiscuous and gullible.

He was tempted to flirt with her, ply her with some more alcohol, then persuade her to leave with him. It wouldn't be difficult. He knew he had the looks and charm, the gift of the gab, and also the right amount of confidence. Women loved him. And she was his type. Slim and pretty.

On another night, Blondie would be easy pickings, but the call from his father had soured his mood and lowered his libido. He had a feeling that tonight he might need more than a quick fuck.

It was the same old shit. Kevin Wiseman was cut-throat and

obsessed when it came to his company, putting work before family and everything else, and he couldn't understand why his eldest son didn't share the same drive, continually picking at him.

Julian had been back in the UK now for nearly a year. When was he going to get his life on track, join the family business and stop taking the piss, using the family name and living on handouts?

His dad spoke as if Julian had never done a day's work in his life, but that simply wasn't true. He had followed his father's wishes, studying and obtaining a degree in business management, then, while living in the US, he had helped oversee his uncle's string of bars. It wasn't his fault that the nightclub venture he had been trying to push forward since coming home had failed. There had just been too much red tape and issues with noise pollution.

Of course, Kevin Wiseman didn't see it that way and now he was making threats about taking away Julian's home and his car, and cutting his monthly allowance if he didn't get his act together and take his place on the board of directors in his property development firm.

Julian couldn't allow that to happen. He was relying on his father until he could find a way to get back on his feet. He just needed to get another business venture going and that was going to take time. Working for Wiseman Homes and having to answer to his father every day wasn't something he was cut out for.

He downed the rest of his drink, caught the eye of the bartender to order another and tried to roll the tension out of his shoulders. He hadn't planned to come out tonight, but after the call from his dad, he was just too damn angry and needed to escape his apartment. He loved living in the penthouse – a perk of having your dad own the building – but knowing his funds could be stopped and he might lose it left him feeling caged.

The only reason he been allowed to live there in the first place was because it was sitting empty, much to his father's annoyance. River Heights had been one of Kevin Wiseman's big visions for the city, but it had been hampered with issues from day one. The build had been problematic and there were frequent power outages and problems with the lifts, plus fire safety issues with the cladding, which all had to be replaced.

The apartments were sleek and spacious, but it had put buyers off, especially for the most expensive homes. Still, his father's misfortune was Julian's gain, and he needed to figure out how to keep the home and lifestyle he loved.

Brooding, he had skulked through the streets, ignoring the groups of pissed-up kids, who were littering the pavements like vermin. The silly little bastards thought they were all so cocky and grown-up, but they had no idea about life. His venue of choice was the Rooftop Gardens, a restaurant and bar that sat atop an office block offering a different view across the city.

As he tapped his card now against the contactless machine and picked up his fresh drink, he noticed Blondie's table was getting ready to go. There was lots of hugging going on, while the most sober of the group gathered up the gift bags and cards.

Now she was standing, Julian could see that that Blondie was wearing a short, tight leather skirt and spiky-heeled red shoes.

His dick stirred. Yes, she was just his type.

She was still looking at him, as though debating whether to come over and talk to him. Not wanting to encourage her, Julian reluctantly looked away.

Sorry, Blondie. Not tonight.

He wasn't sure he would be able to control himself around her. Often, he was satisfied with a quick fuck in a nightclub toilet, but tonight he needed more – and there were far too many witnesses who would see them leaving together.

He also had to be careful with the women he selected. When he had these urges to satisfy, discretion was key. He couldn't get caught.

He didn't know enough about this one. Yet.

He watched her totter away in her skyscraper heels looking disappointed and he wondered if he was making a mistake. But then she was gone and he was left to sip his whisky and ponder his future.

* * *

It was wandering back to his apartment an hour later, having stopped for a late-night kebab, that Julian saw her again. She was in the Tombland area of the city, and stumbling towards him – no doubt to the taxi queue Julian had just passed – and looking suitably worse for wear. And none of her friends were with her.

That last observation piqued Julian's interest. Friends could be cumbersome and sometimes the voice of reason. It was better for him that she was now alone.

Well, it would be if he intended to stop and speak to her, which he didn't.

But then she glanced up and caught his eye, her lips curving up when she recognised him.

'I know you,' she slurred. 'You were in the Rooftop Gardens.'

Julian should ignore her, just carry on walking. He wasn't thinking clearly and Blondie here, with her panda eyes from where her smoky make-up had smeared and her too-short skirt, offered too much temptation.

He lowered his head and went to walk past her, but felt the grip of fingers on his arm.

'That kebab smells really good. Can I have a bite?'

She was looking hopefully at him now – all red pout, a ruby pendant glittering at her throat – and he wanted to tell her no, but instead he paused. She was that delicious mix of sass and stupidity that was so easy to manipulate – and it was making him weak.

'Go on, just one bite,' she pleaded. 'I'm really hungry and my feet are killing me.'

A quick glance around told him they were not being watched. There were people about, but they were either too inebriated or busy looking at their phones. Not that it mattered. He didn't know this woman, so it would just be straight sex. Something to blow off a little steam.

He would have to find a way to control his other cravings.

'Where do you live?' he asked.

'Hethersett,' came the reply.

About six miles out of the city. Too far out to walk back to her place. Could he trust himself to take her back to his apartment?

The whisky was impairing his judgement and this woman was practically throwing herself at him. He just had to behave himself.

To hell with it.

Holding out the kebab, he let her take a bite.

'My place is just up the road if you fancy a nightcap.'

He expected her to jump at the opportunity, so it surprised him when she wavered.

'Thanks, but I should go get a cab.'

Really?

That was unexpected. Perhaps he had her pegged wrong after all.

'You can have my number if you like,' she offered.

Keen, but wary too. He had always liked a challenge, but his true desires and what he wanted to do with her burned a fire deep inside him. That scared him. She was a temptation, but if he got carried away, it could come back to bite him on the arse.

He thought back to six years ago and the murder of Katy Spencer. For a while there, he had been the prime suspect and honestly believed he would end up rotting in prison. His father had been appalled at the shame brought on the family, their reputable name splattered all over the papers, and he had never stopped letting Julian know about it, even though he was eventually released without charge.

In Kevin's eyes, mud stuck, and people would always connect his eldest son to what had happened.

One more fuck-up and he would probably be cut out of the old man's will.

Julian ignored Blondie's request, instead giving her a quick smile. 'I should get home.'

Now he could see she was disappointed, but still he walked away.

'Wait,' she called after him.

Instead of stopping, he ignored her, picking up his pace.

Yes, she was definitely keen, and knowing her eagerness made her vulnerable to his needs, his resolve weakened.

'Hold on, I've changed my mind,' she shouted after him.

Julian kept walking, aware there was a CCTV camera up ahead. But only one. Once he reached the river path, he was safe.

Come along, Blondie, he silently lured.

Hearing the tottering of her heels trying to catch him up, he smiled.

Easy pickings.

4

Nina sat bolt upright on the sofa and for a moment she had no idea where she was or what time it was. As she shook off the haze of sleepiness, she realised the scream had come from the TV, which was now playing a movie.

Hannibal had moved from her lap to the arm of the sofa and was watching her hopefully. Nina knew he would be hoping for some of the bedtime cat treats Dexter often gave him.

Her neck ached from the awkward position she had been lying in and she rolled her shoulders, cursing when she saw it was gone midnight.

Half a glass of the wine she had been drinking sat on the coffee table, and not fancying it, having been asleep, she got up and poured it down the sink, then fetched the Dreamies Hannibal loved.

He purred as he ate them and she turned her attention to the blinking light of the washing machine which had ended its cycle. Although it was late and she wanted to go to bed, her things would be crumpled and smell musty if left overnight, so she quickly pulled them from the machine, shaking out the creases and hanging everything on the clothes horse. Figuring her washing would dry quicker outside, she opened the patio door and pushed the clothes horse out onto the balcony, surprised by how warm it still was.

Down below, the city was still awake, with clusters of lights and bursts of noise penetrating the silence.

Nina was about to go back in when her attention was drawn to the top of the opposite block of apartments.

Penthouse man was still awake.

Was he out on the balcony? She thought the doors were open, though it was difficult to be sure from this distance.

She rubbed at her eyes, suddenly a whole lot more awake, and glanced at the binoculars, her moral compass wavering as she picked them up.

Just a quick peek wouldn't do any harm. She would look to satisfy her curiosity, then put them back inside where she had first found them.

Shaking off her guilt, she trained them on the penthouse, the balcony coming into focus. She had been right about the doors. They were open, though she couldn't see him anywhere. Perhaps he had fallen asleep like she had, though there was no sign of life inside the apartment, which was lit by the low glow of a table lamp.

Nina was about to go back inside when she spotted movement in the doorway at the back of the room and the man stepped into her line of vision. He went straight over to the kitchen, pulling a bottle of wine from the fridge and taking down glasses from an overhead cupboard.

Two glasses.

For the first time, she realised he was talking to someone.

A woman.

Nina could see her now, and that she was pretty. Blonde hair and slim with long, slender legs shown off by heeled red stilettos and a short leather skirt.

The sting of jealousy was unexpected. She didn't even know penthouse man. She had created this whole life for him in her head, but none of it was true.

As she watched, wine was poured and the woman tipped her head back and laughed at something the man had said, a red heart pendant glittering at her throat, before demurely drinking from her glass.

They were moving now, out onto the balcony and giving Nina a bird's-eye view. Realising the light was on behind her and scared they might spot her watching, she called through to Alexa to switch it off. As darkness shrouded her, she felt a little less conspicuous.

This pair were too wrapped up in each other to pay attention, penthouse man now taking the woman's glass and moving behind her, his hands on her shoulders, then moving into her hair, pushing it to one side as his mouth dipped to kiss her neck.

Nina needed to put the binoculars down and go to bed, give this couple their privacy.

She was uncomfortably hot, perhaps in part because of what she was doing, knowing it was wrong, as well as because of the muggy night air. Her neck was damp, and her skin on fire.

She should go in, but it wasn't happening. She was too invested, watching as the man became rougher and more urgent in his actions. One hand tangled in the woman's hair, the other going to her throat and pulling her back. She seemed startled by the change of pace, her eyes widening as he clawed at her top, dragging it up and over her head, then the too-short skirt was being tugged down the woman's long legs, swiftly followed by her knickers.

Hell, this guy didn't waste any time.

One moment Nina was double blinking as the woman stood there completely naked, except the red shoes, the next, her mouth dropped open as she realised penthouse man had dropped his trousers and was pushing the woman down onto her knees. As the woman took him in her mouth, he held her head in place, rocking back and forth on his heels as he stared up at the stars.

Nina really needed to look away. If they realised she was watching, they would be mortified. And so would she. It was wrong spying on them like this.

Except she couldn't bring herself to drop the binoculars.

Instead, she continued to watch. The woman had stopped now, though stayed on her knees, and penthouse man, whose dick was still rock hard, was handing her something.

A condom, Nina realised, watching her put it on him.

No sooner had she finished than penthouse man had pulled her up to her feet and had her pressed against the balcony, one hand tangled in her hair again, the other reaching past her to grip the railing. As he thrust into her from behind, the woman cried out, the sound carrying through the night air.

No build-up or foreplay, just straight down to business.

That was disappointing and not at all how Nina had imagined he would be. In her head, she had painted him as a caring and considerate lover.

The sex didn't last long and penthouse man yanked up his trousers, picked up his wine glass and disappeared inside the moment he was done, leaving his naked companion – whose expression suggested she had been left wanting – to gather up her clothes.

The woman reached to her neck and Nina's initial thought was that the man had hurt her, but then she realised the woman was feeling for her pendant that was no longer there. Had it come loose? She was hunting around on the balcony looking for it when penthouse man came back outside looking for her, his expression impatient.

The pair exchanged a few words, then he reached for the woman's hand, pulling her behind him as he went back inside.

Nina actually felt a little sorry for her.

Was she his girlfriend, or someone he had just met? Either way, he needed to learn some manners. The woman was best shot of him.

They had both disappeared from view now, and realising they weren't coming back, Nina decided to call it a night.

She was lowering the binoculars when she caught a glimpse of movement in the apartment below. Someone else who couldn't sleep, perhaps? The oppressive heat keeping everyone awake and edgy. There was no light on and as she scanned back, she wondered for a moment if she had imagined it, but then she saw it again and the outline of a shadowy figure came into view.

Someone sitting on the balcony, she realised, adjusting the magnification level of each eyepiece for a closer look.

The figure swung more into focus – an older man, bald head, wearing a pair of striped pyjama bottoms and a grey T-shirt, and he held something in his lap. He was looking directly towards her and for a moment she froze, before reminding herself that he couldn't see her.

But then he raised his hand to his face and to her horror she realised that he too was holding a pair of binoculars. Seeing that he had her attention, he smiled and waved.

Had he been watching her all this time?

Nina felt violated.

Add guilty and mortified to that, as she had been spying on her neighbours too, and she understood now just how intrusive she had been.

Her cheeks flamed as she put down the binoculars and quickly fled inside. Had this man been watching her all evening or just while penthouse man and his lady friend were having sex? The apartment was just above him, so he must have heard them and realised what Nina was watching.

She hadn't bothered drawing the living-room curtains before, figuring no one could see in, but now, after locking the door, she pulled them across, wanting privacy.

Hannibal was curled up on her bed in Dexter's spare room and he gave her a superior look that suggested he knew she had been up to no good.

'I didn't know they were going to have sex,' Nina told him guiltily.

She should have gone straight to bed after waking up on the sofa, because now her mind was too active, replaying everything she had just witnessed.

Eventually, the dark quietness of the apartment, broken only by the faint hum of the air-conditioning unit, pulled her under.

Although she slept, her dreams were plagued with penthouse man. In them, Nina had gone to his apartment and she was in his bed, telling him to slow down as he pulled at her clothes.

The dream was interrupted as she awoke with a start and for a moment she was still there in his apartment.

But then the bedroom door opening pulled her abruptly back to reality, and as she realised that there was someone standing beside the bed, she started to scream.

5

The look of horror on the woman's face had been priceless, and as he headed out for his routine late-night stroll, Leonard Pickles revelled in the moment she had realised he was watching her.

Even though she had been sitting in the dark, he had been afforded a clear view of her expression through his high-end binoculars and he had enjoyed watching her squirm, knowing she had been caught spying.

Conveniently, he ignored the fact he was doing exactly the same thing as her, on account that he considered himself to be providing a service for his neighbours.

Well, service might be stretching it, and, okay, it wasn't really for his neighbours.

He was a man who liked to know what was going on and he was selective over who he shared his findings with. One thing he had learnt over the years was that you never knew what went on behind closed doors. Leonard did like to uncover secrets.

His late wife, Molly, had told him he was a nosy old bastard, and she was right. He was sneaky, shrewd and always one step ahead. He also knew what secrets were worth exposing and which ones it might pay to hold on to for a while. The entertainment that ensued when the truth finally did come out, leading to relationships imploding or housemates falling out, was pure gold.

It also went some way to easing his bitterness at how his life had panned out.

His own marriage to Molly had lasted over forty years before she'd succumbed to cancer, just six months after they had both taken early retirement following a lottery win. Their plan had been to see the world together.

Leonard had no inclination to go alone, and given they had been childless, and he was now sixty-two with few true friends, he hadn't wanted to die of boredom, tucked away in their house in the suburbs. He had always been an active man and liked the hustle and bustle of the city, so had ended up selling their modest terrace and sinking all of his money into an apartment at River Heights, the new luxury apartment complex.

He had been the first tenant to move in and he guarded like a sentinel over each resident who had moved in after him, watching their every move. A creature of habit, he used the gym and swimming pool every morning, then, while everyone else was asleep, he headed out for his night-time walk. It was the perfect time for snooping, though he was careful to stick mostly to the lit areas and quieter streets. He was in good physical health and kept himself fit, but he was still wary about who might be around.

As for his neighbours, some of them acknowledged him, while others – especially those who'd had run-ins with him – avoided him like the plague, but mostly all of them were too busy with their lives to pay him that much attention. They knew very little about Leonard, but he made sure he knew everything about them.

He had maps of the two apartment blocks and made it his business to find out who was living in each unit.

If Molly were still alive, she would roll her eyes at him and tell him he wasn't right in the head, but she would laugh with him. She was the only one who ever had.

He had always been this way inclined and perhaps that was in part due to his career as a security guard for one of the city's big department stores. There, his job had been to watch people, and it seemed it was a compulsion he couldn't shake.

Ask him about any of his neighbours and he would have a story. There was Becky across the hall. She lived alone, but Leonard knew she had two different boyfriends – neither knew about the other. Then, on the floor below was Conrad, whose sole interests were women and working out in the gym. In the other block were adulterers, a wife beater and a woman who really needed to draw her blinds before indulging in her sex toy addiction.

And sitting like a king lauding over his subjects in the penthouse apartment above Leonard was Julian Wiseman, one of the most obnoxious individuals he had ever met. The pair of them had fallen out on many occasions and Leonard enjoyed being a thorn in Julian's side. He knew all about Julian's feuding with his father, having overheard many of their phone conversations while sitting out on his balcony, just as he knew Julian had this evening been entertaining female company.

The woman spying on them from apartment 5A had been watching them having noisy sex on the balcony, watching what he could hear. Was that her kink? Was she a voyeur?

She didn't own the place. It belonged to Zac Green, who had moved out long ago, and the tenants were a gay couple, Dexter Fairchild and Mark Chen.

So who was she?

Leonard decided it was time to find out.

6

It took Nina a moment to realise she wasn't the only one making a noise.

Her first reaction on seeing the shadowy figure enter the room had been to scream, and when the intruder gave a startled yelp in response, she had screamed even louder, scrambling back across the mattress in her bid to get away, falling off the bed and landing inelegantly on the floor.

She heard a confused 'What the fuck,' then, before she could get to her feet and flee the room, the sound of shuffling, followed by the click of the bedside lamp.

As light lit up the dark room, she found herself face-to-face with a wide-eyed man, one who was familiar to her, his dishevelled hair standing on end.

The look of shock on his face mirrored hers, but as recognition kicked in, it softened slightly.

'Nina?'

Zac Green. Her brother's best friend.

'What the hell are you doing here?' she demanded, willing her racing heart to slow down.

He took a moment to answer her, looking stunned that they were having this encounter, though his shock quickly morphed into indignation. 'This is *my* apartment, *my* bedroom, *my* bed. What the hell are you doing in it?'

'Yes, but you don't live here any more. Dexter pays you rent.' Nina raised her chin in a challenging stance. 'If you were coming back and wanted to stay, a little notice might have been...' She trailed off, realising that he wasn't paying any attention to what she was saying. Instead, his gaze had travelled southwards.

Looking down, she realised in belated horror that one of her breasts had worked its way free from the camisole nightie she had worn to bed.

'Zac!' she snapped, quickly adjusting the material and poking her boob back in. Her cheeks were burning, despite the air-con, but her skin was goose-pimpled, and her nipples were rock hard beneath the lightweight cotton. She got to her feet, crossing her arms defensively across her chest. 'You are such a pervert.'

The irony that she had earlier been spying on naked people was momentarily lost on her. It seemed to snap Zac's attention back to her face at least.

'Dex knew I was coming,' he told her. Apparently, he had heard some of what Nina had said.

'He knew?' Dexter was aware Zac was coming home. Nina processed that snippet of information. Why the hell hadn't her brother said anything? A little bit of warning might have been nice.

'I told him I would be back sometime late summer.'

Sometime late summer? That was vague.

'Not that I need to give notice. And certainly not to you.' He cocked his head to one side and regarded her through narrowed eyes. 'Why are you here and in my bed?'

'I'm looking after the cat while he's away.'

They both glanced down at Hannibal, who had made himself comfortable sprawled across the wooden floor, one eye open, watching them with lazy interest.

'Dex said you were feeding him, not moving in.'

Nina really didn't want to get into the whole messy break-up with Michael story, certainly not with Mr Arrogant here. She had known Zac Green for most of her life and he had always been a smug shit who excelled at pushing her buttons.

'Well, things changed. He asked me to stay,' she told him, staying on the defensive. 'And thank you for scaring the crap out of me.'

For a moment, he had the good grace to look sheepish. 'It's late and I'm knackered. I've been travelling all day. I had no idea I was going to find you here.'

'Okay, well I am, so can you please go sleep in Dexter's bed?'

Zac looked at her incredulously. 'You want me to leave?'

'Yes. I was here first.'

The corner of his lip twitched. Nina wasn't sure if it was with amusement or irritation.

'It's my room, though.'

'So?'

'So *you* go sleep in your brother's bed.'

'No.'

'Yes.' He was skulking towards her now, looking like he was ready to manhandle her if necessary. 'Look, I'm jet-lagged and I need to sleep. I'm not in a great mood, so I need you to go away and stop annoying me, Ninny Noo.'

Nina bristled at the use of her parents' childhood nickname for her – he bloody knew she hated it. Still, she backed away, very much aware that he was bigger than her. 'Zac, stop it.'

'Get out of my room, Nina, or I'll pick you up and throw you out.'

'You're being unreasonable,' she pointed out, realising from the look on his face that he meant it.

The Zac she remembered had been quite lanky in build, but since she had last seen him – which had to be about four years ago – he had filled out in his arms and shoulders, developing more of a rugby player physique. He wouldn't have any problem tackling her.

'Out, Nina. Now.'

He was edging her closer to the door, and she was annoyed as hell that he always seemed to get the upper hand.

As she stepped over the threshold, she glared up at him. 'You are still such a prick,' she bristled.

The door had already slammed shut in her face before she had finished her sentence.

Seething, she backed away, almost tripping over a pair of discarded trainers.

Closer to the door, she spotted an oversized rucksack and she was briefly tempted to hide it. Teach him a lesson. Truthfully, though, she couldn't afford to piss him off. At least not until she had sorted a plan for where she would go. She couldn't stay here now.

Why was he back? Was it just for a visit or a more permanent thing? Dexter had never really said more than he was travelling. Nina had no idea what his set up was.

Either way, there was no need for her to be here if Zac was home, so where next?

Back to the house she had shared with Michael was out of the question and she knew staying with her friends wouldn't work. Rachel had young twins and really didn't need the added stress, and Charlotte lived with her boyfriend in a cramped one-bed flat. Tori had the space, but Nina didn't want to make things awkward for her and Kyle.

That left going home to her mum and dad. Aurora had offered for her to stay, but Nina honestly didn't think she could cope living under the same roof as her mother. Could she stay here for a few more days? Dexter had invited her to stay, but still, it was Zac's apartment.

Tomorrow she would look at the rental market and see if there was anything in her budget. Even if it was just a bedsit or a room in a shared house.

Sorting her living situation had just become a lot more urgent.

7

Their faces might be different, but they fit a type: pretty, vacuous in personality and believing they can go through life taking whatever they want without having to answer to anyone because of how they look and who they are.

But when you strip back the layers, they are filthy whores, and they need to be punished.

The only way I can cope with the fucking is knowing that once the deed is done I get to expose them for who they really are.

I love showing them that their beauty is only skin deep, and the moment of realisation when they understand they have made a terrible mistake helps ease the pressure building in my head. Taunting them as they beg, as they plead for me to let them go and promise me they won't tell a soul, knowing I will never let them leave, is a soothing balm.

You picked the wrong man to go home with, I tell them.

Cheap, dirty sluts. They deserve everything that happens to them.

8

Although he had only managed a few hours of sleep, Zac Green forced himself to get up on UK time. He had enough experience now of travelling between time zones and was aware he needed to get back into a routine.

Glancing at Dexter's bedroom door, which he had heard slam shut not long after he had kicked Nina out of his room, he guessed she was still sleeping. It was 8 a.m. on a Sunday morning, so that was reasonable, and tempting though it was to make enough noise to wake her, he was relishing this quiet time alone with his thoughts before she interrupted his peace.

Because if he remembered one thing about Nina, it was that she would be spoiling to continue their fight from last night.

Wanting to delay that until he had at least drunk one cup of coffee, he crept about the apartment, trying not to make too much noise as he showered and dressed, fed Hannibal, who was stalking his every move, then took his coffee and the pizza he found in the fridge out onto the balcony.

He had heard the UK was having a heatwave, but it was still a pleasant surprise to feel the sun on his face as he pulled out a chair at the patio table. A different type of morning to the ones he had recently experienced in South Africa. There, it was the middle of winter, and although the daytime temperature still reached a sunny eighteen degrees, at this early hour it was chilly outside.

As he sipped his coffee and enjoyed his impromptu breakfast, exchanging messages with a handful of people to let them know he was home, the fragrant scent of fabric conditioner wafted pleasantly in the air. Glancing over to the end of the balcony, he realised Nina had put her clothes out to dry.

She was certainly making herself at home.

He cast his eye over the garments, realising there was a pair of cotton knickers among them. She would be mortified if she realised he was sitting out here with a full view of her underwear.

Knowing that improved his mood slightly.

Nina baiting had always been a favourite hobby of Zac's. Although there was only nine months between them, he had been in the year above her at school and she had always been Dexter's little sister to him.

Well, apart from that brief moment last night when her boob had poked out of the armhole of her nightie. Disgusted with himself and more than a little worried when he had felt his dick stir, he had been quick to throw her out of the bedroom before he embarrassed them both.

Not only was she his best friend's sister, but she was the closest thing he had to one too. She could be annoying and a pain in the arse, and make him roll his eyes so hard at times he thought he might lose them, but he was also fiercely protective of her.

Not that he would ever admit to that last bit. Certainly not to Nina.

He wondered now what she was really doing here.

Didn't she live with her boyfriend now? How had Dexter managed to persuade to stay here for the whole month? And why wasn't the boyfriend with her?

Matthew, no, Michael. That was his name. Zac had met him a handful of times back when Nina had started dating him, and while he was nice enough in a bland kind of way, he didn't have much of a personality or sense of humour.

Michael wasn't Nina's type. Or at least he wasn't what Zac had expected her to go for. She could do better.

But she had chosen him. So why was she here hanging out at her brother's place instead of at home? Was there trouble in paradise?

As he mused over the question, enjoying the cold pizza and coffee, he glanced at the binoculars sitting on the table.

What were they doing out here? Had Nina been checking out the view?

He picked them up and scanned the perimeter, realising he could see clearly into the windows of the other apartment block.

Had she been spying on his neighbours?

No, she was too straight-laced for that.

Or at least the Nina he remembered was.

As he placed them back on the table, he heard movement inside the apartment; the running of the tap, then the sound of the kettle boiling. He took a sip of coffee, then another bite of pizza, readying himself for round two. He had no problem with her staying here, but he would be damned if she thought she could just take over.

If she stayed, there would be rules. And the first one was that she had to stay the hell out of his bedroom.

'Do you want another coffee?'

The question came from inside and was so unexpected, Zac's head shot round.

She was offering to make him a drink? And her tone was affable, not defensive as he had expected.

'Okay,' he agreed warily.

Unable to shake the suspicion she was up to something – perhaps planning to put laxatives in his cup or spit in it – he got up and took it through to her, leaning back against the counter and watching while she made it.

She was still wearing the little cotton nightie from last night, though had thankfully covered it with a robe, and her dark hair was loose and in need of a brush.

'You still take it milk, no sugar, right?'

'Yeah, thanks.'

Who was this woman and why, after their last interaction had been him shutting the door in her face, was she being so civil?

He had expected fireworks and a teeny part of him was disappointed he wasn't getting them. Fireworks he could cope with, but Nina being demure and polite? Damn, it was a little unsettling.

'You sleep okay?' he asked, watching her. His tone was a little goading and he could see that Nina knew it. Still, she gave a tight nod, refusing to bite.

He thanked her as she handed him a fresh cup of coffee, somewhat disconcerted that she wasn't bantering with him like she normally did.

'Actually, I need to ask you a favour,' she began, and Zac could feel the tension bouncing off her.

Okay, so this sounded serious. He was both worried and curious.

Was this why she was acting weird? Did it have to do with why she was here?

'Sure thing. What's up?' he asked, heading back out onto the balcony and hearing her footsteps as she followed.

That was the moment old Nina returned.

'I can't bloody believe you!' she stormed, staring at the empty pizza box. 'That was *my* breakfast.'

'I didn't know that. I assumed you were done with it.'

'Why the hell would it be in the fridge if I was done with it? It was my food. You had no right to help yourself.'

'Your food, *my* fridge,' Zac pointed out. Why was she making such a big deal of it? It was just a couple of slices of pizza. 'And, as I just said, how was I supposed to know you still wanted it?'

'You should have asked.'

She glowered at him, seeming to briefly forget whatever was bugging her, and he relaxed a little. Maybe whatever she wanted wasn't such a big deal after all.

'Consider it me doing you a favour.'

'How is that?'

'Well, you have a barbecue at your mum's in a few hours and you know she always does far too much food.'

Nina hesitated, for a moment seeming unsure how to respond. 'How do you know about that?' she asked carefully.

'Because I'm going too.'

'What? Mum never said anything about it yesterday.' She was flustered now. 'Wait. She knows you're home?'

'I sent her a WhatsApp this morning to let her know I'm back.'

It was the first message he had sent. He had known Toby and Aurora Fairchild for most of his life and considered them his second family. After his parents had died, their role in his life had become even more significant, so he had been delighted when Aurora had replied, inviting him over.

'Well, this is just great,' Nina grumbled.

'I figured we might as well ride over together.'

She looked disgusted with his suggestion.

'I need to go get dressed,' she announced haughtily, before muttering something that sounded derogatory under her breath.

'Wait.' Zac stopped her, keeping his tone pleasant. 'You said you wanted to ask me a favour.'

Nina glared at him, her hazel eyes so similar to her brother's. She hadn't changed over the last four years. Her dark hair was a little longer and the crease in her forehead when she frowned now cut a little deeper, but essentially she looked exactly the same as before he had left.

'Forget I asked,' she muttered. 'It's nothing important.'

That was annoying. He had hoped to find out why she was really here. But instead she was putting up walls and behaving like a brat.

He picked up the binoculars.

'Nina?'

'What!'

'I wouldn't leave these outside. They look expensive.'

She snatched them from him, but Zac didn't miss her look of guilt.

'They're Mark's,' she told him stuffily.

'Does he know you're using them to spy on people?'

'I am not!'

Her reddening cheeks were enough of a giveaway, but the fact her eyes were darting everywhere to avoid looking at him confirmed he was on the money.

'Liar,' he taunted.

Nina's pretty face scrunched up. 'You are such a dick. I don't know why my brother is friends with you,' she snapped.

Ouch.

Okay, if she wanted to play mean, the gloves were off.

Snatching the knickers from the clothes horse, Zac held them up, delighted when her expression turned to one of horror. She had clearly forgotten they were there.

He held them out of her reach when she made a grab for them, enjoying her look of mortification.

'Give those here,' she demanded.

Zac mentally patted himself on the back as she bit, glad she was reverting to type. This was the Nina he remembered and knew how to deal with. His best mate's petulant little sister. 'Do me a favour and keep your underwear out of my way, okay?'

He tossed them to her, unable to hide his grin as she caught them and quickly brushed past him to scoop up the rest of her stuff from the clothes horse. As she stomped back inside, though, the smile slipped and he sipped at his coffee, wondering what was up with her.

He knew Nina Fairchild well enough to realise when something was off. Whatever was bugging her, he was determined to find out.

9

It was the turning of the key in the lock that had Julian leaping out of bed.

He had ignored the persistent ringing of the doorbell, his head pounding with the hangover from hell as the events of the previous night had gradually come back to him.

Blondie in his apartment – he had never asked her name, and couldn't care less who she was, but he recalled how they'd had sex on the balcony before his darker desires had taken over.

He had promised himself he could be strong. A quick fuck, then send her on her way, but then they had gone inside and they were in his bedroom. That was when he had lost control, giving into his cravings.

Afterwards, he felt sick, realising he had made a terrible mistake. If the press got wind of what he liked to get up to behind closed doors, he would be screwed. They'd had a field day with him before, back when Katy had died. That was why his father had sent him away. Out of sight, out of mind, and all that. And although Julian had grown to enjoy his time in the US, being shipped off like he was a shameful secret had been hard for him to deal with.

Burying his head under the pillow, he had ignored his caller, even as the ringing was accompanied by a loud knocking on the door. It wouldn't be about Blondie. Not yet. It was too soon, surely. But then, after a short period of blissful silence, someone was letting themselves into his apartment?

What the actual fuck?

'Julian, are you ready?'

Tabitha Percy's plummy voice echoed down the hallway and shock had him quickly scrambling into a pair of jogging bottoms, then stumbling out of the bedroom, trying his best to appear sleepy-eyed and surprised, like he had just woken up.

'Tabs? What are you doing in here?'

Her lips pursed, then formed an O of disapproval, and Julian couldn't help thinking that the orangey lipstick she wore looked ridiculous against her pale, powdered face.

'We have your dad's charity event, remember?'

He had completely forgotten about it, last night with Blondie erasing everything else from his brain.

His father's party.

Every August, on the first Sunday of the month, Kevin Wiseman hosted a garden party at the family home. There were caterers and live music, while magicians and face painters kept the kids amused, and guests were invited to dig deep into their pockets, in support of whichever charity had been chosen. There would then be a big public display where Kevin matched the grand total raised.

Last night on the phone with his father, Julian had refused to go, but both of them knew it was a lie. He had managed to avoid it for the last few years while living overseas, so this year his presence was expected. His younger brother, James, always attended, and Julian was expected to be there too. At least he would if he wanted to keep his lavish lifestyle.

He wondered now if his mother's best friend, Grace, would be in attendance.

Hopefully so. She was a free spirit and at least things were never dull with her around.

He certainly hadn't planned on going with Tabitha, and he had ignored her WhatsApp message the previous day asking if he wanted a lift, and the repeated calls when his phone had rung earlier this morning, guessing it might be her.

If he had known she was going to show up uninvited, he would have answered.

Since he had moved back to the UK, she was getting far too involved in his life.

Julian had known her all of his life. Her father, Giles, was his dad's doctor and his best friend. Julian and Tabitha had been born six weeks apart and had grown up together. He knew their parents had hoped they might eventually get married.

It would never happen. Tabitha might come from money and move in the same circles, but she was a world away from the type of woman he was attracted to.

The clothes she wore were ill-fitting and frumpy, her make-up plastered on too heavily, and her hair, even though she'd had it lightened from mousy brown to blonde, always looked like it needed a good comb.

And don't get him started on her high-pitched chortle of a laugh.

The perfect man was out there for Tabitha, but it wasn't Julian.

They had fucked a few times when they were younger, simply because she was often around and it was easy to get her into bed. Not in a long time, though. She was too squeaky clean for Julian's taste and would be shocked if she learnt some of the antics he got up to.

And she worked for Wiseman Homes as his father's personal assistant. Blurring those lines between personal and professional wasn't a good idea, especially if Julian did end up being forced to join the family firm.

It bothered him that she was still single. James had made a joke shortly after Julian had returned home that Tabitha had been waiting for him. At the time, Julian had laughed, but now he couldn't help but worry, just in case it was true.

When he had first moved to the US, she had hinted about going with him and for the first year at least she had regularly sent him messages – half of which he hadn't replied to – and at one point she had even suggested flying out to see him. No thank you. Eventually, though, the messages had dwindled, and although she still stalked his social media, liking everything he ever posted, he assumed she had moved on.

Perhaps not.

It seemed she had the wrong idea about their relationship, which in his eyes was non-existent, and she was getting above her station. Especially when she said things like 'we have', as if they were attending the garden party as a couple. And what was with this whole letting herself in Julian's apartment, as if he had given her a key?

Which, come to think of it, how did she get a key?

He asked the question now, bristling with annoyance when she did the irritating laugh. It sounded condescending, as if she couldn't believe he was asking such a stupid question.

'From the maintenance office, silly.'

Julian knew they kept copies down there, but Tabitha had no right to go in there and help herself.

'It's supposed to be locked,' he pointed out, eyeing the key in her hand. He wanted it back before she left. The idea that she could let herself in her at any time brought him out in a cold sweat.

Thank God he had already got rid of the woman he had brought home last night.

If Tabitha had walked in and seen...

No, he couldn't even bear to think about the drama that would have unfolded.

'Don't worry,' she told him, drawing his attention back to the subject of the maintenance room. 'I made sure I locked up when I was finished.'

'You have a key for the maintenance room?'

'Of course. I have keys for all of your father's buildings.'

Dear God. Julian needed to have a word with his dad and get her access revoked. Surely she was breaching all kinds of privacy laws. There needed to be some boundaries set.

'Well, I'd appreciate it if you didn't let yourself in here again.'

'I knocked and rang the bell. You didn't answer.'

'Because I was asleep. That doesn't give you the right to just let yourself into my home, Tabs.'

He could see she wasn't getting it, staring at him like he was being completely ridiculous, and he sighed, shoving a hand back through his hair.

'Look, this is my place and it's private. You don't live here and you don't have the right to just to come inside uninvited, okay?'

'You should be grateful I did show up,' she said a little huffily. 'The garden party starts in an hour and you know your father will be mad if you're not there.'

'That's not the point.'

'Just go get dressed, Julian. We can't be late.'

He wasn't getting through to her at all, and he was getting fed up trying to reason with her. His dad would have to talk to her, he decided.

Knowing he would struggle to get her out of his home until they left for the garden party, he turned on his heel and headed back into his bedroom. 'Do me a favour and make me a coffee while I shower,' he told her, before slamming the door, then locking it for good measure.

He sucked in a breath and glanced about the room to check there was no trace of his late-night visitor. He hadn't even known Blondie's name. But he did remember her face, and especially her expression when he had opened the safe and taken out his leather case, showing her what was inside.

He should never have brought her here. It had been a big mistake.

Hopefully, it was one he wouldn't live to regret.

10

So, as well as having to put up with Zac in Dexter's flat, now Nina had to tolerate him at her parents' house too? The man hadn't even been back a day and it seemed there was no getting away from him.

She honestly thought she had mellowed where he was concerned. It had been over four years since she had seen him and he was what, thirty-six now? A few months older than her, she remembered. Except, no, here he was, living and breathing, and reminding her of every reason why she detested him.

And that was ridiculous. They were mature adults now and the rivalry from their childhood was long behind them. Yet, he was making her behave like they were thirteen again.

Nina had been in the year below Zac and Dexter at school, but Zac was younger than her brother and closer to her own age. That was why it had always rankled so much that he treated her like a kid sister.

She insisted on being the one to drive to her parents, even though Zac offered to take his hire car, and as soon as she started the engine, she put the radio on loud, trying to ignore that he was sat in the passenger seat beside her.

This afternoon was going to be a nightmare. Aurora loved Zac, and he could do no wrong in her eyes, and she was bound to mention Nina's break-up with Michael, and that it was the reason why she was staying in the apartment.

Nina couldn't stand the idea of him seeing her at her most vulnerable and she definitely didn't need him using it as leverage over her. After their exchange this morning, she believed he still had the lack of morals to stoop to that level.

As expected, her mother fawned over him the moment they arrived.

'Zac. How are you?' Aurora cooed, cupping his face between her hands as he bent down to kiss her cheek, then blushing when he handed her the huge bouquet of supermarket flowers he had insisted stopping off for on the journey over.

If there was one bright side to Zac being here, it was the distraction he provided, meaning Nina's parents weren't focused on the break-up of her relationship. There were four years of his travelling to cover, which took up most of the conversation as they sat around the patio table in the large, shaded garden, and although she would never admit it to him, listening to the journey he had been on kept her interest.

She knew he had travelled around Europe and also that he had spent some time in the US before heading down to South Africa, but she didn't realise he had visited some of Asia and South America too. And she'd assumed he had been staying in five-star hotels, living the high life, when in reality he had mostly been working.

That surprised her. It wasn't as if money was a problem for him and the Zac she remembered had expensive taste and liked an easy life.

But no, he had tended bars, worked on farms, and for the last two years he had been part of a conservation team, helping with the scaling and upkeep of the savannas and shrublands. And that was why he was now back here. He was taking a job as a ranger on the Norfolk Broads, the series of rivers and waterways that ran through the county. A hands-on role that would involve safety, education and maintenance.

It was far removed from the IT job he had quit before leaving and on a much lower pay grade, but she supposed it wasn't about the money. It seemed Zac had changed a fair bit in the time he was away.

It also meant he was planning on staying in Norfolk.

What would happen with his apartment now he was back?

It affected her in the short term, but what about Dexter and Mark? Zac's decision to return was going to have a far bigger impact on them. Surely he wouldn't want to live there with the two of them, and Dexter wasn't going to like that scenario either.

Would Zac force him out? Dexter loved where he lived.

He knew Zac was back. Perhaps they had already discussed it. Though, if so, Dexter had given no indication of what decision had been reached.

Nina was so caught up worrying about her brother, she didn't at first hear the conversation change topic. Her ears pricked up, though, as she heard Michael's name mentioned, the forkful of potato salad she had speared pausing midway to her mouth.

'Hasn't she told you?' Aurora was answering a question Zac had asked, and all eyes turned in Nina's direction.

She didn't need to be a genius to work out what question had been asked or what it was she hadn't told him, and as her mother proceeded to give the full details of Michael's proposal,

Nina's decision to end their relationship, and how it was all a terrible shame, Nina's cheeks glowered.

At first, she tried to put across her side of things, asking why her mother thought she should marry a man she wasn't in love with, but years of experience had taught her she was wasting her time arguing with Aurora Fairchild, and eventually she fell quiet, regretting her decision to drive, and wishing she could pour herself a glass of the red wine she had brought.

Thankfully, her mother didn't mention that she had offered for Nina to move back home, which was one small grace, as it would have given Zac the perfect opportunity to throw her out of his apartment. It didn't stop her scowling at him across the table, though, and she would have kicked him if his leg had been in reach. Not that it was his fault. He hadn't done anything wrong. He just always seemed to bring out this side of her.

He didn't really make much comment on her break-up, which surprised her a little, and on the occasions he glanced in Nina's direction, his expression was unreadable. That threw her too. She had expected him to gloat at her mess of a life. After all, he had the perfect opportunity.

It was unsettling and she found herself zoning out of the rest of the lunch.

* * *

The journey back into the city was uncomfortable and Nina's shoulders were tight with tension, her hands gripping the wheel, as she waited for Zac to say something about her leaving the apartment. He didn't, instead mostly looking at his phone, as, outside the car, black clouds gathered. They had been lucky with the weather and it had stayed dry all afternoon, but now the promised storm was looming, the sky darkening by the second and suiting Nina's mood. It was still uncomfortably humid and she had cranked the air-con up as high as it would go.

'You need to tell him you're back for good,' she blurted, finally pulling into the complex car park and into one of the two allocated spaces.

Zac glanced up, looking confused by her sudden outburst. 'Sorry?'

'You need to tell Dex you want the apartment. He loves living here, and he and Mark are happy. Now you're back and you're going to ruin everything for them.' Nina's tone was accusatory. Although she was worried about her brother, her last sentence was unnecessary and mean, but she couldn't help it. She was still smarting from having her relationship dragged over the coals and Zac, who she blamed for bringing the subject up, was an easy target.

She watched as his expression went from surprised to carefully neutral.

'Why would you assume I haven't already spoken to him?' he asked coolly.

'You have?' So why hadn't Dexter said anything?

'Honestly, it's none of your business anyway, Nina. And regardless of how much your brother likes living here, it's my apartment. I can do what I want with it.'

Shaking his head in irritation, Zac opened the car door and got out, leaving Nina open-mouthed.

He was right. Of course he was. And it might seem unfair on Dexter, but this place did belong to Zac. All she had managed to achieve with her little rant was to piss him off.

Nice going, Nina.

Unsure if she still had somewhere to sleep tonight, she

quickly followed after him, struggling to keep up with his long-legged stride.

She should apologise for jumping to conclusions and for the nasty comment she had made about him coming home and ruining everything. She knew she should, but the words were stuck in her throat.

Instead, they walked in silence across the car park towards the courtyard gardens that led to the apartment blocks, as the first rumble of thunder sounded overhead.

Spotting two figures on the path ahead of them, Nina's eyes widened.

One of them was penthouse man, but the woman he was with, although blonde, wasn't who he had been with last night. They were talking and the man looked frustrated, while the woman kept touching his arm each time she spoke. Was she his girlfriend? Wife, even? Had he been cheating on her last night?

Hearing approaching footsteps, they both paused their conversation, glancing towards Nina and Zac.

Penthouse man nodded towards them, then smiled in recognition. 'Hey, I know you.'

Did he remember Nina from when they had passed on the bridge or had he seen her on the balcony spying on him?

Panic skittered through her before she realised he wasn't looking at her. He was addressing Zac, the two of them now shaking hands.

Nina listened as they spoke, realising they had a shared past. Penthouse man was familiar with Zac's late parents from how they spoke, though had no idea they had passed away, and he offered his condolences, before introducing the woman who was with him, who was eagerly hanging on to every word.

'This is Tabitha,' he told them both, and the woman smiled, though it slipped at his next words. 'She works for my dad.'

It was clear Tabitha didn't like that description of their relationship.

Zac didn't bother introducing Nina, pointedly ignoring her as she stood by his side, even though penthouse man and Tabitha were looking at her, so she decided to do it for him.

'I'm Nina,' she said, thrusting out her hand. She didn't expand on her relationship to Zac, and he said nothing either. She could tell penthouse man was curious, though, by the way his gaze lingered on her face in a mildly flirtatious way.

Tabitha noticed too and didn't seem happy. She had been introduced as an employee of his father's, but the way she kept looking at him suggested he was more to her than that. Were they involved? Lovers, perhaps? There was definitely something going on between them.

Nina was picking up on a vibe that Tabitha was more into penthouse man than he was into her. He definitely hadn't been thinking about her last night, she recalled, the image of him yanking his companion's skirt down before taking her roughly from behind etched in her mind.

Her cheeks burned. He had no idea she had been watching him and it felt wrong standing here having a conversation with him after witnessing what he had been up to. She was glad when moments later heavy spots of rain splashed down and, realising the downpour was imminent, they said their goodbyes.

Things were uncomfortable with Zac and she knew he was annoyed with her, but Nina's curiosity got the better of her as they headed into their building, wanting to know who penthouse man was.

'I didn't realise you knew him,' she said.

Zac pressed the button for the lift and for a moment she didn't think he was going to answer her, but then he shot her a look and she could tell from his narrowed gaze that his interest was piqued too. 'Why? Do you?'

'I've seen him about,' she admitted, though didn't elaborate in what capacity or that she knew he occupied the top-floor apartment. 'I don't know his name, though.'

Zac didn't speak again until they were in the lift and Nina wondered if he thought she was interested in penthouse man. Not that it was any of his business.

'He's Julian Wiseman. His father owns this building.'

Wiseman Homes. They were a well-known developer around East Anglia, the region that comprised Norfolk and its surrounding counties, and Nina had often seen Kevin Wiseman's name in the local press.

So penthouse man was called Julian and his dad owned Wiseman Homes. Interesting. It certainly explained why he had the flashy top-floor apartment.

'So how do you know him?' she asked, keen to find out if they were friends or passing acquaintances.

'Through our parents. They were in the same social circle and I used to sometimes get dragged to along to the events they organised, as did Julian. He's a few years older than me, though. I don't know him that well. I've seen him maybe twice since we were kids.'

The lift pinged and the doors opened on the fifth floor.

As Nina followed Zac out into the hallway, silence fell between them again and awkwardness had her wringing her hands together as she waited for him to unlock the door, not liking to pull her own key out since she was now technically his guest until he decided otherwise.

'I'm sorry for what I said in the car.'

The words she had tried to find for an apology suddenly came tumbling out, surprising them both.

She did regret what she had said to him, but right now she was worried about where she might sleep tonight. She didn't want him to say she couldn't stay.

Whatever animosity there was between them, here in the city was an infinitely better option than staying with her parents.

Zac acted as if he hadn't heard her, pushing the door open and stepping into the dark hallway. Outside, the downpour had started, heavy rain pounding the windows, and he flipped on the light switch, instantly brightening the space, before waiting for Nina to follow so he could close the door.

'If this is about you keeping Dex's room until he's back, it's fine, it's yours,' he said, once they were both inside.

'No, of course it's not...' Nina trailed off as he gave her a withering look and rolled his eyes.

'Save your apologies until you mean them, okay?' he suggested.

Patronising git. She opened her mouth to tell him that, then closed it again. He had seen right through her. Best to not push it as he was letting her stay.

'Thank you,' she managed, trying not to choke on the words, even as relief sagged her shoulders.

'I was always going to let you stay, you know,' Zac said, mellowing as he headed through to the kitchen and scooped up Hannibal, who was on the counter waiting for his dinner. 'And, for the record, I think you did the right thing breaking up with Michael. I never thought he was right for you.'

'You didn't?' Nina was surprised he even had an opinion about it.

'He's a bit dull, Nina.'

Zac thought that? She had thought she wasn't on his radar enough for anything about her to matter to him.

When they had been kids, it had bothered her that he was

only interested in hanging out with Dexter. She had tried so desperately to join in, hating that Zac always wanted to exclude her, but then, over the years, she had found her own group of friends.

She became closer with Dexter as they grew into adulthood and that was good, because he was her brother and mattered. As for Zac Green, she didn't care what the hell he thought.

But he had noticed Michael and he thought she could do better.

'He's a good person,' she said now, feeling the need to defend her ex-boyfriend, even if things weren't great between them at the moment.

'I'm sure he is,' Zac agreed. 'But good isn't enough of a reason to spend the rest of your life with someone.'

Nina chewed over his words as she fed the cat, surprised that for once she was in agreement with him. For now, they had reached a truce of sorts, but given that they could both be hot-headed, there was no guarantee how long that would last.

The rain had already stopped, the heavy shower passing quickly and the thunderstorm they needed to clear the air having amounted to nothing. Deciding she would go for a swim to burn off some of the calories she had eaten, Nina grabbed her towel and costume and headed down to the leisure centre in the opposite block.

As she crossed the courtyard gardens that separated the two buildings, there were a few puddles on the ground, but they were already drying; evidence of the sudden rain storm disappearing as quickly as it had arrived.

She glanced up at the penthouse suite, but there was no sign of Julian or Tabitha. They must be inside.

Movement below the penthouse caught her attention and

she realised there was someone on the balcony in the apartment. The apartment, she realised, where the man had seen her spying.

Zac's sudden appearance last night had distracted her and she hadn't given the man much thought, but now she did, and although he was five floors up, she could see his shiny bald head as he peered over the balcony and, she realised, he was waving.

At her?

Nina glanced around, certain it must be at someone else, but she was the only one on the pathway.

Did that mean he recognised her from last night?

She had hoped the binoculars and the fact it was dark might have helped hide her identity and didn't like how vulnerable it made her feel.

Was he really expecting her to wave back?

Ducking her head, her cheeks heating, she hurried into the building and down the stairs towards the leisure club.

She hadn't been the only one spying on people. This man had been watching his neighbours too, so really it was tit for tat. Still, that didn't really make her feel any better.

He hadn't been the one watching Julian Wiseman having noisy, rough sex, though – and given that his balcony was directly below, this man must have realised what Nina was watching.

What if he was friends with Julian? They lived in the same building, so it was quite possible they knew each other.

If he told Julian what had happened last night, how would he react?

Stupid, Nina.

She should have minded her own business.

Embarrassed that she had been caught out and a little

panicky that there could be grave consequences if Julian ever found out what she had done, she decided she would start looking at rentals first thing in the morning.

11

As personal assistant to Kevin Wiseman, one of the most successful businessmen in the region of East Anglia, Tabitha Percy took her role very seriously.

He might be her godfather as well as her boss, and almost like a second father to her, but she had worked hard to earn this role and knew she had more to prove because of their personal connection. She had heard the whispers that she had been favoured, but, truthfully, she knew she was the best-qualified person for the job and she went over and above every single day, taking care of her business duties, running errands that were outside of her remit and making sure she was there for Kevin's son, Julian.

He was on her mind as she drove out of the city, having dropped him off after the garden party, heading back to her home in Newton Flotman. The three-bed property was set on the outskirts of the village and was far smaller than the house where she had grown up, but it was all hers and at forty-one she was mortgage free. She was proud of that fact, despite her father joking about it being a shoebox. It wasn't and Tabitha looked after her home. It was a sanctuary to come back to after working hard all day. She just wished she had someone to share it with.

No, correction. Not just someone. She wanted Julian and no one else.

She had been worried about him since his return to the UK and she knew his parents were too. It had been Kevin's idea to send him overseas – a decision which, at the time, had broken Tabitha's heart. She knew Julian had seen it as his father banishing him as a punishment, and yes, there had been anger at the press intrusion, but, truthfully, Kevin was worried about him. They all were.

Julian had always been close with his mother, Jemima, and he had a healthily competitive relationship with his younger brother, James. As for Kevin, Tabitha knew he cared deeply about his son. When it came to business, Kevin was shrewd to the point of ruthlessness, but he had never known how to deal with his firstborn, alternating between frustration and throwing money at him.

Tabitha knew he had hoped that five years away would be enough time for Julian to straighten his life out and for the scandal that had rocked their family to die down. Instead, Julian had returned impulsive and self-destructive, and even almost a year after coming home, he was an empty shell of the man Tabitha remembered.

If she was honest with herself, she had witnessed moments of cruelty in his behaviour which had shocked her.

They had once been close; childhood friends who had become lovers, but then Julian had been arrested on suspicion of murder, and from that moment on everything had changed. It was a story that had rocked the country. Bride murdered on her wedding day. Son of wealthy businessman, who had been having an affair with her, found covered in her blood.

Of course he was innocent. When the time of Katy Spencer's death had been established, Tabitha's alibi had proven Julian couldn't have killed her. The police had been forced to accept the truth, that he had stumbled upon the gruesome scene when Katy was already dead. At the time, Tabitha had wondered if the detectives thought she was lying to protect him, but thankfully one of the groundsmen at the hotel had then been arrested and they realised Julian had nothing to do with the murder.

Still, the reverberations of that day would never leave them and it stung learning that Julian had some deeply serious flaws. Tabitha had been his date and the wedding was supposed to be one of the social events of the year. Instead, Julian's life had been ripped apart and Tabitha – who had truly believed her relationship with him was finally becoming more serious – had learnt the truth about the man she was in love with. That he had already given his heart to someone else.

The shock and betrayal when she discovered he had been having an affair with Katy had floored her, along with everyone else. She had been made to look a fool, as had Katy's husband-to-be, Hugh, who also happened to be one of Julian's friends, and Tabitha was ashamed to admit that – before the groundsman was arrested – there had been a moment when she had considered going back to the police and telling them she had lied. That she hadn't been with Julian when Katy died. He should suffer for what he had done, but when it came down to it, she didn't have it in her to hang him out to dry, so she had stood by him then, just as she stood by him now.

An ocean had separated them for too long. Now he was back and the realisation that she was still desperately in love with him, that no other man would ever come close, had almost knocked her sideways.

Okay, so he hadn't reacted in the way she had hoped, but the old Julian was still there. She knew it. He had been through a lot and this new reckless and colder side to him was because he had put up walls.

She could break them down. It would just take a little time.

Patience was key. He would eventually realise they were meant for each other.

That's what Tabitha had told herself today at the garden party as she'd painted on a bright smile and mingled with the guests, relieved the rainstorm which had threatened to derail the event had held off until after it was finished.

It had been purely a social event for her and there was no work to do, as the garden party was Jemima's project and she always took care of everything, but it never hurt to put on a business face.

Despite being tired and grumpy on the ride over to his parents' house, Julian had managed to put on a civil if subdued performance at the party. There were no sharp words between him and Kevin and he had dutifully mingled with his father's guests. That had been a relief to Tabitha, as she knew his mood could have ruined everything.

Still, it had dismayed her how many times Julian had tried to sneak away from her. At one point, she had even caught him seeking sanctuary with his mother's best friend, Grace.

Tabitha had never been able to get the measure of that one. She knew Grace had been married and divorced twice, but apart from that she was a mystery. Old-school, but glamorous, with a sleek, dark bob and cat's eyes that followed you everywhere, she had this unnerving way of making you think she knew all of your secrets. And despite being a woman who seemed very comfortable in her own skin, she was always dressed for winter. Even today, on one of the hottest days of the year, she had been wearing all black, with a polo-neck collar and long sleeves.

Tabitha wasn't a fan, if she was honest, but Grace was almost a second mother to Julian, so she made the effort. It was just a shame that Julian couldn't return the favour. It was as if he was embarrassed to be seen in her company and that had stung more than his insistence she return the spare key to the maintenance room before she left after dropping him off.

Did he not trust her?

Although she had promised she would return it, the key was still in her purse for now. Having it there made her feel a little bit closer to him.

She understood the penthouse apartment was currently his home and that she didn't live there, but it was his father's property and Julian wasn't paying any rent. Besides, it wasn't as though Tabitha hadn't seen him naked. They had been as intimate as two people could be.

It made her wonder what other secrets he might be hiding.

12

Over the week that followed, Nina gradually settled into life at River Heights.

She hadn't seen anything more of Julian's downstairs neighbour and with each day that passed she hoped to put the encounter behind her, and despite their differences, she and Zac had quickly settled into something of a routine. Zac made himself scarce during the day, meaning Nina was able to concentrate on work, for which she was appreciative, and during the evenings, if they were both at home, she tended to watch TV in her room to give him space.

Still, she had registered on the books of every rental agency in Norwich and had been to view a handful of properties. None of them had been right, but at least she was actively looking.

Dexter and Mark had arrived safely in Hong Kong and her brother appeared to be having the time of his life, declaring his love for Mark's welcoming family, as he and Nina WhatsApped, and telling her they were planning a few days in Vietnam.

She had grumbled about the Zac situation initially, but Dexter had pointed out that Zac hadn't given him specific dates for his return. He seemed as surprised as she was that he was back so soon and when he called her, worrying she was annoyed at him, Nina had felt bad.

Yes, it wasn't an ideal situation, but it was only until the end of August, and it wasn't Dexter's fault. She didn't want to ruin his holiday, so she resolved not to mention Zac again.

To be fair to Zac, he had been a considerate housemate, and he surprised her when neither of them had plans on Saturday night, by offering to make her dinner.

Okay, that was perhaps exaggerating it a bit. It was a last-minute invitation as he had overbought on ingredients. It was either feed Nina or struggle to find room in the overpacked freezer. Still, she appreciated the gesture.

Deciding that if he was sharing his food with her, she should make an effort to join him in the kitchen, she poured herself a glass of wine, offering Zac one too, though he was happy with his beer.

'It will just be another five minutes. Okay?'

'Yes, that's fine.' Nina took her drink to the table, which he had already set, and sat down.

The TV was showing *Sky News* and she would have preferred to have music playing instead, but Zac seemed to have one eye on the headlines, while adding the finishing touches to his dish and making small talk with her, so she didn't say anything.

He served the food, joining her at the table as she took her first bite, and she had to stop herself from making a yum noise. The fusion of flavours worked perfectly together. Chilli adding a kick to the rich cheese sauce, and was that lemon she could taste?

'How is it?' he asked, winding his fork into the linguine.

'Really good,' Nina admitted. 'I didn't realise you could cook.'

'I have a lot of talents you don't know about.'

He winked at her and grinned, and it was probably just the chilli flakes she had watched him sprinkle liberally into the pan, but her skin suddenly heated up despite the air-con.

She had never thought of Zac Green as anything other than Dexter's annoying friend, but now she grudgingly admitted that the time away had refined him. He had always looked a little bit geeky, but over the last four years, his face had matured, and fine lines and stubble now added an edge of roughness that seemed to complement his clear sea-green eyes.

Seeing his attention was on the news, she snuck another look, this time lingering.

Yes, he was now a man who women – other women – *might* find attractive.

Not her of course, because Zac would always be an irritant, no matter how much he had changed, but if she had any single friends, she might have considered trying to hook them up.

His gaze had narrowed now and he stopped eating, fully focused on the news.

Nina glanced at the TV, where the story of a missing woman in Norwich was being covered. Police divers were searching the River Wensum in the area where the woman was last seen, as initial suspicions were that she might have fallen in.

As the screen changed to show the face of the woman who had vanished, Nina swallowed the wrong way, choking on a prawn, and Zac's attention flipped back to her, his eyes widening.

'Are you okay?'

She managed a nod, eyes watering as she continue to cough and splutter, and he disappeared from the table, returning moments later with a glass of water, which she took gratefully.

After a few sips, she swapped it for her wine glass and downed the alcohol.

She pointed to the woman on the TV screen, the one who had disappeared and whose name was printed below her image. Peyton Landis. 'I know her.'

Zac stared at her. 'You do?'

Well, not know exactly, but Nina had certainly seen plenty of her.

She thought back to the previous weekend when she had been spying on the residents of the opposite apartment block. The blonde woman who had been in the penthouse apartment with Julian Wiseman.

She was now missing.

There was no doubt in Nina's mind it was the same woman.

Did Julian know she had vanished? Nina was still unsure what his relationship was with Peyton. If she was his girlfriend, he was going to be worried.

Ignoring Zac who was still waiting for an answer, she focused on the newscaster's voice, picking up snippets of the story.

'Out for a meal with friends.'

'Went to catch a taxi.'

'No one has seen her since Saturday night.'

Was that when she went missing? The night Nina had been watching?

Had Julian Wiseman been the last person to see Peyton Landis alive?

A dark thought crept towards her subconscious. Had Peyton Landis ever left the penthouse apartment?

No. Stop it. What she was thinking was ridiculous. She didn't even know Julian Wiseman. She had no right to assume he was involved in the woman's disappearance and the newscaster had said the police thought the woman might have fallen in the river. If she had, that was an accident, nothing sinister.

'Earth to Nina.'

Zac clicked his fingers in front of her and, focusing on the TV again, she realised the story had changed.

'You said you know her, the woman who's missing. Is she a friend of yours?'

'Not exactly,' Nina murmured, putting her fork down in her bowl. Suddenly her appetite was gone.

'So who is she then?' he pushed.

This was getting awkward and she inwardly cursed her big mouth for blurting out that she recognised Peyton. What she had been doing, spying on the neighbours, was wrong. She should never have been privy to what had happened on that balcony.

But she had been and now she was potentially one of the last people to see Peyton Landis before she vanished.

'I, um, I saw her with Julian Wiseman.'

'You did? When?'

'Last weekend.'

Zac's eyes widened. 'When she went missing?'

'Yes.' Nina didn't elaborate where.

He was silent for a moment. 'You're sure it was definitely her?'

Oh yes. Nina had seen Peyton Landis in great detail and the memory of what she had witnessed was still etched in her brain.

'Yes,' she repeated, a little more impatiently.

Why was Zac looking at her like he was doubtful.

'So where did you see them?' he asked after a moment, and Nina fell quiet.

She had known she would have to come clean, but how bad

was it going to look that she had been spying on the other residents?

When he arched an eyebrow, waiting, and looking more and more by the second like he was starting to doubt her, she blurted the truth out.

'There was a power cut before you arrived back and I was bored, so I got Mark's binoculars. I only meant to look out at the city and see what was going on, but then I realised the lights were back on in the other block.' She paused for breath and could see now that she had his interest. Not wanting to admit that she had still been watching after the blackout had ended, she left out that little detail.

'So you were spying on them in Julian's apartment?'

He made it sound so sordid.

'Do you think she's his girlfriend?' Nina asked, dodging the question.

'Are you sure it was her?'

'Of course I'm sure. I watched them, you know... They were being intimate.'

The moment the sentence was out, her cheeks heated.

'You were spying on people having sex?' Zac asked, amused.

'I didn't mean to.'

'Well, you could have stopped watching, Nina,' he jokingly chided.

She ignored his comment, aware it already sounded bad enough. 'I need to tell the police, don't I?'

Zac studied her for a moment and she could tell he was taking his time picking the right words. 'You do, as long as you're absolutely certain it *was* Peyton Landis?' he asked.

'You already asked me that and I said yes!'

'I know. I just need you to be sure before you involve the police. If you have the wrong person—'

'I don't have the wrong person. Besides, if Julian has done nothing wrong, why hasn't he spoken to the police himself?'

'You don't know that he hasn't,' Zac pointed out. 'How do you know he hasn't been cleared from their enquiries?'

'But he was with her.' Nina fell silent. 'I have to tell them what I witnessed. She's missing.'

'As long as you're certain beyond a reasonable doubt that it was Peyton.'

Nina tried not to take offence at his hesitancy. 'Why are you so unwilling to believe what I saw?' she asked, trying to keep her temper in check.

It was a valid question, but Zac huffed a little as he answered. 'I never said I didn't believe you.' He paused. 'Look, this is about Julian, not you.'

'I'm aware of that.'

'A few years ago he was a suspect in a murder case.'

'What?' Nina's eyes widened. 'Well then, I definitely need to tell them if he's already killed someone.'

'No, he didn't kill anyone, but he had been having an affair with the victim. He was eventually released without charge and the police realised one of the groundsmen who worked for the hotel was guilty, but the press had a field day. You must remember it. Katy Spencer, the bride who was murdered on her wedding day?'

Yes, Nina did. It had been a huge news story. Katy had been bludgeoned to death with a shovel and when she was found, she was in her wedding dress. Nina remembered reading that a man had been arrested and then released, but she hadn't really paid attention to the details of who he was.

'That was Julian?' It would explain why he was wary.

'I heard it's why he moved to the US,' Zac said. 'To get away from the negative publicity.'

'Jesus. I had no idea.'

'Which is why you need to be certain of what you saw. The police seem convinced she's fallen in the river. Don't bring trouble to his door and make them think otherwise unless you're absolutely certain it was Peyton Landis in his apartment.'

Zac's scepticism was making Nina start to doubt herself and it didn't help that she had been spying. If she went to the police, what would they make of that? Would she be in trouble?

Perhaps she should stay quiet and see if Julian came forward of his own accord. If Zac was right and there was an innocent explanation, she didn't want to cause trouble for him.

She fell silent as she ate the rest of her meal, the pasta which had started off tasting delicious now sitting heavy in her stomach.

Zac didn't push the subject and she suspected that deep down he was wondering if she had it wrong. Instead, he continued to eat, one eye on the news and making small talk, to which Nina gave monosyllabic answers.

Finally, after pushing the last few mouthfuls of food around her plate, she gave up and set her fork down.

'Are you done with that?' he asked, starting to get up.

'You cooked, I can clear,' Nina told him, getting up from the table abruptly and picking up both of their plates.

After washing everything up, she went through to her bedroom and changed into her pyjama bottoms and an old T-shirt. Hannibal had settled himself on the bed and yawned lazily as she tickled him under his chin.

'What should I do?' she asked him, knowing deep down that it had been Peyton she saw. She could be hampering the investigation if she didn't say anything.

And besides, Peyton wasn't dead, she was missing. What if she was alive somewhere and relying on someone finding her?

Nina had to do the right thing and report what she had seen to the police.

Wandering back through to the living room for her phone, she looked to the open patio door. Zac was outside leant against the railing and she realised he was looking at the other apartment block with Mark's binoculars.

Hearing her approach, he lowered them and turned to face her.

'What are you doing?' she asked, even though it was pretty obvious exactly what he was up to.

'These give a pretty clear view into the apartments,' he commented without answering her question.

'I know. You can see everything.'

Zac was silent as he raised the binoculars again.

'Are you 100 per cent certain it was her?' he asked eventually.

Nina nodded solemnly. 'Yes. I watched them out on the balcony. They weren't exactly discreet and I had a clear view of Peyton Landis's face and what she was wearing. Whether he's innocent or not, I have to tell the police.'

This time, he didn't try to stop her. Instead he nodded.

'Okay.'

13

They always have hope at first.

Even with the odds against them, they truly believe they will figure out a way to get free. Perhaps I will take mercy on them and let them go, or they will manage to somehow escape.

As the days pass, that hope slowly evaporates. Muscles ache from where limbs are held in place, sores begin to bleed where rope rubs against skin. As the body weakens, the days become longer, the agony of their ordeal more intense.

I am stripping back the layers. Exposing the ugliness that hides beneath their perfect flesh.

Towards the end, they are begging to die, but as much as I despise them, I am not a murderer. Well, not since that first time.

But a person can atone, right?

Instead, I talk to them and I clean up their mess, and I let nature take its course.

As I unlock the door now and step inside, Peyton barely raises her head and I know the time is near. She has been here a week and it has been three days since she begged me for release. That's three days without food or water.

She sits and waits, tied to the chair in the middle of the room, and her face is gaunt, her lips parched and dark shadows haunt her eyes. In the early days, they were red raw from crying, but now she barely makes a sound.

I pull up a stool and sit before her, studying her, fascinated by this process. I am not a murderer, but I do have a rage inside me that has to be satisfied. The pain I inflict cannot be helped, but I am honest with them from the start when they wake up here.

They can fight to stay alive, but I will punish and torment, both physically and psychologically. Not enough to kill, but I make sure they are in constant pain and fearing what comes next.

I will also ensure they are fed and watered, because I am not a monster.

No one goes hungry under this roof.

Well, until they decide they've had enough. When the suffering becomes too much and the hope has faded inside of them. When they finally understand I am never going to let them go and they plead with me to let them die, that is when everything stops.

No more torture, only kindness, but no more food or water either.

I lean forward and touch Peyton's knee, and she flinches slightly, her bare toes with their chipped nail polish scrunching against the plastic sheeting beneath the chair.

'Not long now,' I tell her, watching a single teardrop slide down her cheek. 'It will be over tonight.'

When we met, she had shown herself to be a desperate whore. She had been so pathetically grateful when I said I would drive her home, completely unaware of the horror that awaited her. Now she is nothing more than a meat-coated skeleton waiting for the end.

It's exactly as it should be.

14

The police had taken Nina seriously when she called them first thing Sunday morning, sending two detective constables out to take her statement. DCs Wilson and Broom were both younger than her and very sombre, neither cracking a smile during their visit. Wilson had asked her a lot of questions, while his colleague typed onto his laptop. Their expressions remained neutral when Nina had cringed, confessing to spying on her neighbours.

Zac had gone out, so it was just the three of them. Well, apart from Hannibal, who decided to join them and kept trying to climb onto DC Wilson's lap. She suspected he wasn't a cat person as he kept ignoring the Ragdoll and, after apologising and removing Hannibal half a dozen times, Nina had eventually locked Hannibal in her bedroom.

She had shown the detectives the binoculars, watching as Wilson stood on the balcony and used them to view the other block of apartments. Then Broom had asked her to read through the statement he had been typing, before they both left, thanking her for her time and telling her they would be investigating further.

A short while later, she spotted them from the balcony window, crossing the courtyard towards Julian's apartment block.

Nina needed to go out. She had been invited to lunch at Rachel's and would be late if she didn't leave now. She couldn't leave, though, until she found out what was happening.

She fired off a quick message, apologising that she was running a little behind, figuring Rach would understand, then turned her attention back to Julian's apartment. She wanted to use the binoculars, but didn't dare, so instead she watched his building like a hawk and waited.

Were the detectives speaking with him right now?

Despite knowing she had seen him be intimate with Peyton Landis on the night the woman had vanished, guilt stabbed her. She had spied on a private moment and it was possible the encounter she had witnessed had been entirely innocent. What if he had nothing to do with Peyton's disappearance?

But then, if that was true, he would have already come forward and spoken to the police, telling them he had been with her that night. Nina had read all of the articles she could find online. Peyton had last been seen on CCTV in the city. Julian's silence was too suspicious.

Eventually, the two detectives emerged from the building, but, to her surprise, they were alone. They must have spoken with Julian, so why hadn't they arrested him? She had expected to see them take him away in handcuffs.

The ping of her phone was a noisy distraction as she watched them cross the complex, heading towards the maintenance room, and glancing at the screen, she saw she had a message from Rachel.

> Are you on your way? I need to dish up dinner.

Realising she was now over half an hour late, Nina guiltily replied.

> Yes, be there ASAP. Xx

She didn't want to piss Rachel off. Her friends were already annoyed that they had found out about her break-up via Michael. Apparently, he had told Kyle when they were at the gym, who, of course, had told Tori, and the news had quickly made its way around the rest of their group.

Grabbing her bag and keys, she let herself out of the apartment.

There was no sign of the detectives as she crossed the courtyard, but the door to the maintenance room was ajar, so she assumed they were inside.

It was just as she had turned on her engine that she spotted Julian. He was crossing the car park at a fast pace, a scowl on his face, and Nina's heart pounded, certain he was heading towards her car.

Did he know she was the one who had called the police?

But then he diverted his path, crossing to where a silver Porsche was parked and quickly climbing inside.

She let out a trembling breath of relief. For a moment there, she had thought he was going to confront her, and the enormity of what she had done hit her hard.

Julian wasted no time pulling out of the car park and steadying herself. Nina followed.

She was behind him at the lights, but then as they reached the next junction, they veered off in different directions, Julian speeding off into the distance. Wherever he was going, he was in a hurry to get there.

Nina wondered what the police had said to him. He hadn't looked happy.

Whatever he had said to them must have proven he was innocent. Knowing that brought a fresh wave of guilt and by the time she pulled into Rachel's drive, Nina was beating herself up, wishing she had never made the call.

* * *

Someone had told the police that Blondie had been in his apartment.

Although Julian hadn't been arrested, shock had reverberated through him when he saw the two detectives standing on his doorstep, and his stomach had dropped when they'd told him they would be back in touch if they had any further questions.

It had been such a stupid idea bringing the woman back here, but he had done it anyway. Now the police knew she was missing and he was on their radar.

After that night, he had tried his best to do some damage control, his first worry being that he and Blondie – or Peyton Landis, as he now knew she was called – had been caught on the complex security cameras. But, in what he had considered a stroke of luck, the cameras had been down thanks to the power cut.

At the time when it had happened, Julian had been royally pissed off. He had been on his Xbox when the screen went blank, and frustrated, he had headed straight down to the maintenance room to complain. That little twerp, Dylan, had been on the receiving end of his temper. It wasn't Dylan's fault, he knew that. He was just the gopher, but Julian needed someone to sound off to. How ironic that what had been an inconvenience then might now be his saving grace.

The regular blackouts across the complex always sent the shitty security system into a meltdown. Julian knew it was the bane of his father's life, but then that was what happened when you tried to cut costs.

After he had finally managed to get rid of Tabitha the following day, he had spent time going through the footage, making certain there was nothing of him and Peyton. No one ever questioned his motives when he went down into the maintenance room. He was the boss's son and they assumed he was keeping an eye on things for his father.

He had heaved out a huge sigh of relief when he'd realised the cameras hadn't been working all night.

So he was safe with the cameras and he hadn't bumped into any of his neighbours as they'd headed up to his apartment. But one of them had seen him.

Julian would put his money on it being that nosy fucker, Leonard, who lived on the floor below him. The old man was always lurking where he had no need to be. He must have seen Julian and Peyton as they crossed the courtyard.

This was bad, but it was Leonard's word against his, and in a moment of panic, Julian had lied to the police.

Telling them the truth wasn't even an option, so he had strongly denied bringing Peyton home with him. Yes, he had been in the Rooftop Gardens – no point in pretending he hadn't – but, no, he hadn't spoken to her. And if they checked the CCTV footage in the city, they would catch them on that one camera he knew was near the Maids Head Hotel, but not together. He had been careful about that.

He tried to be amenable, letting the detectives in to look

around, despite the fact they didn't have a search warrant, hoping to convince them he had nothing to hide.

Julian knew he couldn't be caught anywhere near this. His father had exiled him once. He wouldn't get another chance. So when they asked if there was someone who could vouch for his whereabouts, he had panicked.

A witness had claimed they had seen him with someone, so there was no point pretending he had been home alone. Thinking of the one person who was always desperate to please him, who wouldn't hang him out to dry, he had blurted out her name.

Tabitha Percy.

She was clingy and read too much into things, and mostly she annoyed the hell out of him, but he was in a real bind here and she had helped him before. Besides, he knew she had been on the complex that evening, helping the maintenance team as they sorted out the blackout. He had seen her on his way out, ducking behind a bush when she had glanced in his direction, not wanting the irritation of talking to her.

He'd told the police she had come up to his apartment after he'd returned home. Both Tabitha and Peyton were blonde – though that was where the similarities ended – so it was possible, he'd suggested, that whoever had seen them might have muddled the two women up.

He just hoped like hell she had gone straight home after leaving River Heights that night, because if anyone had seen her, he was going to be in a whole heap of trouble.

The police were going to check he was telling the truth, which meant he needed to get to her before they did. They were still on the complex at the moment and he had watched them go into the maintenance room, where no doubt they were talking to whoever was on duty and probably wanting to view the cameras.

Picking up his phone, he went to call Tabitha, but then had a light-bulb moment of realisation. It would look suspicious if there was a call log between them.

He would have to go over to her house.

The detectives hadn't told him he had to stay put and he was a busy man. There was nothing suspicious about him heading out; still, he moved quickly and discreetly, worried that if they spotted him they might follow.

As he raced over to her address in his Porsche, his mouth dry and sweat beading on his forehead, despite the car's ice-cold aircon, he hoped to hell that she was home.

* * *

'I've tried to keep everything warm,' Rachel told Nina as she opened the door, ushering her inside.

Nina hadn't thought she was hungry, but the aromas coming from the kitchen had her stomach rumbling. 'I'm sorry I'm late,' she apologised, as she followed Rachel into the kitchen, where her husband, Nick, and their five-year-old twins, Oscar and Lucas, were already seated at the table.

Conversation was light as they ate, but Nina was distracted by the morning events, and Rachel seemed to pick up on it. She waited until lunch was over, then sent Nick out to the park with the boys. Once they were gone, she gently probed as Nina helped her wash up.

'Are you having second thoughts about breaking up with Michael?' she asked, going down the wrong track. 'Tori and Kyle have said he misses you. It's not too late to go back.'

'God, no,' Nina blurted, her over-the-top reaction earning her a frown from her friend.

That's what Rachel thought was on her mind?

Truthfully, Nina hadn't thought much about Michael at all over the last few days, which was a sure sign that they shouldn't be together. Still, she softened her reaction. 'I'm not in love with him any more, Rach. And he deserves someone who loves him back.'

Of her three friends, Rachel was the most understanding that she wanted to move on. Tori could only see how their break-up affected their little friendship circle, while Charlotte had always been a big Michael fan. He was steady and secure, and she didn't get why Nina no longer wanted to be with him.

'Are you still staying in Dexter's apartment?' Rachel asked.

Nina nodded. 'Till the end of August.'

'And what will you do then?'

Honestly, she still didn't know. She had been looking for an affordable rental, but properties were being snapped up as soon as they came on the market.

'I'm keeping an eye open for somewhere.'

Rachel was thoughtful for a moment. 'My cousin, Chris, has a few rental properties. Do you want me to have a word and see if he has anything free?'

'Yes. Please.' Nina would take anywhere, as long as she could afford it. 'I'd really appreciate that.'

'Consider it done,' Rachel said, putting plates and cutlery away, while Nina scrubbed at a baking tray. 'So,' she asked lightly, 'if it's not Michael playing on your mind, what is it? I've never seen you as quiet as you were over dinner. Even Nick looked surprised.'

Nina managed a laugh and tried to shrug off her mood. She hadn't planned on saying anything about Julian Wiseman; too embarrassed that she had spied. Rachel could tell something was up, though, and Nina knew she wouldn't let up until she finally found out what was going on.

'I might have got someone in trouble with the police,' she eventually admitted, before the whole story about how she had watched Julian and Peyton have sex came out, and how she had called the police.

Of her friends, Rachel could sometimes be the most straight-laced and Nina expected her to take a reproachful tone. Instead, she surprised her.

'As we're talking about Julian Wiseman, it wouldn't shock me at all if he was involved in that woman's disappearance. I've never liked him.'

'You know him?' Nina asked, surprised.

'My dad worked for Wiseman Homes for a while.'

'He did?' She knew Rachel's dad was a carpenter by trade, but hadn't realised he had worked for a big firm like Wiseman Homes.

Rachel nodded. 'He didn't like Kevin Wiseman much, but at least he was by the book. Julian was always swanning about, living off his dad's money and driving his fancy cars, looking down on everyone. There were plenty of rumours going around.'

'What kind of rumours?' Nina asked, curious.

'That he is an entitled brat who thinks he's above the law, and that he can be a bit of a pervert.'

'Really?' Nina's eyes widened.

'Remember, this is all hearsay,' Rachel pointed out. 'I'm only going by what Dad said and we're talking a long while ago.'

Shit.

Nina thought back to the first time she had seen Julian, when they had passed on the bridge. At the time, she had fancied him, but that first impression had quickly changed when she had seen how selfish he had been with Peyton.

'And you know about Katy Spencer?' Rachel asked.

Nina nodded, remembering what Zac had told her. 'The police released him without charge, I thought.'

'They did, and someone else was charged with her murder, but I know I'm not the only who wondered if he was really guilty.' Rachel shrugged. 'He moved away shortly after that, and who knows, maybe he has changed. I wouldn't bet on it, though.'

Learning of the reputation Julian had helped ease Nina's guilty conscience. Still, she was surprised the police hadn't taken him in for questioning.

Unless Peyton Landis had shown up safe and well, and the online news headlines had yet to be updated.

It was possible, she supposed, though deep down she didn't believe it.

15

Tabitha lived on the edge of the village of Newton Flotman, her modest house sitting on a mature plot surrounded by high hedgerows.

Relief eased some of Julian's tension when he spotted her Range Rover parked in the driveway, and he almost pulled to a halt behind it before common sense kicked in. Instead, he continued down the lane, pulling off the road down a woodland trail that offered privacy, then sprinted back to the house, aware he needed to talk to Tabitha then get the hell out of there in case the police showed up.

Standing on a doormat that read 'Please wipe feet and paws', he used the brass knocker to announce his arrival, tapping his foot impatiently as he waited for Tabitha to answer.

Seconds ticked by. He was sweating profusely now and although the warm day and his impromptu run didn't help, he knew it was mostly down to the urgency of the situation. The sickness churning in his belly was not helped by the strong sweet scent of the jasmine that was trailing up the walls of the house.

Where the fuck was she?

He rapped the knocker again, this time more aggressively.

In the distance, he could hear the sound of a car engine approaching.

Shit. Was it the police already?

If so, he was screwed.

He couldn't go to prison. The very thought of being behind bars had fear shuddering through him.

Just as he was debating whether he should hide, the door swung open. Tabitha wide-eyed in surprise. 'Julian? What are you doing here?'

She seemed in part flustered, but also delighted, and he didn't waste any time pushing her back into the house and stepping over the threshold, quickly shutting the door behind them.

Tabitha's brief look of shock quickly dissipated as she took in his appearance. 'What's wrong?'

She went to reach her hand to his face and Julian swatted it away.

'I need your help, Tabs.'

'Okay. Tell me what I can do.'

He went to speak, but for a moment struggled to breathe, the enormity of everything catching up with him. As he tried to gather himself, swallowing noisily, he shocked both of them by bursting into tears.

'Julian. You're scaring me.'

Tabitha tried to put her arms around him and he backed away, shaking his head. He already felt suffocated.

'Look, come through to the kitchen and let me get you a glass of water,' she offered.

'No, there's not time. I need to tell you.'

'Tell me what?'

'Last weekend, on the Saturday night, we were together.'

Her lips quirked. 'No, we weren't. The garden party was Sunday, remember?'

'No, Tabs. Listen to me. If anyone asks, we were together on Saturday night. I went out for a drink, but then you came over to my apartment about midnight.'

'But why?' She sounded worried. 'I don't understand? What's going on, Julian? That's not what happened.'

'Please, it has to be. They think it's me.'

'Who thinks what is you?'

'The police.' Julian's tears were falling harder now. Panic, he realised, at the mess he was in. 'They think I have something to do with that missing woman. I'm innocent. You believe me, don't you?'

Something akin to fear briefly crossed Tabitha's features. Was she doubting him? She had always been gullible and easily persuaded. He needed to be able to count on her support and in that moment he would offer her the world to have his back.

'Please, Tabitha. You're the only one I trust. The only one who has never let me down. If you help me, I will be in your debt forever.' He managed a smile, forcing himself to reach for her hand.

It seemed to do the trick. Although she still looked wary, he could see she was wavering.

'I think you need to sit down and tell me everything,' she told him, her cool fingers tightening around his clammy ones. 'I need you to be honest with me.'

There wasn't time for this charade, but he couldn't afford to piss her off, so Julian dutifully let himself be led into the kitchen, taking a seat at the table when instructed. His knees knocked together as he trembled, and while Tabitha busied herself putting on the kettle, he glanced around the room to try to distract himself.

It was a bright and airy space, and traditional in style. Cream shaker units and powder-blue walls gave it a country cottage feel. All of the accessories were bee related; they were on tea towels, utensil pots and also on the two mugs she took down, with the slogan 'Bee kind', while vases of flowers and green trailing plants adorned the windowsill and wall shelves, giving a homey feel. Everything in the room was cheerful and tidy. No clutter at all.

A sudden knock at the door had Julian almost falling off the chair.

He gulped for breath, looking to Tabitha for support, and for a moment she was frozen in place, her blue eyes ridiculously wide. But then she spurred into action, putting the mugs back in the cupboard and pulling him up from the chair.

'It might not be the police, but go wait upstairs in my bedroom, just in case.'

Would it not be better for him to sneak out of the back door?

He wanted to suggest that, but she was already pulling him into the hallway.

'Go,' she urged, turning him towards the staircase. 'I'll give you ten seconds to get settled before I answer.'

Another knock at the door had him scuttling up the steps, and he paused on the landing, trying to remember which one was her bedroom. He hadn't been here in a long time. One door was closed, but the others were open, and he could see a bathroom with slate blue walls, while the other two had beds in them. He took a chance on the larger one that was mostly pink. Floral wallpaper covered the wall behind a traditional wrought-iron bed that was covered in cushions. Yes, this was Tabitha's room.

Pushing the door closed, he went and sat on the bed. Down below, he heard the door open and Tabitha's far too loud and jolly greeting. Quickly ascertaining it was indeed the police, he clutched one of the cushions in his lap and squeezed the material between his fingers like a stress toy.

Please don't let her fuck this up.

It was too hot in the room and it felt like there was no air, but Julian didn't dare move from the bed, terrified of making any kind of sound in case they decided to come upstairs. Although he was pretty certain they would need a warrant for that, fear had him worrying irrationally.

They must have moved through to the kitchen, as, annoyingly, although he could still hear the noise of voices talking, they were no longer clear enough to make out the actual conversation, meaning he had no choice but to sit and wait, the silence of the room broken only by the perpetual ticking of an alarm clock.

Eventually, the voices grew louder again and he heard the front door open and close, then a few minutes later the sound of footsteps on the steps.

Had they gone? He thought so, though didn't dare move in case he was wrong.

His chest tightened as the doorknob turned. As Tabitha stepped into the room, her expression was unreadable.

'What did you tell them?' he demanded.

For a moment, she seemed distracted, staring at him sitting on her bed, an almost faraway look on her face, but then she gathered herself.

'It's okay, I said we were together last Saturday. That there's no way you could have been with anyone else.'

'Did they believe you?'

'Of course, silly. Why wouldn't they? The sex we had was mind-blowing, if they ask.'

She winked and her high-pitched peal of laughter that

followed had Julian unsure if she was joking or not, so he ignored the comment, swallowing down his irritation and reminding himself that she had just done him a huge favour.

He was impatient to leave, but aware that he needed to keep her sweet. It was also important to find out exactly what she had said to the police as their stories needed to be consistent, so he accepted her offer to finish making the tea, grilling her with questions as he followed her downstairs.

'Relax, Julian, it's going to be okay,' Tabitha assured him. 'You know you can always count on me. You secret is safe between you and me now.'

How the hell was he supposed to relax? Did she not realise the trouble he was in?

He thought back to that night with Peyton and how he had tried to walk away. He had known from the start that it wasn't a good idea, but even then, he hadn't realised quite how far things would spiral out of control.

If only he had been strong enough to say no.

Now this one mistake could haunt him forever.

* * *

After Nick and the twins returned from the park, Rachel made everyone ice cream cones and they sat in the garden, the boys splashing in the paddling pool, while the adults soaked up the heat of the late-afternoon sun. By the time Nina eventually left, she was stuffed full of food and certain she wouldn't be able to eat for another week.

Pulling into the car park back at River Heights, she could see a black Audi in one of the two spaces that belonged to Zac's apartment. She slid her car in beside it, wondering if it was a cheeky neighbour or if the Audi belonged to a friend of his.

Julian's Porsche was also back in its parking space and she crossed the courtyard keeping a wary eye out for him. Having given her witness statement to the police, she would feel uncomfortable if they bumped into one another, though, after what Rachel had told her, she had no regrets in doing so.

There was no sign of him, but another resident, an older man wearing a navy tracksuit, was exiting the leisure club. Spotting her, he deviated from his path, heading her way.

There was something familiar about him, but it wasn't until he was closer, grinning broadly at her, that she clocked who he was and her heart sank.

It was the man who lived below Julian, who had seen her spying.

'Well, hello, neighbour,' he greeted her, his tone jaunty.

'Hi.' She smiled back, deciding to play dumb as she went to continue past him.

'Bit of excitement we had here this morning, wasn't it? Not often the police come by to question us all.' When Nina didn't react, he added, 'Two detectives knocked on my door as I was making lunch, asking questions about that missing woman.'

'Were they?' Nina asked.

He narrowed his eyes at her, as if trying to decide if she was being on the level with him, and she inwardly squirmed. There was something about him that reminded her of her old maths teacher. Pleasant enough on the surface, but sneaky underneath. She had always felt like he was trying to wrong-foot her and catch her out.

'Of course, I had to tell them I didn't see a thing. I heard Mr Wiseman with a lady friend. Difficult not to when his balcony is right above mine and they were making so much noise, but I couldn't tell them who she was,' he continued. 'But you saw her, didn't you, missy?'

Nina's cheeks heated and she opened and closed her mouth. 'What?' she managed to squeak.

The man grinned and made Os with his thumbs and forefingers, raising them to his eyes to mimic binoculars. 'You're a nosy girl.'

He could talk. Remembering that she hadn't been the only one with binoculars, anger pushed her embarrassment to one side.

'Pot, kettle, black,' she snapped. 'You were spying on me too.'

'Watching you watching everyone else.' He seemed highly amused that he was pushing her buttons. 'I like to keep an eye on everyone. Call me the neighbourhood watch. I make no secret of it. But you, you like to spy on your neighbours. Watch them getting up to private things.'

'I do not!'

'You're the one who called the police, aren't you?'

He knew that? How the hell had he figured out it was her?

'I saw those detectives in your apartment this morning,' he told her, as if reading her mind. 'And you were on your balcony watching when they went upstairs to talk to Mr Wiseman. You gave him a bit of a headache, I tell you.'

Nina wasn't sure how to react. Should she cling to denial and tell him to mind his own business, or come clean and admit it was all true, then hope to hell he didn't tell Julian it had been her? At a loss of what to do, she stayed quiet.

'I know your type,' he said instead. 'I'll be adding you to my chart. Nosy girl in 5A.' He waggled white eyebrows at her. Beneath them, his blue irises were bright and alert. 'I'll be keeping my eye on you.'

She wasn't quite sure if he meant that as a threat or if this was just a game to him and for a moment she expected him to try to blackmail her. But then he was on his way, wishing her a good evening as if they had simply exchanged pleasantries, whistling as he crossed the courtyard.

Nina had no idea what to make of him.

Unsettled by the encounter, she headed upstairs, hoping like hell he didn't go blabbing to Julian about what she had done.

16

Zac could see Nina was rattled the moment she returned home.

He was lying on the sofa watching TV and, ignoring his hello, she tore through the apartment like a whirlwind, slamming her bedroom door.

That would be her fiery Spanish temper. She had Aurora to thank for that. But what had poked the beast, he had yet to find out.

Eventually, she emerged, wearing a pair of striped pyjama bottoms and a T-shirt that didn't quite cover her midriff. As she moved about in the kitchen, grumbling under her breath, he glanced in her direction, trying his best to ignore the appealing curve of her arse through the thin material as she reached down into the cupboard for Hannibal's biscuits.

He really didn't want to think of Dexter's sister that way.

'I already fed him,' he told her, earning a grunt and a muttering under her breath in response. He was pretty sure there had been a swear word or two in her reply as well.

Leaving the cat food, she turned her attention to wine, emerging from the kitchen moments later with a glass of red in one hand and the bottle in the other, heading back towards the bedroom.

Okay, this looked serious enough for an intervention, and while part of him didn't need that, especially as he was starting his new job in the morning, he was also curious to know what the hell was going on.

She had been out most of the afternoon, with friends he assumed. Had something happened with them that had upset her? Or was this to do with the police visit this morning?

Zac had gone out before they had shown up, but given that he had bumped into Julian Wiseman as he'd returned home, he gathered no arrest had been made.

Nina had promised him that it was Peyton Landis she had seen in Julian's apartment, but had she had been mistaken?

If so, he had little sympathy for her, as he had warned her to be careful before pointing the finger. He didn't remember much about Julian Wiseman, and word on the street was he was a bit of a wanker, but the man didn't deserve to have his name dragged through the mud again if he was innocent.

Pulling himself up from the sofa, Zac stretched, grabbed himself a wine glass from the kitchen cupboard, then headed down the hallway to Nina's bedroom, knocking on the closed door.

It didn't surprise him when there was no response, but instead of walking away, he pushed down the door handle, letting himself into the lion's den.

'Do you mind?' She glared up at him from where she was sat on the bed, phone in one hand and wine glass in the other. Her eyes widened when he ignored her.

Grabbing the wine bottle from her bedside table, he dropped down onto the mattress, pulling his legs up so he was sat facing her, back rested against the footboard.

'What the hell do you think you're doing?'

'Pouring a glass of wine,' he told her, careful not to spill any on the duvet as he recapped the bottle and set it on the floor beside him.

'Zac, get the hell out of my room.'

'Tell me why you're in such a foul mood first.'

'Because some arsehole is disturbing me and won't leave me alone.'

He grinned at her comment, which seemed to make her more annoyed. 'You were stomping and slamming doors before I came in here—'

'I wasn't stomping!'

'I disagree.' He took a sip of his wine and studied her. The edge of her temper had pinkened her cheeks and heated the flecks of gold in her hazel eyes, and tendrils escaped the loose knot she had tied her long, dark hair in, framing her face. In that moment, he was the kid who wanted to pull her hair to provoke a reaction, but he also felt oddly protective of her, as well as something else that he didn't care to define. 'So, as I like to take credit for all of your bad moods, I'd like to know who or what my competition is.'

'Go away.'

'Talk to me and I will.'

Nina's scowl deepened. 'I have no idea why my brother is friends with you,' she grumbled.

'Well, he is and I'm here,' Zac said amiably. 'So I'm afraid we're stuck with each other. Look, can we please talk about what's bugging you? I'm rather fond of my doors and hate to see them getting hurt.' He chanced another smile, and although she didn't return it, the scowl softened slightly.

'They didn't arrest him,' she said after a moment of contemplative silence.

So this *was* about Julian.

'I know. I did tell you to be sure you weren't mistaken.'

Nina looked up. 'I wasn't mistaken,' she said coolly. 'I'm guessing they must have evidence that Peyton was okay after she left Julian's apartment.'

Or she was never there – Zac kept that last thought to himself. 'So is this why you're annoyed? Because they didn't arrest him? It's innocent until proven guilty, remember?'

'I know that, and no, of course not. But I do feel bad for calling the police. It was Peyton, but if I hadn't been watching them...' She trailed off.

'You thought you were doing the right thing,' Zac pointed out diplomatically, though he was starting to wonder if Nina perhaps needed glasses for long-sightedness as well as working on her computer.

'There's this man,' she blurted, abruptly changing the course of the conversation.

'What man?' Now Zac was frowning.

'He lives in Julian's block, an older guy. He just stopped me downstairs. He knows I was the one who called the police.'

'What? How?'

'He saw me talking to the detectives this morning. They spoke to him and he heard them talking to Julian.' For a moment, she looked like she was going to say something else, but then she fell quiet.

'Did the police not come up here and talk to you in privacy?'

Silence, then, 'Yes.'

'So how did this man see you?'

This time the silence dragged longer.

'It doesn't matter,' Nina said eventually. 'But he knows it was me. If he tells Julian, then I'm going to look like a dick.'

It did matter, but he decided not to push it. 'Did he say he was going to tell him?' he asked instead.

'Well, no, but he made a point of letting me know he knew it was me. He was really smug about it. Why would he tell me he knew it was me if he wasn't going to say something to Julian?'

Zac had been racking his brain, trying to figure out who it was she was talking about, now a face appeared in his mind. 'Wait, you said older guy, right?'

'Yes.'

'In his sixties, bald head, always wears a tracksuit?'

Nina nodded.

'That will be Leonard Pickles,' he said, remembering his officious neighbour. 'He likes to stick his nose in everyone else's business.'

When he had first bought the apartment, he'd had a couple of run-ins with the old man who was far too meddlesome for his own good. Leonard liked to stir shit, but he generally let things reach boiling point first.

At the end of August, Nina would be gone and hopefully would avoid any fallout.

He didn't say so in case he was wrong, not wanting to give her false promises. She seemed so miserable and, despite doubting her, he felt sorry for her. It was obvious she believed what she had seen, and it had backfired on her spectacularly.

'Leonard,' she sniffed. 'Yes, he looked like a Leonard. And talking of sticking things where they don't belong, someone has nicked your parking space.'

Zac smiled. 'No they haven't.'

'Last time I looked, your hire car was a Nissan Juke, not an Audi.'

'The hire car's gone back. The Audi's mine. That's where I went this morning: to pick it up.'

'Oh, right. I thought you only drove spanking-new cars? That one's at least six years old.'

There was sarcasm in her words, the comment a dig, and he guessed he deserved it. For so long, he had valued material things, but losing his parents so suddenly had adjusted his outlook.

He didn't much care for other people in those early days following their deaths, and he cared even less for himself. Losing their loved ones so abruptly might have made some people want to stay close to home, but not Zac. He travelled as far away as he could, visiting country after country to try to find some meaning for why he was still here.

When he looked back, he didn't like himself much then and that first year he had been away, he remembered very little of. He had blown through a small fortune, staying in the best hotels and eating in the fanciest restaurants, visiting the whitest beaches and swimming in the clearest seas, but he didn't find happiness.

It was the simplest encounter that changed everything. While walking back to his hotel in Mexico one night, he had given chase to a street thief who had stolen a woman's handbag.

Zac had managed to get the bag and a black eye in the process, and the family of the woman had invited him to their house for dinner the following evening.

Initially, he wasn't going to go, but they seemed so indebted, and not wanting to let them down, he had enjoyed one of the best home-cooked meals of his life.

They were humble people, but proud too, and despite the language barrier – they spoke more English than Zac did Spanish – he enjoyed himself for the first time in a long while.

After that night, he changed his approach. Smaller, more intimate lodgings, and he became less aloof, making the effort with the people he met, wanting to learn more about them and their culture. He started helping out in some of the places where he visited. Initially lending a hand in a small family restaurant, then, with experience, graduating to bar work.

And eventually, as his travels took him across continents, he developed an interest in conservation, thanks to Ava, a woman he became involved with. In turn, his own life suddenly felt like it had purpose and he felt richer than he had done in a long while, and although his relationship with Ava had broken down, he was now in a much healthier place.

He had left the UK as a hot-headed and reckless man, angry at life for the hand he had been dealt, but now he would be willing to give up the fortune he had inherited just for one more day with his parents. He was a different person to the man Nina remembered, and while she still had the ability to push his buttons, and he would always get a kick out of winding her up, he wasn't quite the self-absorbed arsehole she still believed him to be.

While he was here and Dexter still away, he felt it his duty to step into the big brother role. That's why, after finishing the rest of his wine, he got up from the bed and held his hand out.

'Come on.'

Nina looked dubious. 'Come on where?'

'I figure we need something stronger than wine to cheer you up.'

She seemed wary, though didn't completely dismiss the idea. 'Don't you start your new job in the morning?'

'Yes, but I don't need to be there until late morning,' he lied. 'And you're self-employed, so can always start and finish late.'

Her mouth opened and closed, and he could tell he had just crushed her next excuse.

'What are we drinking?' she asked, still not moving.

'I have a bottle of tequila for emergencies.' He gave her an easy grin.

'Salt and lime?'

'No can do, but it's good tequila. You won't need it.'

He watched as she wavered, realising that he wasn't doing this just for her. It was for him too. He wanted her to say yes.

'Come on, Nina. One drink.'

Eventually, she nodded. Draining her glass and setting it down on her bedside table, she reached for his hand and let him pull her to her feet.

'Okay then. One drink.'

17

The woman staying in 5A was called Nina and she was the sister of Dexter Fairchild, who was currently out of the country.

Leonard had managed to find that information out quite easily, having struck up conversation with Dylan Hargreaves who worked on the maintenance team. He was one of the newer members of staff, so wasn't yet wised up to Leonard, and a few probing questions soon revealed Nina's identity. Dylan remembered her from when she had first shown up, planning to stay in her brother's apartment, and he had helped her with her luggage.

And Zac Green was back too, arriving a few days after Nina.

His was a familiar name and face, and Leonard remembered Zac, even though he knew he hadn't lived here in a long time. The two of them had been among the first to move in to River Heights and they'd had their share of run-ins. Leonard had been glad to see the back of him when he'd moved out. Apparently he had gone travelling after his parents had died, which was another reason to dislike him. Leonard still bitterly used Molly's death as the reason why he had never had the chance to see the world. It was easier to blame her than accept he was too scared to go alone. Watching Zac head off to live the dream that should have been his really sucked.

So Zac was back and Dexter Fairchild's sister was staying with him. Were he and Nina in a relationship? Had she been travelling with him?

It annoyed Leonard that she had been the one to see Julian the night that young woman, Peyton Landis, went missing. Leonard had known Julian had female company. He had heard them talking on the balcony above him. It had been the woman's moans that had really caught his attention, though.

He had been locking up, getting ready to go out for a late-night stroll when the noise came from above. Loud, disgusting sex groans and grunts that had him muttering under his breath and wondering if he should call out to them to shut the hell up.

It was while standing in the dark, shaking his head in irritation, that he had spotted what he thought was a glint of movement on the balcony of the opposite block.

Losing all interest in what was going on above him, he had picked up his binoculars, catching his first glimpse of Nina Fairchild.

Nosy bloody cow, he had raged, ignoring the irony of his words.

At least she knew now that he was on to her. He had caught her red-handed spying on Julian, plus he knew she had called the police.

At first, he hadn't been certain it was her, but the look of guilt on her face had soon confirmed his suspicions.

She was getting herself involved in everyone else's business.

He didn't like the idea of someone else snooping, nor certainly knowing that she could see inside his apartment.

Hopefully his little warning that he was on to her had now deterred her.

If not, he had his bargaining chip, aware that Julian would lose his shit if he found out who had called the police on him. Leonard would keep that titbit stored away for possible later use.

In the meantime, he was curious to know if there was any truth in Nina's accusation.

The police had asked Julian if Peyton Landis had been in his apartment, which he had strenuously denied. Leonard knew as he had been eavesdropping from his balcony, and Julian's patio door must have been open because he had heard plenty.

There had definitely been someone with him that night and Julian had told them it was a friend of his, Tabitha Percy.

Leonard knew who she was. The plummy girl who worked for Julian's dad, Kevin Wiseman. She had been on the complex that night, so it was possible he was telling the truth, and it was obvious that she fancied him from the way Leonard had seen her coo over him.

Was the Fairchild woman mistaken? Had she muddled Tabitha up with Peyton Landis or was Julian a liar?

Leonard was determined to find out.

18

Nina was sprawled on her back when she snorted herself awake and for a moment her times were out of sync. Was it morning, evening? Weekend or weekday?

Her head thumped and the cloak of sleep threatened to pull her back under, but she was conscious enough to grasp for straws and as memories slowly surfaced, she recalled getting drunk with Zac as they ploughed their way through a bottle of tequila. He had been trying to coax her out of her bad mood; his plan to ply her with alcohol working rather too well.

She remembered they had been laughing together as he did a rather uncanny and hysterically funny impression of Dexter, and she had a vague recollection of them having a limbo dancing competition in the living room.

After a few drinks, she had forgotten it was a Sunday night and they both had to work the next day. Now, though, she was aware of the thread of sunlight cutting through the curtains.

Monday was already here.

And moments after that realisation hit, her focus zoned in on the duvet.

It wasn't Dexter's.

His was a pale blue. This cover was dark grey.

Her brain kicked up a notch, racing through the gears.

This room had curtains. He didn't have those either. Dexter had blinds. And the window was on the wrong wall. The dresser at the foot of the bed instead of beside it.

It was different, yet also familiar.

She had been here before.

That was the moment the penny dropped.

She was in Zac's room.

What the fuck?

She sat up abruptly, the sharp burst of pain in her head making her wince, and glanced around warily. Her heart was thumping in her chest, even though she could see he wasn't in the room, and her mouth was incredibly dry, though that was probably more to do with the alcohol than sudden nerves.

Where was he? The en suite was empty, the door wide open. Unless he was in the main bathroom or had gone to make coffee?

And why was she in his bed?

Oh God. Had they...

She glanced down, relieved to see she was still wearing her T-shirt and pyjama bottoms. That didn't prove anything, though, she realised. She wouldn't be in his bed if nothing had happened.

How did she not have any recollection of getting here?

They had been sat on the sofa at one point, she remembered that, but her memories were hazy. Still, she was pretty sure she would know if she had kissed Zac or, God forbid, done anything else.

Pushing back the covers, she clambered off the mattress,

eager to sneak back to her own room before he returned from wherever he was.

This whole situation was going to be so awkward. How could she stay living here if they had slept together? Zac Green was her arch-nemesis and, okay, she would grudgingly concede that over the last week of living together they had found some common ground and he had surprised her by being more bearable to be around than she had expected.

And yes, somehow while he was away he had become a whole lot more attractive, but she would only admit that in her head. She would never confess it to him or to anyone else, and she sure as hell had never planned to have sex with him.

Noise came from the other side of the door and Nina froze, her eyes widening.

Shit, he was coming back and she was just standing here like an idiot.

Did she have time to dive under the duvet again and pretend to be asleep?

She wasn't ready to have this conversation.

Except it was too late. The door nudged open.

Instead of Zac, a fluffy feline face poked its head through the space and Nina heaved out a relieved sigh. As Hannibal pushed his way into the room, meowing a greeting that she was fairly certain translated to 'Feed me', she glanced through the widening crack.

The hallway was empty and, seizing the opportunity, she crept past the cat and out of the bedroom. Hannibal would have to wait for a bit for his breakfast.

Zac had work today, she remembered. He was starting his new job and would surely be leaving soon. All Nina had to do was lie low until he was gone.

Hopefully he was feeling as awkward about this as she was

so would be grateful she had removed herself from the situation. Being self-employed meant she could set her own hours, editing into the evening if needed. Once Zac was gone, she would work out what the hell she was going to do.

She could see the main bathroom door was open and he didn't appear to be in the living room either. In fact, the whole apartment was silent, which had Nina risking a peek into the kitchen area.

There was no Zac, and she could see he wasn't on the balcony either.

So where the hell was he?

It was at that moment she happened to glance at the wall clock. The hands telling her it was 10.40 a.m.

She double-blinked, and looked again, certain she had misread the time.

No. It was still correct.

She had assumed it was much earlier. Around 7 a.m., as that was the time she usually woke up. But then she supposed she didn't usually stay up late drinking tequila.

Zac must have already left for work.

Belatedly, she wondered what sort of state he had been in. Did he have a throbbing headache too?

Nina double-checked the apartment again, just to be certain he was gone, but her shoulders were already relaxing, aware she now had the rest of the day to figure this out.

As she went to put on the kettle, she spotted that Zac had left her a note.

You were out of it, so I didn't wake you. Hope your head's not too sore.

P.S. Did you know you snore like an angry rhino?

Z.

Nina humphed at his cheek. She wasn't that bad, and if he was here right now, she would have taken exception to the comparison. He wasn't, though, and right now she was more distracted by his wording, which her mind suggested worst-case scenario.

I didn't wake you.

There would have been no need to wake her if they had been sleeping in separate beds.

Nina stewed over things all morning, unable to settle with work and her headache, still throbbing away. Snatching her phone up when it rumbled on the table, she expected it to be Zac with some clue as to what had happened, and was bitterly disappointed when she saw instead it was Dexter.

Should she tell him what had happened?

No. Her brother would find it highly amusing and Nina would never hear the end of it. Instead, she replied to the photos of places he had visited and kept their conversation focused on his trip.

Eventually, deciding she was too distracted to work, she gathered her swimming things. She would take a little time for herself and then work later.

Being a Monday lunchtime, the leisure club was quiet. As she passed the door to the gym, she could see there were a couple of guys in there. One of them she recognised from her previous visit. Hearing her approach, he glanced up and gave a brief nod of acknowledgement as she passed.

The pool was completely empty and as she got into the water and started swimming, her thoughts returned to Zac. She still hadn't decided what her approach would be when he returned home from work. Initially, her instinct had been to flee. She hadn't wanted to return home to her parents, but perhaps it would be for the best. As the day had worn on, though, she decided she was overreacting. Zac's note had seemed chilled, like he was his usual annoying self. Perhaps they could just laugh about it and agree to pretend it had never happened.

Assuming something had happened.

Nina didn't feel like she'd had sex, though all of her limbs ached as if she'd had a good workout.

And they had been in the same bed. They must have been intimate in some way for that to happen, even if it had just been a kiss and a fumble.

Had she initiated it?

Dear God, she hoped not.

Alcohol always brought out her flirtatious side and Zac, with all those new muscles in his arms and shoulders, and his annoyingly pretty sea-green eyes, might have unleashed the monster in her.

If it was her doing, he was going to be smug forever.

Banishing the thought, she concentrated on getting her lengths in, deciding if she managed to reach a hundred, she would head into the city afterwards and feed her hangover a Big Mac.

Nina had been in the water for about ten minutes when she heard the door to the changing room open and, glancing up, she saw the man from the gym. He had changed into a pair of budgie smugglers that left nothing to the imagination, and with only the trunks on, she could see he was all oversized muscle and no neck.

He smiled in her direction, and Nina nodded in acknowledgement before refocusing on her goal.

Moments later, there was a huge splash as he jumped in, a wave of water hitting her in the face and going up her nose. As she choked and spluttered inelegantly, he ignored what he had done, creating another tsunami as he broke into a messy crawl.

Regaining her composure, she angrily shouted at him. 'Hey!'

She tried three times before catching his attention and once she had it, she pointed to the sign on the wall.

'No jumping. Can't you read?'

He looked at the sign and then at her. 'Sorry,' he shrugged, not sounding at all apologetic. The smile he followed up with wasn't contrite either. If anything, it was slightly lecherous and her cheeks heated as his gaze dropped to her cleavage. 'I'm Conrad,' he told her, wading towards her, as if he thought this was an invite to have a conversation.

'Okay, well, Conrad, can you stick to your side, please?' Nina kept her tone civil, though it was obvious she was still pissed off.

'I've seen you about,' he said, instead of moving. 'What's your name?'

She had no intention of telling him, especially since he was still staring at her tits and not even trying to be discreet about it.

Creep.

'Can you leave me alone? I came in here to swim.'

Conrad grinned, revealing a gold capped incisor. 'Sorry.'

Determined not to let on that he was making her uneasy, she shook her head in irritation and swam away from him.

Just a few more lengths, because she felt it important to show he wasn't bothering her, not wanting to give him any level of control, but then she would get out. She swam to the end of the pool, then back again, but she was no longer enjoying the exercise; her belly was now rumbling with nerves instead of hunger.

Although he watched her, Conrad stayed where he was. Nina still didn't like it, though, conscious they were probably the only two in the building and that in a few minutes she was going to have to climb out of the pool in front of him. When she heard the sound of voices, spotting two women about her own age coming through from the changing room, her shoulders sagged with welcome relief.

One of them, a skinny brunette who she had seen coming out of the other building before, glanced in her direction and smiled as she set her towel down on one of the poolside loungers.

Nina chanced a glance at Conrad, who was now noisily splashing his way back and forth across the pool. He seemed oblivious to the newcomers and the fact he was taking up so much space, and there wasn't going to be much room for them all if they wanted to swim.

She was about to get out, but then he beat her to it, pulling himself up out of the water and shaking himself off like a wet dog, before snatching up his towel.

Spotting the two women, he grinned at them. 'Hello, ladies.'

Both of them greeted him back and as he headed to the changing room, Nina felt a bit bad. Had she misjudged him? She had assumed he was hitting on her, but perhaps he was just overly friendly and not very good at respecting boundaries.

Although the two women proceeded to get in the pool, they didn't seem interested in swimming, their conversation taking precedence.

Nina ignored them at first, swimming another half a dozen lengths, but then, as she approached the end where they were standing, she heard the brunette mention a name.

Julian Wiseman.

She wanted to stop and eavesdrop, but it would have been too obvious, so instead she slowed to a gentler pace, straining to listen over the lapping of the water.

Even then, it was possible only to pick fragments of their conversation, so as she doubled back on herself, she stopped midway, her back to the women, as she made a show of readjusting her hairband and retying her hair into a knot.

'It was mistaken identity then?'

'Apparently so.' Nina was pretty certain it was the brunette woman speaking now. 'Whoever saw them thought it was Peyton Landis, but they were wrong. He was with that woman who works for his dad.'

Thank God Nina's back was to the women because her look of surprise would have alerted the women that she was listening.

'Who?'

'You've seen her about,' Brunette was saying now to her friend who didn't appear to know who the woman was. 'Blonde lady, maybe in her early forties, always says hello and she's quite well-spoken. She's friends with Julian.'

'Tabitha Percy.'

'Yes, that's her.'

Nina cast her mind back to the Sunday afternoon she and Zac had bumped into Julian and his friend. Tabitha. Nina remembered he had introduced her as an employee of his dad's, though at the time she had wondered if Tabitha thought more of their relationship.

'I think they might be more than friends,' the other woman in the pool laughed now, before her tone turned sombre. 'But, oh my God, how awful for him, someone mixing them both up. The poor man has only been back a year. People need to be careful jumping to conclusions. This could have destroyed his life. Especially after what happened before. Thank goodness Tabitha was able to tell the police they had been together that night.'

The pair of them fell quiet, probably thinking about the murder of Katy Spencer that Julian had been caught up in, and Nina forced herself to start swimming again, concentrating on the water, frightened that if she looked up the two women would see it written all over her face that she was the culprit.

This was not good. People were sympathising with Julian Wiseman and speaking badly of the person who had called the police.

She thought of Leonard who had seen her with the detectives. Had he been the only one? What if he let her name slip or someone else figured out it was her?

But that wasn't the worst bit.

Julian was claiming he had been with Tabitha that night, but Nina knew he was lying.

She had watched him with Peyton Landis and no matter how far she stretched it, Peyton and Tabitha were not that similar.

Yes, they were both blonde, but Peyton was shorter and slender, her facial features daintier than Tabitha's. And she had been wearing the same outfit she had gone missing in. Nina remembered the red shoes.

So Julian was lying and Tabitha was too.

Nina understood Julian wouldn't want trouble with the police, but he just had to be honest. Peyton Landis was missing and could be in trouble, perhaps even dead, and he was likely the last person to see her.

If he had nothing to hide, they would be able to eliminate him from their enquiries, surely.

Unless, of course, he had done something to her.

And if he had, was Tabitha in on it too?

She had given him a foolproof alibi, lying to the police. Why would she cover for him like that? Something was missing here.

Exactly what were they both up to?

19

Trouble follows Julian.

Kevin Wiseman's words were ringing in Tabitha's ears. The friendly warning he had given her that morning both unexpected and sincere.

Julian had wanted to keep the news that he had been questioned by the police quiet from his father. It wasn't like last time he had promised her. They hadn't hauled him into the station and made him sit in a cell between round upon round of questions. And he hadn't needed to call his father's attorney. It had just been a friendly chat and no one would ever have to know it had taken place.

He had been wrong about that. Tabitha could have told him that rumours spread like wildfire. It only took one neighbour to see the police at his door and word would get out.

Although she had been right, it had still shocked her when she had arrived at the office on Monday morning to see Kevin waiting for her, wanting to have a chat.

Somehow he had already found out about the witness who claimed to have seen his son with Peyton Landis, and he was worried about Tabitha, urging her to stay away. They might not be flesh and blood, but Kevin had always doted on her like a daughter and she knew he had her best interests at heart.

He wanted to be certain that she hadn't been coerced into doing anything she shouldn't. His legal team had been speaking with the police and Julian had been drinking in the same place where Peyton Landis and her friends had been dining. Currently, Tabitha's alibi was the only thing saving him from further questioning. If she was covering for him, then she needed to come clean. Lying to the police could have serious consequences. Kevin didn't want to see her manipulated. If Julian had been with Peyton or, God forbid, had anything to do with her disappearance, he needed to step up and face the music.

Tabitha's stomach had twisted in knots as she'd promised Kevin that Julian was telling the truth, sticking to the story she had told the police. The words she had rehearsed with Julian the previous day had flowed easily. Now, though, she was certain guilt was written all over her face.

Could Kevin see through her?

She felt awful lying to him, but she had no choice. She had to protect Julian.

That was why she was now on her way over to River Heights in her lunch break. She was desperate to see Julian and in need of reassurance that now the lie had been told, they would stick by one another like glue.

Kevin was wrong about his son. Tabitha knew he was innocent. And it wasn't just blind faith. She understood him better than anyone else and she refused to give up on him, even though she knew some of their family and friends viewed her with pity.

She had heard what they had to say, usually when they thought she was out of earshot.

He strings that gullible woman along.
She's a fool if she believes he will ever love her back.
Poor thing. She's wasting her life waiting for him.

The gossip stung, but it didn't sway her. Tabitha didn't need anyone's concern or sympathy; she was too proud for that, and she wasn't stupid either.

She knew Julian slept with other women. Dear God, look at him. He was a beautiful man.

He was getting it out of his system, though. She truly believed that. And when the time was right and he was ready to settle down, she would be there waiting. He would see her for who she was. The one person who had been there for him, always.

That's what she had told herself this morning as Julian had ignored the WhatsApp message she had sent him asking if was free for lunch. It hadn't even blue ticked to show he had read it, which had made her bristle as she could see he had been online.

Eventually, she had resorted to sneaky tactics, sending another message telling him they needed to talk about the night they'd spent together and it was urgent.

That had caught his attention and he'd responded immediately, saying she could come over.

Tabitha didn't want to show up empty-handed, so she stopped by one of her favourite delis on the way, picking up baguettes stuffed with smoked salmon, cream cheese and dill and two New York cheesecake slices. She could make a pitcher of iced tea if Julian had lemons, and, as it was another gorgeous blazing hot day, they could eat outside on the balcony.

She also bought some cleaning supplies. Cloths and sponges, bleach and antibacterial wipes. Julian had insisted he had cleaned the apartment thoroughly, to get rid of any trace of Peyton ever being there, but Tabitha wanted to be sure.

Pulling into the parking space beside Julian's Porsche, she gathered her purchases.

Normally, her first stop on a visit to River Heights was to the maintenance room. She always liked to check in with the staff on duty in case there had been any problems. Today, though, she was so eager to see Julian, she barely gave the building a glance.

When he had shown up on her doorstep yesterday, he had panicked the life out of her. She had watched him unravel right in front of her and he had been so vulnerable, at first it had left her feeling helpless. But then, when he had broken down, her instinct to protect him had kicked in and she knew she had to be the strong one. Somehow she had managed to gather herself when the police knocked on her door, letting them in and answering their questions, managing to keep it together even though she was quaking inside.

Now she was invested in Julian's lie, and an accomplice, and it scared her what might happen if he wavered or was wrong-footed. She wanted to help him, but could she trust that he would never tell anyone else their secret? If he did, it wouldn't be just his neck on the line. Tabitha would be in a lot of trouble too.

She was pensive as she rode the lift up to the sixth floor, considering the implications if they were caught out. She had been so eager to help, but she hadn't really thought things through. When the lift stopped, she was so caught up in her own little world, it took her a second to realise she wasn't on Julian's floor. Instead, the lift had stopped on the fifth level – the one where that nosy old man, Leonard Pickles, lived, and she caught a glimpse of him in the doorway before he pushed the door shut. Not all the way, mind. When she looked again, she could see it was still open a crack.

Knowing Leonard, he was probably wondering why she was on his floor.

So was Tabitha, and at first she assumed she must have pressed the wrong button, but then she spotted Dylan Hargreaves closing the door to apartment 5G.

He gave her an easy smile as she stepped back to let him enter. 'Sorry, I was the one who called the lift, but then I realised I hadn't locked Miss Johnson's door.'

Becky Johnson. Young, pretty and probably close in age to Dylan. Was he sleeping with the residents on work time?

Dylan must have gauged from her expression what she was thinking, because his eyes suddenly widened. 'She's away on holiday,' he spluttered. 'I'm just watering her plants for her.'

Oh.

Tabitha's cheeks reddened, realising she had jumped to the wrong conclusion about him. Here she was judging Dylan for doing a nice thing for one of the residents, when she was lying to the police and covering up for Julian. Was it her own guilty conscience? Just because she had done something bad didn't mean she could tar everyone with the same brush.

She looked to the floor, avoiding eye contact as the doors closed again. As the lift ascended, she forced a cheerful smile on her face. 'That's kind of you,' she managed, wanting him to know she believed him and he wasn't in trouble.

Thanking him as the lift stopped on the sixth floor, she stepped out, grateful when the doors closed, taking him back down to ground level.

Drawing in a breath, she went to Julian's door and rang the buzzer, trying her best to hold it together. Here she was worrying about him crumbling under the weight of his lie, but she was a mess too. She hoped that once she had spoken with him and they had gone over everything again that she would feel better about things.

There were two penthouse suites, though the apartment

opposite Julian was currently empty, meaning he had the floor to himself. When he took his time answering the door, Tabitha grew impatient, shifting her bags into her right hand while she fished in her trousers pocket for the key with her left. Yes, he was going to be annoyed that she hadn't yet returned it to the maintenance room like she had promised, but she was jittery and needed to see him.

She was about to jam it in the lock when the door opened, and she quickly closed her hand around the key so he didn't see it.

Not that Julian would have noticed anyway. He had dark smudges under his eyes and he was dressed in a pair of old joggers. He barely registered Tabitha before turning his back on her and leaving her to follow him into the hallway and through into the main room of the apartment.

He stopped in the kitchen area, turning to face her as he leant back against the counter. The apartment was dark, the blinds still shut, and the air-con cranked high, though she could see a light perspiration on his skin. An empty tumbler and bottle of whisky sat on the side and she could smell the faint whiff of alcohol and sweat on him.

'You said you had something to tell me,' he demanded, his tone impatient.

The panicking and overly grateful man she had helped yesterday was gone and she barely recognised the version of him standing before her. His eyes were dead.

'Have you been drinking?' she asked, deciding that being assertive with him was the best way forward.

He shrugged. 'So what if I have?'

'It's 1 p.m., Julian.'

'And?'

He rolled his eyes and she noticed how bloodshot they were.

Ignoring his reaction, wishing it didn't sting after everything she had done for him, she put her bags down on the counter, then moved through the apartment, clearing away rubbish and drawing the blinds back to let light into the room.

Julian didn't like that and he shielded his eyes with his arm against the sun as if he was a vampire.

'Hey, what are you doing?' he grumbled.

'Trying to tidy this place up,' she huffed back, unlocking the balcony door and stepping outside. The apartment needed some fresh air to help shift the stale odours.

Julian stomped out after her, his voice raised in anger. 'What is it you need to tell me, Tabitha? Just say it and go.'

Ouch.

She reminded herself it was probably the alcohol talking, but perhaps it was time for some home truths.

'You stink, Julian. Go have a shower,' she snapped. 'I brought lunch, but I'm not going to eat it with you while you're like this. I did a huge thing for you yesterday. You showed up at my house and begged for my help. I lied to the police for you and this is your response? To get drunk and be rude to me? I put my neck on the line for you, so you're going to get your act together and prove to me that I made the right call.'

He pouted a little, but stayed silent, making no attempt to move, so Tabitha pressed on.

'Your father was waiting for me when I arrived at work this morning.'

That got his attention.

'Why?' he demanded. 'What the fuck did you say to him?'

'Nothing!' she snapped back, shocked at the ferocity in his tone. 'I didn't need to say anything. He already knew all about the police coming to question you and he's not happy.'

'No surprise there.' Julian's eyes flashed angrily and Tabitha was relieved to see there was at least a spark of the man inside who she knew and loved. 'Tell me what he said.'

'I will, but first I want you to go shower and put some fresh clothes on,' she insisted. 'I'll tidy this place up a bit and get lunch ready, then we can talk and I will tell you everything.'

He glared at her, but seemed to rein his temper in. 'You'd better.'

'You have my word,' Tabitha promised him, her tone cool. 'I think I've proven my loyalty to you, Julian. It's time you start trusting me.'

For a moment, he made no attempt to move, watching her through suspicious eyes, but then he nodded, leaving the room without another word.

Tabitha sucked in a breath, aware her heart was racing.

She had seen this side to him before, but never this angry. He was usually either indifferent to her or all over her. Though that was generally when he wanted something. But this? He had briefly looked like he wanted to throttle her.

Foolishly she had believed that yesterday was a turning point. After he had cried all over her and she had soothed him, promising to make everything better, she had thought he was going to start appreciating her more. He had even agreed to go to her parents' wedding anniversary with her as her date. Well, okay, he hadn't actually used the word 'date', but it was close enough and things were looking up.

Until today, when he was back to acting like a spoilt and ungrateful jerk, and the flashes of temper he had just displayed had genuinely scared her.

It wasn't him. It was the situation. It was the alcohol. She tried to convince herself it was the truth as she unpacked the bag of cleaning products and started to scrub the worktops and doors. Julian was a flawed man and this was a side to him she didn't like, but then she remembered the good, kind and lovely person he could be, where he made her feel needed and important, and she tried her best to cling to that. It was when she saw that side of his personality that she felt special. When he dropped hints that one day her waiting on the sidelines for him would pay off. He just had things to work out of his system. She had to be patient.

By the time Julian emerged, every surface had been tackled, the scent of detergent clinging to the air, and the glass coffee table on the balcony was fancily set for lunch with glasses, plates and cutlery, as well as a pitcher of iced tea and the lunch Tabitha had brought.

To her relief, Julian was looking perkier. His hair was damp from the shower, but he was dressed now in smarter clothes. He eyed the table, a sardonic smile curving his lips. 'You know food isn't going to solve any of this, right?'

Despite his scepticism, he took a seat and picked up one of the baguettes, sniffing at it, while Tabitha's stomach churned.

By giving an alibi for Julian, she had placed herself under scrutiny from the police. She needed him to keep their secret, aware she could be in a huge amount of trouble if they found out she had lied.

The problem was, she had never been good at depending on others and preferred to be in control of every aspect of her life. And Julian could be so bloody unpredictable.

If he slipped up...

No. She couldn't think like that. He was just having a wobble and she would talk him around. He had more to lose than she did. If the truth did come out that they had lied, he could end up in a lot of trouble.

The thought of losing him to prison was almost too much to bear.

'It's going to be okay,' she promised him now. 'We just need to make sure we both stick to the same story. Best-case scenario, Peyton Landis shows up safe and well and you won't even need my alibi.'

She smiled brightly, aware she was giving him false hope, but needing him to believe everything would be okay.

She knew Julian Wiseman. Yes, he could be unpredictable, but she still understood him better than anyone else, and she truly believed that underneath the selfishness and the bad temper was a vulnerable, but ultimately good man, desperately needing someone to understand him.

He wouldn't let her down or hurt her. She had to believe it.

20

Did Julian Wiseman have something to do with that missing woman after all?

It was fortuitous that Leonard had decided to stay home after seeing Julian's lady friend, Tabitha Percy, heading up to his apartment. He had been planning to go for a walk, but eavesdropping was always a more attractive pastime and the acoustics out on the balconies meant that he could usually hear much of what was going on upstairs.

If only Julian knew.

The lift had stopped on the fifth floor for that sap, Dylan, who had been looking after the apartment of Leonard's neighbour while she was on holiday. Leonard would have happily watered Becky Johnson's plants for her, but she didn't trust him, and he guessed he didn't blame her, because he wouldn't have been able to resist snooping.

Still, it was lucky Dylan had offered, because it meant Leonard had seen Tabitha going to visit Julian and that he had been home to witness the mother of all conversations, as

Tabitha had admitted she had given the police a fake alibi to cover for Julian.

It was so crazy that Leonard had actually wondered at one point if his ears were deceiving him.

This was far bigger than anything else he had stumbled across since moving into his apartment and he knew he would have to go to the police.

The problem was, all he had were snippets of a conversation between Julian and his lady friend admitting she had covered for him. It would be Leonard's word against the two of them, and given that they had already lied once, he didn't doubt they would do it again.

No, before he could report this, he needed to dig deeper for some kind of proof. If Julian had done something bad, there had to be evidence somewhere.

Leonard just had to find it.

21

Zac's first day in his new job had gone smoothly and was surprisingly satisfying, considering he was nursing the hangover from hell. There had been a lot for his tired mind to absorb, but the painkillers he had taken, along with three cups of strong black coffee, had helped, and his new work colleagues seemed like good people, while the work was interesting. He was ready for this new challenge, knowing he would take everything in his stride, and tonight he intended to be in bed early so he was better refreshed for his second day.

Getting drunk on a Sunday night had never been part of his plan, but it had ended up being good fun. Nina had needed cheering up and what he had intended to be two or three drinks had ended up turning into a whole lot more.

As he let himself back into the apartment, he wondered how her head had been this morning. She had confessed to him last night after downing half a dozen shots that she had never drunk tequila before, and Zac had briefly questioned the sensibility of his decision to give it to her.

That had been somewhere between her feeling the need to

prove she could still get into the crab position – apparently she could, and he had tried his best not to stare as she'd arched her belly up while on all fours and the thin fabric of her pyjama bottoms had slipped down to reveal her navel – and her insisting on getting into his bed, which she assured him was far more comfortable than Dexter's. He had tried his best to stop her, aware it could lead to a slippery slope, but of course this was Nina and she had refused to listen.

He found her now at the dining table, those cute little glasses she wore when she worked slipping down her nose as she concentrated on the screen. The radio was on and the noise had perhaps masked his return as she didn't seem to realise he was there until he spoke.

'How's your head?'

A simple enough question, but one that had her jumping, the glasses sliding completely off her nose as she looked up in horror, her eyes bug wide.

'Hi.'

She sounded flustered and looked a little trapped, as if she wasn't sure where to run to, which surprised him, given how close they had been with each other last night. It wasn't quite the reaction he had been expecting.

'Did you have a hangover this morning?' he rephrased, since she was now sitting there staring at him like a rabbit caught in headlights and not saying a word.

'Um, yes. Did you?'

'A little bit. Perhaps not my wisest move pulling out that bottle of tequila the night before starting a new job.' He winked at her and grinned, and her cheeks flushed pink.

'No,' she agreed robotically.

'I had fun, though,' he told her, still perplexed by her reaction. Things had been a little awkward the first few days of living here together, but last night he thought they had really connected. 'Did you?' he asked now, unsure if he had read her wrong.

'Um, yes,' she repeated, picking up the cup beside her and taking a sip. It was the least enthusiastic yes he had ever heard.

'Did you ache this morning? That was one hell of a position you managed to get yourself in.'

It appeared he had said the wrong thing again, Nina managing to choke on whatever it was she was drinking before he had even finished talking. Her cheeks had now gone from pink to scarlet and her expression to one of pure mortification.

Zac quickly fetched her a glass of water and she snatched it from him, gulping greedily.

'Are you okay?' he asked after a moment and she nodded slowly. Although the choking had subsided, he knew she was far from okay.

Why was she acting so weird?

She hadn't even asked him how his first day had gone.

Rude.

As he wasn't getting any conversation out of her, he left her to sip at the water while he went to get in the shower.

He had just tugged his T-shirt over his head when the bedroom door burst open, Nina charging into the room.

Now it was Zac's turn to look shocked. 'Do you mind?' he blustered.

Ignoring him, she sat herself down on his bed, for a moment seeming fixated on his bare chest until he self-consciously pulled his T-shirt back down.

'We need to talk about last night.'

Okay, not what he was expecting. Was she mad at him for getting her drunk?

'Look, I'm sorry. You should have told me sooner you'd never had tequila.'

'It's not about the tequila,' she snapped.

'So what is it? You seemed to be enjoying yourself fine at the time.' He chanced a grin, but it only seemed to fluster her.

'We should never have slept together,' she blurted.

Zac stared at her, dumbfounded. 'What?'

'It was a mistake. It just makes everything complicated.'

She thought they had slept together, here in this bed? Wait. Was she referring to sex? Did she mean that kind of sleeping together?

He wasn't sure if he was offended that she thought so little of him to believe he would have sex with an unconscious woman or if he should be amused that she had got this so very wrong.

'We didn't,' he told her matter-of-factly.

'Didn't what?' Now she was the one who looked confused.

'We didn't sleep together, Nina. There was no sex, no sharing a bed even. You passed out in here and I couldn't wake you, so I went and slept in Dexter's room.'

'You did?'

'I did.'

'But you said...' She trailed off and he could see she was switching through the gears, realising she had misinterpreted everything in their conversation. 'It didn't happen,' she said to no one in particular.

'It didn't,' Zac agreed, fighting hard now to keep the smirk off his face. She looked so confused, it was adorable. 'But, you have my promise, if we *do* ever have sex, I will make sure you remember it.'

He had wanted her flustered again, he realised, and his wish was granted.

Now if he could just see her back in that crab position.

Damn it. Stop thinking about that.

She had no idea how to react to his comment, seeming annoyed, then embarrassed, but mostly like she wanted the ground to swallow her up, and while part of him had been joking, wanting to get her to bite, now the thought was in his head, he couldn't say he entirely disliked it.

This wasn't good. She was Dexter's sister.

'Now we've cleared that up, scoot. I need a shower.'

He swatted at her with his towel and she grumbled a few choice swear words as she scurried off the bed.

'You're very full of yourself,' she muttered, stopping by the door.

Needing her gone, not liking the reaction she was suddenly having on him, he resorted back to insults. 'Says the woman who snores like an angry rhino.'

'I do not!'

Okay, he was exaggerating. She had been making cute little grunting sounds, but as she had been asleep she didn't know that.

Doing his best angry rhino impression, he skulked over to her, pushing her through the door, before closing and locking it. Then he went into his en suite and turned the shower dial to cold.

Stepping under the spray, he wondered what the hell he had started last night.

* * *

Nina was mortified after her misinterpretation of the previous night, but knowing she hadn't slept with Zac, she was determined to put it behind her.

She had been drunk and, yes, she had just made a fool of

herself, but she really needed to stay living here for a little bit longer. She had more property viewings lined up over the coming days and was hoping to hear soon from Chris, Rachel's cousin, but she didn't want to be pushed into accepting something that was out of her budget or not right for her.

She and Zac could get past this, she promised herself, even as the comment he had made about her not forgetting it if they ever did have sex played on a loop in her head.

At least he was bantering with her again. Well, making insults about her snoring.

Deciding they needed a start over to this evening, she cleared her work away and turned her thoughts to dinner. She had the ingredients for a mushroom risotto recipe that Charlotte had given her and figured she would make enough for Zac.

A peace offering of sorts.

While she cooked, she asked Alexa to turn up the volume on the radio, enjoying the banter of Johnny Vaughan and his team, and their indie playlist on Radio X. Zac was taking forever in the shower – either that or he was avoiding her – and the risotto was simmering, delicious smells filling the kitchen, as the 7 p.m. news came on.

The Peyton Landis story received a brief mention and Nina bristled as the newscaster announced that police were still focusing their searches on the river.

She had called the police station after overhearing the two women talking in the pool, asking if there was any update to her witness report, but the officer she spoke to had been cagey with information, telling her they were still actively following up enquiries, and essentially fobbing her off.

It was obvious those enquiries no longer involved Julian though. His friend had given him an airtight alibi.

Needing to offload, she told Zac what she had overheard

while they ate. Things had still been a little uncomfortable between them when he had finally emerged from his room and Nina was quick to try to move forward. Julian and Peyton Landis's disappearance gave them something else to talk about and help them forget the awkwardness of their earlier encounter. Plus she could do with another perspective. Julian lying to the police was really starting to bother her.

'They are both blonde,' Zac pointed out now, referring to Peyton and Tabitha. 'Is it not at all possible you got them mixed up?'

'No. Peyton's younger and smaller in build, and she doesn't look like Tabitha facially. Besides, she was wearing the clothes in the description the police have issued,' Nina pointed out.

'Maybe Tabitha has a similar outfit.'

'I know who I saw, Zac,' Nina assured him, her tone firm.

'Then how do you explain Tabitha saying it was her?' He took another mouthful of risotto, then washed it down with a drink of water. No alcohol for either of them tonight. 'This is good. I didn't realise you could cook.'

'I have my moments. And honestly? I don't know.'

'From what I know of her, she's quite straight-laced and takes her career seriously. I very much doubt she would throw it all away to cover for Julian.'

'She works for Wiseman Homes.' Nina paused eating. 'For Kevin Wiseman, right?'

'Yes.' Zac's eyes narrowed. 'Why? Please don't suggest he has something to do with Peyton Landis's disappearance too.'

'Is it really that far-fetched?'

'Yes, Nina. It really is.'

He had the nerve to roll his eyes at her and she fumed a little. Knowing she wasn't going to persuade him to consider her theory, she changed the subject, but still, what she had seen the night Peyton disappeared played on her mind.

Peyton Landis had been in Julian's apartment and both Julian and Tabitha had lied to the police. Nina had to find a way to prove it.

Zac insisted on clearing away the dishes and leaving him to it, so Nina went to her room, taking her MacBook with her.

As she made herself comfortable on the bed, Hannibal, who had followed after her, jumped up beside her, and she picked him up, making a fuss of him while waiting for the machine to load.

'I know I'm right, even if no one else believes me,' she told the cat, kissing his soft head and feeling the vibrations as he purred against her chest.

Setting him down beside her she opened Google, typing Julian Wiseman's name into the search bar.

There were a few articles about him, mostly in connection to his dad, though a few were about his various business ventures and there was some negative press. A bar fight he had been involved in when he was younger, another time when he had crashed his car after drinking and driving, and unsurprisingly there was mention of the Katy Spencer murder.

Nina read everything she could find, learning that Julian had been having an affair with Katy and that Katy's husband-to-be, Hugh, was one of Julian's closest friends. Julian had been the one to discover Katy's body, which was why the police had originally suspected him, but then it had been proven that he couldn't have been with her at the time of her death, as an alibi put him elsewhere, and he was released without charge.

Convenient that. Another alibi. There was nothing to say who had provided it, the focus shifting when one of the groundsmen who worked at the hotel, a man called Eric Grogan, was arrested and charged with murder after the shovel that had been used to bludgeon Katy was found in the boot of his car.

Was Grogan really guilty?

Some of the press articles painted Julian as entitled and self-absorbed, saying he wasn't a particularly nice person, but, other than the Katy Spencer story, there was nothing to suggest he might have a more sinister side.

Rachel had said she thought Julian might still be guilty of Katy's murder and that Eric Grogan had been set up, and a search of the man's name in various chat forums showed Nina that there were others who believed the same. But, ultimately, there was no hard evidence to confirm anything. It was all just rumours, with nothing solid to back that theory up. It did seem coincidental, though, that Julian had been at Katy's wedding and now a woman was missing who had last been in his apartment.

No one knew the fate of Peyton Landis, and it was possible she was safe and well and might show up in a few days, but Nina couldn't shake the worry that she was already dead and had never left Julian's place after she had seen her.

If Rachel's theory was right about Katy Spencer and Nina's suspicions about Peyton Landis were correct, Julian Wiseman had killed two women and managed to get away with it.

22

It was Tuesday evening and Julian was on his way out when he bumped into Leonard Pickles, the lift stopping on its way down at the fifth floor to pick him up.

He had been in a good mood until he saw Leonard's smug face, but now he was immediately irritated. After the panic of Sunday and his bad temper on Monday, which Tabitha had received the brunt of, he had finally found a more positive headspace and now he feared this idiot was going to ruin it.

Generally, he used the service lift at the back of the building to avoid running into his neighbours, but it was having maintenance work done. Just his luck he would bump into Leonard.

'Well, well, well. If it isn't the almighty Wiseman Junior,' the old man greeted him as he stepped back to make room. 'Coming down from your tower to hang out with the common folk, are we?'

It was the jaunty tone that annoyed him more than the words. Julian couldn't give a shit what Leonard thought of him, and in a way he was right. He was a commoner and Julian did look down on him. The man frankly looked ridiculous in an unflattering burgundy tracksuit, his bald head shiny and his belly sticking out. Not as far as his nose, though, which was always into everyone else's business.

'Leonard,' he responded, acknowledging him. Just his name, mind. He didn't deserve a hello or a good evening. Especially not when Julian was still convinced he had been the one who had called the police.

'Off somewhere nice, are we?' the old man asked, eying his linen shirt and chinos.

He was being sarcastic, Julian knew that. He wasn't dressed any differently to normal, though he always made an effort with his clothes. He had put on aftershave too before leaving his apartment. Something he always did for his lady friends.

Instead of answering, he smiled tightly.

When he realised he wasn't going to get a reaction, Leonard changed tack. 'So that was a nice bit of Sunday entertainment you gave us, having the coppers over to visit,' he said, sounding amused. 'They didn't find that missing woman under your bed, then?'

Julian's nostrils flared, his good mood fading fast as he turned on him. 'I bloody knew it was you, poking your nose in where it doesn't belong.'

'Didn't have to get Daddy to bail you out again then?'

'I answered their questions and they know it was a troublemaker who made the call.'

Leonard didn't seem threatened. 'A troublemaker, eh? Actually, it wasn't me, but I wish it had been.'

Was he lying? Usually Leonard liked to claim his victories with glee. If he had called the police, he would have probably been gloating about it.

'Well, who the hell else would it be?' Julian demanded.

'Do you think I'm the only one around here watching

things?' Leonard tapped his finger against the side of his head. 'You know, if you used this a little bit more, you might one day be as smart as your daddy. How would I be watching you and your lady friend when I live on the floor below you? You need to be looking a little further afield.'

Was he suggesting it was someone in the other block who had seen him with Peyton Landis?

He scowled at Leonard. 'You know who it was, don't you?' he growled.

'Now, what would be the fun in me telling you that?'

Julian wanted to throttle him. 'There's a special place in hell for people like you,' he muttered.

Unfortunately, his comment only seemed to amuse Leonard, his smug smile widening.

'I guess I'll have to save you a seat then, because we both know you'll be joining me down there.'

'What the hell is that supposed to mean?'

Leonard leaned in close, his voice dropping to a conspiratorial whisper. 'You know, when we're both out on our balconies, I can hear everything.' He waggled his eyebrows before repeating, '*Everything*.'

Was that a hint of a threat? What did he mean he could hear everything? What was he referring to? As Julian scrambled his brain for answers, the lift doors opened and Leonard stepped out.

He started whistling as he walked away, hands in his pockets, and for a moment Julian was tempted to follow and try to force him to answer. The infuriating man wouldn't tell him anything, though. Instead, Julian left the building, staring up at the other block as he crossed the courtyard.

Someone had been watching him and they had called the police.

But just how much had they seen that night?

Panic fizzled in his gut as he realised just how badly things could have turned out.

But it was okay. The police had seemed satisfied and Tabitha had come through for him.

Recalling her visit to his apartment yesterday, he froze.

He was pretty certain they had been out on the balcony when they were talking about her lying to the police for him.

Was that what Leonard meant? Had he overheard their conversation?

Julian's neck started to sweat, the collar of his shirt suddenly too tight, and when he swallowed, his mouth was dry.

It was bad enough that someone in one of the other apartments had seen him with Peyton Landis, but if Leonard knew Tabitha had given a false alibi he was in deep shit.

Part of him was tempted to head back up to his apartment and figure out a way to deal with this problem, but there was little he could do. The damage had already been done.

And even as the fear of being caught coursed through him, rage was building in his gut. Anger at Leonard for being such a nosy bastard and at whoever had called the police.

He needed an outlet for it, which is why he continued to the car park. He had been heading out because he had an itch to scratch. Once he had taken care of it, his head would be clearer.

Still, paranoia had him looking over his shoulder now, and when he got into his Porsche, pulling out of the car park, he kept a cautious eye on his rear-view mirror.

He couldn't risk anyone following him or finding out where he was going.

Leonard's words had scared the shit out of him, and they haunted him as he drove out of the city. The old man liked to play games and it was possible he could be bluffing, but Julian didn't think so. Not this time.

He tried to push the meddlesome man from his thoughts now, deciding he would figure out a way to deal with him later. Pulling into the driveway of the big, secluded house, he killed the engine. The first lick of excitement heated his veins in anticipation of what awaited him inside, and it momentarily pushed his fear to one side.

Leonard's eyes would be on stalks if he knew where Julian was right now and what he was about to get up to.

The old man had no idea what went on inside Julian's head or the things he did behind closed doors, and if he knew the truth, it would shock the hell out of him.

23

After exhausting her search on Julian Wiseman, Nina had googled his father, Kevin, and the rest of his family. There were far too many articles to wade through – some on news sites, others on social media and YouTube – but she had viewed the ones she thought might be interesting or helpful, gaining a little more insight into the Wiseman family's life.

Opinions on Kevin Wiseman varied greatly. There were several people who admired him for what he had achieved, given he had come from nothing, while others found him sly and ruthless. Pretty much everyone agreed, though, that he was tenacious, and think what you want of him, he was prolific in helping out good causes, especially those that affected the city.

He had clawed his way to the top and his background, growing up in a council house and wearing hand-me-down school uniforms, was well-documented. He had started with his boots on the ground, getting a job in construction straight out of school, and in his early thirties he had set up his own company.

His wife, Jemima, was also from Norfolk; the daughter of a farmer who had been working on one of the beauty counters in the Norwich department store, Jarrolds, when they met, introduced by a mutual friend, and aside from Julian – who, at forty-two, was their firstborn – they had a forty-year-old son, James, who was on the board of directors of Wiseman Homes.

By all accounts, Julian was the black sheep of the family, and if Facebook was to be believed, he had been in and out of trouble ever since he was at boarding school. After Katy Spencer's death, he had moved to the US for an extended period and since his return home a year ago, he had the failed venture of a new nightclub behind him, but seemingly now was between jobs.

Finding nothing to support her theories, she had called it a night, but over the following days what she had seen continued to play on her mind.

There were occasions where she was starting to doubt herself. Perhaps she had been mistaken and it really had been Tabitha with Julian that night. But then she would have a moment of clarity and be certain of what she had seen.

It just made no sense. Why would Julian lie if he had nothing to hide?

And Tabitha was in on the deception too. She was taking a huge risk lying to the police. What was in it for her?

It was a question she posed to Rachel, Charlotte and Tori when they met for a drink on Thursday night.

They were sitting outside at the Ribs of Beef pub, and although it had already gone 8 p.m., a sticky heat was still clinging to the air. The traditional drinking hole was a favourite of theirs and they had been lucky to get one of the outdoor tables, which were on a narrow balcony that ran between the pub wall and the river.

Nina hadn't planned to bring the subject of Julian up, but then Rachel asked if she had heard anything more from the police and Tori and Charlotte had piled in with the questions, demanding to know what was going on.

'This Tabitha woman works for his father, right?' Charlotte asked now. 'Maybe she's been asked to cover for him.'

'But that would mean Kevin Wiseman is involved.' Rachel was dubious. 'I know he's not supposed to be the nicest of people, but I don't think he would help give Julian a fake alibi.'

'Perhaps she's in love with him then. People can do strange things when the L word is involved.'

Charlotte had a point and it was something Nina had considered herself. But if Tabitha was in love with Julian, would she really give him an alibi knowing he had been with another woman?

Still, it did seem the most plausible suggestion.

'You really have it in for this poor guy,' Tori commented.

It was the first time Nina had seen her since her break-up with Michael and she had been quiet all evening.

Both she and Charlotte had reacted with surprise that they were only just finding out what Nina had witnessed, but while Charlotte was intrigued and excited to have something to gossip about, Tori seemed miffed and a little put-out that Nina had spoken to Rachel about what she had seen before her.

'I don't know him well enough to have it in for him,' Nina pointed out diplomatically. 'And I can only go by what I saw that night.'

'What if you are wrong?' Tori challenged. 'You were still a distance away, even if you did have binoculars.'

'I'm not wrong,' Nina told her adamantly.

'But if you are you could ruin his life.'

The words made Nina bristle, reminding her of Zac's initial warning that she needed to be sure before she meddled. Why did everyone keep making her try to doubt herself?

Though, from Tori's sulky stance, it could be more than just Julian that was eating at her. She hadn't been at all happy when she'd found out Nina had ended things with Michael.

When her friend excused herself to go to the loo a few minutes later, Nina got up and followed.

'Are you upset with me?' she demanded, as Tori looked over her shoulder, surprised to see Nina behind her.

'Of course not,' she said a little too quickly.

'Then what's your problem?'

Tori's eyes narrowed. 'There is no problem. At least not with me. I don't know what's going on with you, though, Nina. You're making some really weird decisions at the moment.'

'Such as?'

'Well, first you dump Michael completely out of the blue and move into your brother's place without saying a word to anyone. Now there's all this Julian Wiseman business that you're caught up in.'

'There's nothing going on with me,' Nina said a little sharply. 'And I know exactly what I'm doing.' It annoyed her that Tori was making it sound like she was having some kind of breakdown.

'Do you, though?' her friend accused, but then her bluster simmered down. 'I just worry about you, okay? And I miss you.'

'I'm still here,' Nina promised her. 'I just needed some time to myself before I told the whole world that my relationship was over.'

'I get that. But I'm your friend. I thought we kept each other in the loop and were always there for each other?'

'We do and we are. You're one of my closest friends, Tori. But Kyle is Michael's cousin. I didn't want to put you in the middle.'

They were silent for a moment as Tori contemplated Nina's words.

'Is there no way you will give Michael another chance?' she asked eventually. 'He's a good man and he misses you. He regrets like hell that he proposed. He told Kyle that if he had never bought the ring you'd still be at home with him.'

Nina shook her head. 'Which would be a terrible mistake. It was the wake-up call I needed. And I know Michael is hurting now, but in a few months' time he will realise this was the best decision for both of us. We were both stuck in a rut that we were too lazy to get out of. He deserves better than that and so do I.' She paused and nudged her friend on the arm. 'And this won't affect us. I still care about Michael and I don't want to fall out with him. I just don't want to be with him. You and I can still do stuff. It just won't be the four of us any more.'

Tori's smile was hesitant. 'You promise?'

'I promise.'

To Nina's relief, they hugged it out.

'We're cool with each other, right?' she checked.

'Yeah, we're cool. You don't get rid of me that easily.' Tori grinned. 'Now, I really do need to pee.'

While Tori used the loo, Nina checked her make-up in the mirror, then tied her loose dark hair back in a knot to keep it off her sweaty neck.

'Rachel told me Zac Green is back,' her friend commented from within the stall. 'How's that working out, living with him?'

To Nina's surprise, her cheeks heated, her thoughts returning to Monday morning when she had woken in Zac's bed, certain they'd had sex. She was glad Tori couldn't see her in that moment, scared she might mistake Nina's fluster for something else.

Which would be ridiculous, as there was nothing going on between her and Zac.

After the awkward conversation they had shared Monday

evening, when he had told her she was mistaken, they had settled back into a friendship of sorts, but Nina would be lying if she ignored the slight tension between them that hadn't been there before.

She answered Tori's question as honestly as possible.

'He's not been too bad, actually. I think all that time living abroad has helped him grow up a bit.'

Tori laughed. 'I never thought I would hear you say that. I remember how much you hated him.'

As the chain flushed, Nina considered her friend's words.

Why had she always hated Zac so much?

Yes, he teased her, though if she was honest it was never anything more than harmless ribbing, and it did annoy her how he always treated her as the little sister, even though there was only a year's difference between Dexter and Nina, and even less between her and Zac.

But was that it?

She had it in her head that he was irritating, and at times he really was, but that didn't make him a terrible person. Even growing up together, there had been times when he did nice things for her. Like showing her how to fix a puncture on her bicycle, and hanging around to walk home with her one time when she had been given a detention and missed her bus.

In a way, he had been no different to Dexter; a second brother, she supposed. But she let Dexter get away with things more because he was family. Even though Zac was too.

And it was there that lay her problem.

Since he had been back, there had been moments where things felt different between them, and much as she didn't want to admit to it, there was a spark of something that kept threatening to ignite.

Nina was doing her damnedest to keep these newer and

unwelcome thoughts pushed down and trying to ignore them. Hell would freeze over before she accepted she had any kind of attraction to Zac Green, but that didn't stop her noticing new little details about him. Like how the sun picked out rich tones of gold and chestnut in his thick hair, and how the tiny mole above his top lip disappeared into the crease of his dimple when he laughed. And she found herself flushing whenever he was close enough for her nose to pick up on the subtlety of his aftershave – a clean, appealing scent with a hint of spice.

If she was really honest with herself, after waking up in his bed on Monday morning, she was struggling to push him out of her thoughts.

And that was why she needed to move out of the apartment as soon as possible.

Another reason was Julian's nosy neighbour, Leonard, and Nina found herself looking up towards his apartment as she crossed the courtyard later that night, relieved there was no sign of him. It was late, so hopefully he would be in bed.

Rachel had insisted her taxi drop Nina off at the entrance to the complex, despite Nina's insistence that she could walk the short distance home. Peyton was missing and the police still had no idea what had happened, her friend sensibly pointed out. Regardless of whether Julian was involved or not, it was gone midnight and it wasn't a wise idea walking through the city streets alone at night, despite there still being people about.

When Nina had initially argued back that she would be fine, Charlotte had chipped in.

'She's right, Nina. Listen to her. They still haven't found that other woman who went missing either, have they?'

'What woman?' Nina had asked.

'You know, the one who disappeared last Christmas. They

thought she might have fallen in the river, but she's never been found.'

'Maria Adams,' Tori had said, googling her. 'She lived just out of the city and went missing after her work's Christmas party. The last sighting of her was on the footpath alongside the River Wensum.'

'Yes, that's her,' Charlotte had confirmed.

Nina vaguely remembered the case and she googled Maria's name when she arrived home.

Zac's door was already shut and she assumed he was in bed, though he had been considerate enough to leave the hall light and a table lamp in the lounge switched on for her.

Settling down on the sofa, Nina read a few articles about Maria, wondering if there had been any further developments in her case.

But, by all accounts, she had vanished without a trace.

Just like Peyton Landis.

The thought popped into her head out of the blue and she suddenly found herself considering both women. It was ridiculous to even try to link the two of them together, but now it was all she could think about.

Like Maria, Peyton had, according to the police, been on her way home after a night out. And they had disappeared within eight months of each other.

In both cases, the police suspected they had fallen in the water.

But if that was true, why hadn't their bodies ever been found?

Nina studied a photo of Maria Adams. She was brunette and pretty. A similar slender build to Peyton Landis, though the hair colour was wrong and facially they didn't look anything alike.

There was nothing to connect them to each other. And the police weren't stupid. They would've looked at all of this stuff.

Still, it didn't stop her searching Peyton Landis next, and seeing the woman's familiar face again and the CCTV image of the outfit Peyton had been wearing the night she disappeared only reaffirmed what Nina already knew. Peyton had definitely been in Julian's apartment that night.

There had been a lot more press coverage of her disappearance over the past couple of days as public interest was piqued, everyone coming up with their own theory as to what had happened to her. Some believed, like the police, that she had fallen into the river, while other theories were more outlandish. On X, the former Twitter site, there were threads by armchair detectives discussing drug dealers Peyton was reputed to owe money to, while others suspected her ex-boyfriend. A few even claimed she had faked her own death, though to what end, Nina wasn't quite sure.

Amateur sleuths were stalking the riverbanks and loitering outside her home in the hope of cracking the case, with a couple of TikTokers arrested for breaking and entering, streaming live from her bedroom until the police arrived to shut them down.

It was sick and disgusting how people were trying to exploit her when she wasn't here to defend herself, and Nina completely agreed with the detective who appeared at a press conference calling them ghouls and asking them to stop, while conveniently ignoring that she was also taking far too much interest in Peyton's case.

She read article after article about the investigation, finding out everything she could about the woman and comparing her circumstances to those of Maria Adams.

Peyton was older than Maria. She had not long turned thirty-three, while Maria was just twenty-five. She worked for the insurance giant, Aviva, and Maria for a local independent jewellers called Nix. Both were single, and Peyton came from Attleborough, where she lived alone, while Maria house-shared. Though the woman she lived with had been away the weekend she had gone missing.

Maria had been at her work's Christmas do and had disappeared in December. Peyton was celebrating a work colleague's birthday and had vanished on one of the hottest nights of the year.

Both women had been drinking, which is why the police were so focused on the river.

Street cameras showed Maria heading in the direction of home, but she never made it. And Nina knew Peyton had been in Julian Wiseman's apartment. She just didn't know if the woman had left there alive. And, frustratingly, it wasn't being investigated because of the lie he and Tabitha had told.

She was wasting her time trying to join dots that were too far apart and, stifling a yawn, she decided to call it a night.

It was after she was in bed, the light already out, and Hannibal snuggled up beside her, that a thought occurred, and reaching for her phone, Nina squinted at the screen and typed a new search into Google.

Missing women in Norwich.

The initial results were all about Peyton Landis and Maria Adams, but further down the page amidst the press articles was a link to an amateurish website called Unsolved Mysteries.

It had been updated in the last few days and the homepage Nina clicked on told her it was for an online video series presented by a man named Scott Thomas, who described himself as a private investigator, conducting his own find searches regarding unexplained encounters. They varied from otherworldly to gruesome. Tales of haunted houses and UFOs, to ghost dogs – Norfolk's own black shuck was featured – and serial killers. It was the kind of thing Nina might occasionally watch if she was drunk, but mostly she rolled her eyes at.

The episode on the screen in front of her was about Peyton's disappearance, but what had Nina's eyes widening was the question being posed as a headline.

Is there a serial killer flying under the radar in Norfolk?

Knowing she wouldn't be able to sleep until the question was answered, she clicked play.

24

In hindsight, Leonard realised he shouldn't have goaded Julian when he saw him in the lift on Tuesday night. Not only was the man potentially dangerous, but Leonard had tipped him off that he knew he was up to no good. Now, if there was any evidence to find – and, frustratingly, despite his best efforts, he hadn't uncovered anything yet – then Julian was likely to destroy it.

So far, Leonard had tried everything. Thanks to the blackout, the cameras had all been down the night Peyton Landis went missing, so if Julian had taken the woman up to his apartment then it wasn't recorded anywhere, and he had been up to Julian's floor when he knew the other man was out to have a nose around, but there wasn't much to see. On a whim, he had even tried the front door, but, of course, it was locked, and breaking in, especially with no one to keep lookout, was just too risky.

Instead, he had been trying to strike up conversation with all of the neighbours, in the hope that they might have seen something, though no one had.

Some had given him a wide berth, familiar with his reputation, but a few were sucked in by his gossipy tones when he furtively told them, 'Did you know the police think Peyton Landis might have been here the night she vanished?'

Even Conrad, who lived on the floor below and who usually ignored Leonard, had been curious enough to talk.

'They really think she was here at River Heights? Who do they think she was with?' he had asked, his close-set eyes bulging as he tried to push Leonard to reveal his source.

Leonard was careful not to give any specific information away, and he didn't mention Julian's name either, talking about Peyton's disappearance in a general way, and he could tell that it was irritating Conrad.

Well, tough. It was the first time the man had bothered to give him the time of day. Why should he do him any special favours?

Unfortunately, his reluctance to share information only seemed to make Conrad more curious. 'Was it you who saw her?' he'd asked.

'No, it wasn't,' Leonard had blustered.

'Really? I see you walking around keeping an eye on things, especially late at night,' the younger man had pushed. 'You can tell me if it was you. I won't say anything.'

'I assure you I didn't see a thing.'

Despite Leonard's indignant tone, he got the impression Conrad didn't believe him. Well, that was tough. He was telling the truth, and keen to move on, he'd excused himself.

So far, he had avoided approaching the Fairchild woman.

Initially, he had thought she was a troublemaker, but now he realised they were perhaps on the same side. But would she give him the time of day after their last encounter?

By Friday afternoon, with no avenues left to explore, he was desperate enough to try to reach out. If the two of them could put their heads together, maybe they could find a way together to trip Julian Wiseman up.

25

At Kevin Wiseman's insistence, Tabitha took Friday off work.

Her job came with twenty-five days' annual leave, but she wasn't keen on taking personal time and she had never been a woman who was good at switching off from the office. It was her parents' fiftieth wedding anniversary, though, and on Saturday night there was a surprise party planned.

The party was Jemima Wiseman's idea and at first Tabitha had been unsure. Her parents were not people who liked a fuss and she was already taking them for an afternoon tea at the Assembly House the following weekend.

Eventually, she had caved under pressure and this morning she and Jemima would be going over the final details to ensure everything was in place.

Jemima had at first suggested they host the party at Tabitha's house, but that wasn't a good idea. It wasn't big enough and the layout wasn't party friendly, she had pointed out.

She had been relieved when Jemima then offered to host. The Wisemans' house was far bigger and perfect for entertaining, and Jemima had so much more experience when it came to these kinds of things.

As she drove out to Coltishall, sunglasses on to protect her eyes from the sun burning against the windscreen, Tabitha barely noticed the lovely weather.

One on one or in smaller intimate groups, she was fine, but parties, where she was forced to work a room making polite small talk with people, some she barely knew, made her anxious and was something of an ordeal for her.

It was also a few days since she had heard from Julian.

He had promised her that he would accompany her to the anniversary party, but that had been after the police had visited her house and she had covered for him.

His mood the following day had worried her, though, as had his dismissive rudeness when she'd showed up at his apartment. And even though things had improved before she had left, she hadn't heard from him all week and was starting to worry he wasn't going to turn up.

Needing to put her mind at ease, she called him now on hands-free, fresh nerves surfacing when he didn't answer and the ringing cut to voicemail.

'It's only Tabitha,' she told the answer service, injecting lightness into her tone. 'Just checking you haven't forgotten about the party tomorrow night. Shall I pick you up?'

That was good. End on a question. And offering to pick him up was a smart move too. If he was with her, she wouldn't be worrying as she waited for him to arrive.

Still, she wondered if he would get back to her, knowing how unreliable he was. She had almost reached Coltishall when her phone started ringing. Her heart was a leaden ball in her chest seeing his name flash up.

Please don't let me down.

'Hi,' she greeted him after pressing answer, trying not to sound too excited. 'How are you?'

'You left me a voicemail,' he complained, ignoring her question. 'Couldn't you have just messaged or sent me a voice note like a normal person? Now I have to listen to it to clear it off my phone.'

Tabitha prickled. 'I had to, I'm afraid. I'm driving and on hands-free. I'm heading over to your mother's, actually.'

'Why?' He sounded annoyed now.

'We're going over the final arrangements for tomorrow, silly. These parties don't just organise themselves.' She paused. 'That was what the message was about, actually. I wanted to double-check you hadn't forgotten. Shall I pick you up at six-thirty? Your mum and dad are going to get my parents. They think they're off out for a meal, but your mum is going to pretend she's forgotten something so they have to nip home. We need to be there at the house before they walk in.'

She was aware she was babbling and giving far more information than was needed and she forced herself to stop.

There was silence on the line, and for a moment she thought Julian had hung up, but then she heard what sounded like a huff, and she waited impatiently for his response, concern gnawing at her belly.

'I'll meet you there,' he said eventually.

'It's no trouble to pick you up,' Tabitha insisted. 'I can cut through the city.'

'No, I have plans in the afternoon. It's easier for me to meet you there.'

Plans? He hadn't mentioned anything about plans before. What if they overran or he forgot about the party?

Spiralling panic had her overreacting, her voice becoming high-pitched. 'You're not going to let me down for this, are you,

Julian? You promised you would go and I'm counting on you being there.'

'Okay, chill out. I never said I wasn't going.'

'I helped cover for you and you owe me.'

'I'm aware of that,' he snapped. 'You keep reminding me. Are you going to keep holding that threat over my head, blackmailing me to do things for you?'

Was that what he thought she was doing?

Tears sprang, pricking the back of Tabitha's eyes. 'I'm not trying to blackmail you. Julian, I promise that's not what this is.'

'Don't make me regret asking for your help, Tabs.'

He sounded like he was reprimanding a child and, guiltily, she backed down.

'I'm sorry. You know I will always help you. You're so important to me.'

There was another pause that seemed to drag on and she was about to fill it with more apologies when he spoke again, his tone sombre.

'I'll see you tomorrow night.'

Tabitha released a shaky breath, relief making her giddy. She was about to thank him and promise him again how she would always be there for him, when she realised he had ended the call.

Not on the best note, but at least he was coming.

Her mood had improved by the time she pulled into the driveway of Kevin and Jemima's beautiful home, and even though her mind wandered as they discussed guests and catering, she was able to appear enthusiastic.

'Do you have something nice to wear?' Jemima asked when they were finishing up. She had been showing Tabitha the pretty green and white dress she had bought for the party, that would no doubt look stunning on her slim frame. She was a couple of years shy of her seventieth birthday, though looked at least a decade younger with her salon-sleek auburn bob, her clothes and make-up always perfect.

Truthfully, Tabitha hadn't given much thought to her outfit. Clothes always seemed to hang wrong on her body and dressing up had never held that much appeal.

'Probably my black A line dress,' she told Jemima.

It was her go-to item and one of the few things she owned that she knew flattered her.

Already, Jemima wasn't looking impressed. 'You wear that old dress everywhere, sweetheart. And black does nothing for your complexion. It's your parents' wedding anniversary. A celebration of their life together. Not a funeral.'

Her words weren't said unkindly, but still Tabitha felt the sting.

She wasn't a clothes horse and knew she couldn't compete with younger, prettier women. It wasn't as if she didn't make any effort. She always wore make-up, even following some of the tutorials she had found on YouTube, and last year she had finally conceded and allowed her mousy brown locks to be lightened to blonde.

'We're going to go shopping,' Jemima declared, adding, as she clocked Tabitha's horrified expression, 'Don't look so worried. It will do you good to get a makeover and we can find you the perfect outfit.'

Tabitha weakly protested, pointing out that she had things to do, but Jemima batted away all of her excuses.

'It will be fun,' she promised.

To Tabitha's surprise, she didn't hate the experience as much as she was expecting, and after being made to try on a dozen different outfits, she had a new dress. At first, she had been dubious about the bold blue shade, so unused to wearing colour, but Jemima was insistent it was the one, saying it brought out the colour of her eyes, and Tabitha had to admit the sweetheart necklace and capped sleeves did flatter her. Shoes had come next. A pretty nude pair with a heel she was going to be scared of walking in.

Then it was time for a facial, followed by a manicure and pedicure, and finally a visit to the hair salon, where Jemima persuaded her to have fresh highlights threaded through her hair.

Later that night, Tabitha stood in front of the floor-to-ceiling mirror in her bedroom dressed in her new clothes, surprised with what she saw.

Jemima was right. They did flatter her, and for a change, the reflection looking back showed a woman who seemed confident in her appearance and comfortable in her own skin.

It gave her the belief that she could be that woman if she wanted.

And she really did want to be her.

She was determined that when Julian saw her, she was going to knock him dead.

26

'You were out late last night,' Zac commented when Nina emerged the following morning.

He was leant against the kitchen counter, a plate of toast beside him that he was munching his way through as he watched the news on breakfast TV.

When she responded with a grunt, getting a glass of water that she glugged down quickly, he added, 'Hangover? How late were you?'

'You're not my dad, Zac. Quit it with the questions. My head hurts.'

Truthfully, she had only drunk three glasses of wine, but her night hadn't been an early one as she had stayed up watching the video posted by Scott Thomas and had then been unable to sleep, her tired mind playing over everything he had said.

Her plan last night had been to talk to Zac before he headed off to work, wanting to use him as a sounding board for what she had learnt. But now, in the cold light of day, she knew that would be a mistake. He wasn't the sort of person to just accept what someone said without digging deeper for facts. There would be questions and, damn it, she wasn't ready for those. Not this early in the morning when she was coasting on too little sleep.

No, she decided she would do some research of her own and wait until he came home, when hopefully she would be feeling less irritable.

When he finally left to go to work, she fired up her Mac and typed into Google the name Tammy Helgens. The face of the pretty blonde who appeared on her screen was the same one she had seen last night on Scott Thomas's video.

Tammy had vanished from her home in Poringland six months ago and, to this day, no one knew what had happened to her. Although she hadn't taken her phone with her, her purse had gone and she was being treated as a missing person. An adult who had left home of her own accord.

She had no family, other than a brother who lived overseas, and had not long split up with her boyfriend, and it wasn't the first time she had upped and moved on a whim.

Still, it made no sense. According to Tammy's friends, she was settled in Norfolk and enjoyed her job working at Dunston Hall – a popular hotel and golf club. There had been no animosity in the break-up with her boyfriend; they had simply drifted apart, and she had an active social circle, living life to the full. Her friends had argued that she wouldn't just leave without telling anyone.

Julie Rodriguez was next.

Petite with glossy, dark hair and a megawatt smile, she had disappeared while out running two months ago. Like the other women, Julie was single, and she had recently moved out of the city-centre house that she had shared with three friends, buying a fixer-upper property in Lingwood.

The police were still actively following leads, but given the remote location where she had disappeared from, no one really knew what had happened to her.

So Julian had moved back to Norfolk a year ago and in the last nine months four women had vanished without a trace from around the Norwich area.

It all felt rather coincidental, but was that because Nina was making it so?

The police didn't think the cases were connected, Scott had said.

Peyton and Maria had both gone missing after a night out, but they had been inebriated and walking routes that took them by the river. Meanwhile, Julie had disappeared while out running in the countryside and Tammy had vanished from her home.

Scott hadn't pointed the finger of suspicion at anyone in particular. He was just asking questions and joining dots. Nina was almost tempted to call him, wondering what he would think learning that Peyton Landis had been in Julian Wiseman's apartment.

Would her information spark a change of direction for his investigation or would he accuse her of trying to wreck an innocent man's life?

Unsure what to do, she continued looking into Julie Rodriguez, turning to the woman's social media.

It was going over Julie's Facebook profile, which fortunately had lax privacy settings, that Nina made a connection. Under the woman's 'About' information, she had listed all of her places of work and one of her employers had been Wiseman Homes.

It had been over seven years ago and, according to the timeline, only for a few months. And Nina had no idea if Julian would have ever come into contact with the woman. As far as she could see, he had never actually worked at his father's firm.

Still, it was a connection. Albeit a tenuous one.

She carried on down her rabbit hole for a while longer, though, try as she might, she could find nothing else that might link Maria Adams or Tammy Helgens to Julian.

Eventually, she clicked off from the internet, knowing she had work to do.

Before opening the manuscript she was editing, she messaged her brother, curious to know what his thoughts on Julian were. She kept her question vague, not wanting to worry him, and wasn't surprised when he thought her interest in Julian was personal.

He's a bit of an entitled arsehole, Nina, came his response. *I don't know him well, but what I do know of him I don't like. I'd stay clear if I was you. You're too good for him. x*

So Dexter wasn't a fan either.

The black marks against Julian kept stacking up.

Nina put her phone to one side, and trying to keep her mind focused, she worked solidly throughout the rest of the afternoon.

She had no plans for tonight and hoped Zac didn't either, as she really needed to talk through what she had found with someone else. Rachel had her sister visiting this weekend, while both Tori and Charlotte could be prone to flights of fancy. As irritating as Zac was at times, he was logical in his approach. He might not always tell her what she wanted to hear, but he would make sure she stayed grounded.

On a whim, she picked up her phone and sent him a WhatsApp message.

> Are you about tonight? I'm cooking and didn't know whether to include you.

His reply came quickly.

> Yeah. Sounds good.

Pleased with his answer, Nina glanced at her watch. It was nearly 6 p.m. and she needed some ingredients for the paella she wanted to make. Deciding it would be quicker to drive to the supermarket instead of walking, she headed down to the car park, dismayed when she saw Leonard exiting his building. Keeping her head down, hoping he hadn't spotted her, she hurried over to her car, tensing when she heard the crunch of footsteps behind her. She had just clicked her fob when she heard his voice.

'Wait a minute. I need to speak with you.'

Nina didn't have the time or the inclination for a conversation with him. She'd seen him from the balcony talking to different neighbours over the last couple of days and had no idea what trouble he was stirring now.

'I'm running late,' she told him. 'I don't have time.'

'I'll be quick. It's important.'

There was something in his tone that had changed from their previous encounter. Before, he had been taunting and smug. A proper busybody who seemed to relish having one up on her, but now he just sounded desperate.

Well, tough. He would have to find someone else to bother.

'I'm sorry. I've got to go.'

She opened the door, tossing her handbag inside and climbed into the driver's seat.

'It's about Julian Wiseman,' Leonard tried again.

Nina rolled her eyes. She was sick of this game. 'Tell him what I did if you have to. I no longer care. I called the police because I thought it was the right thing to do.'

'It was. You were right.'

She had already slammed the door before his words registered. They still took a second to sink in and, as they did, she wound the window down, staring up at Leonard, who was still standing by her car.

'What do you mean, I was right?'

'You were right that he was with the missing woman the night she disappeared.'

Nina already knew that, but was he being straight with her?

'Why do you say that?' she asked warily, worried this was some kind of trap to try to catch her out.

'Because I overheard him talking with his lady friend, the one who vouched for his whereabouts.'

'Tabitha?'

She was trying hard not to get her hopes up, but couldn't extinguish the tiny spark of excitement in her belly that someone might actually believe her.

'Yes, the one who works for his dad. They were arguing and she was angry with him because she said he didn't appreciate the sacrifice she had made in covering for him.'

'You really heard her say that?'

'Yes,' Leonard told her impatiently. 'My hearing works fine. It was Monday lunchtime and I saw her going up to Julian's apartment. I went out onto the balcony so I could hear what they said.'

'Monday? That was five days ago!' Why on earth was he only just telling her this now? 'Have you gone to the police?'

'And told them what? That I heard a conversation?' He was getting ratty now. 'It's my word against theirs. We know how that worked out for you,' he added sarcastically.

'It doesn't matter. You have to tell them.'

'No. What we need to do is gather more evidence.'

Was he serious?

'You and I?' Nina asked, her tone so dubious he glared at her.

'We're the only two who know the truth. You need to work with me here. There has to be some physical evidence somewhere. I'm thinking if we can maybe get inside Julian's apartment—'

'Whoa, hold on. That's breaking and entering.'

'No worse than what he's done,' Leonard sniffed.

This was certainly a turnabout of events. Before, the old man had been hell-bent on trying to catch her out. Now he wanted to be partners in crime?

It was the fact he was coming to her and not going to the police that bothered her, paranoia creeping in as she wondered if this was another one of his games.

Was he trying to set her up?

'So, what do you say then? They keep copies of the keys in the maintenance room. One of us needs to be a lookout.'

No. Nina didn't like this at all.

'I think if you really heard them talking, then you need to go to the police,' she said firmly, starting to wind the window up.

He looked dismayed. 'You're making a big mistake.'

'I don't think so. Goodbye, Leonard.'

He remained where he was as she backed out of the parking space, a scowl on his face as she pulled away, and as she drove down to the supermarket, she thought over what he had told her.

If he was being level with her, then the police needed to know. He couldn't go breaking into Julian's apartment. Exactly what he thought he might find, she wasn't sure. Julian had lied about Peyton being there, so he was hardly going to leave any trace of her for Leonard to find.

She decided she would mention the conversation to Zac tonight and get his take on it. For now she focused on the dinner she was going to make, getting carried away in the supermarket aisles as she bought dessert and wine, along with the ingredients she needed to make the dish.

It was going to be quite some feast, she realised, looking at her basket as she waited in the queue for the self-service checkout, and she wondered why she was going to so much effort. She was only cooking for Zac, after all.

To try to keep him sweet, she tried to convince herself, though she wasn't entirely sure that was the only reason.

'What are you making me for dinner, then?'

The deep voice came from behind her, pulling her from her thoughts, and she swung around, surprised, then disappointed to find Conrad grinning at her.

She hadn't bothered to change before leaving the apartment and still wore the casual yellow sundress she had been working in all afternoon. It had thin shoulder straps and dipped a little low in the cleavage, and now, seeing the way he was leering at her, she wished she had grabbed a cardigan that covered her up a bit more.

He had annoyed her when she saw him in the pool, refusing to leave her alone, and she wasn't in the mood to make small talk with him now. Still, she couldn't bring herself to be outrightly rude when all he had done was ask her a question.

'I'm making paella, but I'm afraid it's not for you.' She offered him the ghost of a smile and turned away.

'Aw, that's a shame. I like a woman who's good in the kitchen.'

Really? Nina rolled her eyes, cringing at his comment and deciding to ignore it.

When he didn't get a reaction, she felt him lean over her shoulder to peek in the basket again, and the warmth of his breath brushed her bare shoulder.

'Maybe you can cook for me another time?' he asked, his tone hopeful.

'I don't think so.'

'Aw, that's a shame. Do you have a boyfriend then?'

'Yes, yes, I do,' Nina lied. Thankful when after another 'aw' he fell silent.

Not for long, though, and in the end it was the most innocuous comment that had her temper boiling over.

'You have pretty eyes,' he said.

'How would you know?' she snapped, turning on him. 'You're standing behind me!'

For a moment, he seemed surprised at her tone.

'Well, I can see them now,' he told her defensively. 'And they're pretty.'

Nina shook her head at him, rolling her eyes.

Behind Conrad, an older lady who was listening to their exchange chastised her.

'Don't be so rude to the young man. He just paid you a compliment.'

Nina reddened. Was she overreacting? Conrad was irritating, a little like an annoying fly and he was getting on her nerves, but he hadn't done anything really to warrant her temper.

Spotting a checkout had come free, she hurried over, keen to be away from the awkward situation, quickly scanning her items through.

She smiled at the store assistant who came over to approve her wine.

As the woman tapped at the screen, Nina absently watched, looking at her blood-red nails and the ruby ring on her little finger. The way it glittered reminded her of the pendant Peyton Landis had been wearing.

The one she had been hunting for before she had disappeared inside with Julian.

Was it still on Julian's balcony?

If so, it would be proof that Julian was lying. That Peyton had been with him that night.

Nina considered the implications as she headed out of the store. Should she call the police and tell them or would she be wasting her time? Julian might have already found and disposed of the pendant.

Unsure what to do, she loaded her bags into the boot of her car, heading round to the driver's door.

'Hey, I didn't mean anything.'

Distracted by the voice, she looked up, her heart sinking when she saw Conrad. He was parked in the bay opposite, and as they made eye contact, he took it as an opportunity to wander over.

'I was only trying to be friendly in there,' he said, sounding genuinely upset.

Had she overreacted?

She had been a little bit rude, she guessed.

'I know. I'm in a rush and not in a good mood. I'm sorry I took it out on you, though,' she told him. It was a halfway apology as she didn't want to encourage him.

His grin widened, reminding her of a child who had just been praised. In that moment, she realised he was probably harmless, though perhaps not the sharpest tool in the box, and he might be a bit of a flirt, but he wasn't a sex pest.

'It's okay,' he told her, before chancing his luck again. 'You can make it up to me by cooking me dinner sometime.'

Nina started to shake her head, about to reiterate the boyfriend lie, but then he winked at her and she realised he was joking.

'Is everything okay here?'

A new voice, and both Nina's and Conrad's heads shot round.

Julian?

Nina's eyes widened.

He stood there in his trademark outfit of linen shirt and chinos, looking authoritative and unflappable as he glared at Conrad, and for a moment, she worried Conrad might get confrontational. Instead, he surprised her by backing off immediately.

'We were just talking.'

He looked hopefully at Nina to back him up and she nodded.

When Julian made no attempt to leave, looking like he wanted to talk to her, nerves crept into her belly. Had he found out she was the one who had called the police?

Now she wanted Conrad to stay, but he was already stepping away in the direction of his car.

Nina watched him go, very conscious that she was alone with Julian, her mind racing ahead of her. Had Leonard said something to him?

No, that was ridiculous. He had no way of knowing he would find her here.

Besides, Julian didn't look mad or like he planned to confront her. If she was honest, he seemed pleased that they had bumped into each other.

'Are you sure everything is okay?' he asked, sounding genuinely concerned.

'Yes, I'm fine. We were just talking.'

'The man is an idiot.' Julian rolled his eyes. 'I know what he's like.'

'You know him?'

'Only in passing. He lives two floors below me. We've had a couple of run-ins.'

Julian didn't elaborate what sort of run-ins and Nina didn't push.

Was he really just here because he had seen her talking to Conrad?

Given that she had spent a fair amount of time googling Julian and his family over the past few days, and she felt she knew him better than she actually did, she was terrified she might slip up and give away some detail she wasn't supposed to know.

'You were with Zac Green?' he commented now, as if only just recalling they had met briefly, even though Nina had the impression he remembered exactly who she was.

It made her uneasy. What else did he know about her?

As she nodded, he probed further. 'Are you his girlfriend?'

'No, we're just friends,' she told him. 'He's actually my brother's best friend. I'm staying with him while Dexter's away.'

Stop babbling, Nina.

Julian smiled politely. 'Interesting.'

He seemed down to earth; nice and unassuming. She found it hard to reconcile he was the man described as entitled and a spoilt brat.

An unwelcome image popped into her head. Of Peyton Landis on her knees as Julian looked up at the stars.

Oh God. Nina had seen his dick.

Her neck flushed and her cheeks burned in mortification.

'So you're single then?'

Wait, what?

Why did he want to know that?

'Um, yes,' she answered, still unable to shut the picture show off that was playing in her head.

He was rocking from one foot to the other now and, unless she was mistaken, he seemed a little nervous.

'I know this is wholly inappropriate after you've just had to deal with Conrad Mackenzie, but if you ever fancy having a drink with me, I would love to take you out sometime.'

Belatedly, Nina understood. He was hitting on her, and as her jaw dropped, he gave her a coy smile that if she didn't know better suggested he wasn't used to doing this sort of thing. It was an act, because he hadn't been at all bashful around Peyton Landis, and Nina had read enough about him to know he was a confident, to the point of arrogant, man.

So Julian Wiseman wanted to take her out for a drink. For a moment, she had no idea how to react. Was his invite genuine or was there an ulterior motive?

He faltered a little. 'I'm sorry. Perhaps I shouldn't have asked.'

But he had, and now she had a dilemma. Because although she suspected he had done something bad to Peyton Landis, he could also provide her with answers.

Was Peyton's ruby pendant still on his balcony?

If she went on a date with him, would she get an invite up to his apartment?

That could be dangerous. But it was legal and far better than Leonard's suggestion.

What she should really do was give him a polite but firm no, then get the hell out of there. Instead, she found herself smiling back at him.

'No, it's okay. I'm glad you did. In fact, I would really like that.'

27

'You did what?'

Zac's tone was incredulous and Nina watched his nostrils flare, knowing he was trying to steady his temper.

After her encounter with Julian Wiseman, she had returned to the apartment and cooked the paella. She had opened the wine to let it breathe and asked Alexa to select a chilled playlist, ignoring that, minus candles, this was everything she would do in preparation for a real date.

It wasn't, and the motions she went through were just because she needed Zac to be on her side. At least, that's what she'd told herself.

He had been impressed when he'd arrived home. Surprised at the effort she had gone to, and appreciative too. And for a while, it had felt like their trajectory had changed; both of them negotiating an unknown territory, and there was a carefulness between them that caught Nina off guard. She sensed Zac felt it too. The teasing and banter was still there, but it was gentler. Neither one of them wanting to overstep boundaries. And what was it with her reaction all of a sudden whenever he made her laugh, a warmth spreading inside of her, and the way her skin sizzled on the occasions when he caught and held her stare.

She had only drunk a couple of glasses of wine, but she felt intoxicated.

Which was ridiculous.

This was Zac. Annoying Zac. Her brother's best friend and her childhood tormentor.

She did not have feelings for him.

Well, certainly not *those* kind of feelings.

Forcing herself to focus, she had told him about her day. Starting with the video she had watched late last night, irritated when she saw he was biting his lip to stay quiet, and reminding herself this was never going to be an easy sell.

From there, she explained everything, from Scott Thomas's theory about a serial killer, her encounter with Leonard and how she had remembered Peyton's pendant. Then she told him that she had bumped into Julian at the supermarket and how he had asked her out. That was when Zac's expression had gone from mildly irritated to annoyed.

She had always known she would have her work cut out trying to win him over and she had her argument carefully prepared, but the sudden change in him from mellow to angry genuinely caught her off guard. She had expected scepticism, but not this kind of reaction and she needed to get him back on side.

'Look, just hear me out, okay?' she told him, trying to calm things down.

'You've agreed to go for a drink with a man you're determined to try to pin a murder on,' he raged. 'I don't need to hear you out to tell you you're out of your mind.'

Nina bristled a little. 'You make it sound like I'm trying to set him up.'

'Can't you just accept that maybe you got it wrong? That maybe it really was Tabitha with Julian that night.'

'No! Because it wasn't. And it's not just me. Leonard heard them talking too. Tabitha is covering for him. She admitted it.'

'According to Leonard,' Zac muttered sarcastically.

'So you don't believe him either?'

'No, I don't believe him. He's a bored old man out to cause trouble. If he was telling the truth, he would have gone to the police. As for you, it's not that I don't believe you, Nina. I just think you need to accept you may have been mistaken.'

'But I'm not mistaken. Regardless of what you or anyone else thinks, I trust my eyes. I know what I saw.' She tried to keep her voice calm. There was no point in both of them yelling. 'Tabitha is covering for him and that means he is hiding something.'

'Well, if you are right, then you need to stay the hell away from him.'

'But he asked me out. If I can get inside his apartment, then maybe I can find that pendant, which will prove it was Peyton Landis there that night.'

'For fuck's sake, Nina. You're not Nancy Drew.' Zac shoved his hands back into his hair, looking like he was going to start yanking it out at the roots. Getting up from the table, he paced into the kitchen area, then back again. 'Why would you think this is a good idea?'

'Because it's the only way we can catch him out.'

'*We*? There is no bloody we.' Zac was shaking his head in disbelief. 'I'm not on board with any of this. You don't even know for certain that Peyton Landis is dead. At the moment, she is still a missing person.'

'As are Maria Adams, Tammy Helgens and Julie Rodriguez. These women vanished into thin air, Zac, and all over the last twelve months since Julian Wiseman returned home.'

'Do you not think the police have investigated all of this? That if there was a link they would have found it?'

'Scott Thomas says—'

'Who?'

'The investigator with the video channel who I just told you about? Zac, weren't you even listening?' Nina huffed in frustration, but he wasn't paying attention to her, muttering under his breath as he tapped into his phone. 'What are you doing?' she asked.

'Scott Thomas,' Zac read aloud. 'Solves the mysteries others give up on.' He was silent for a moment as he studied the screen. 'Are you serious, Nina? He posts about bloody aliens. This is the guy you want to believe?'

'That's just one thing. And it has nothing to do with this case.'

'He's an opportunist.'

'But he makes a good point.'

Zac shook his head in disgust. 'I need to call Dexter and get him to talk some sense into you, because you're sure as hell not listening to me.'

No, Nina didn't want him talking to her brother. She had asked Dexter for his views on Julian, but she hadn't told him why she wanted to know, letting him assume her interest was romantic. Dexter would kill her if he knew the truth.

She pushed her chair back, following Zac as he paced back into the kitchen, and trying to grab for his phone.

'Don't involve him in this,' she pleaded when he held it out of her reach. 'Zac, please. All you will do is make him worry and I'm going to meet Julian either way,' she challenged. 'You can't stop me.'

When he glared at her but made no further move to call her brother, she tried again.

'Please, sit down and talk to me. Let's have a rational conversation.'

'There's nothing rational about any of this,' Zac growled, but he did relent, leaving his phone on the counter and following her back to the table.

'Look, it's just a drink,' Nina tried to reason. 'And it's not like I'm teaming up with Leonard and trying to break into Julian's apartment. I'm doing this the sensible and legal way. I'll be fine.'

'You seem very sure about that.'

'I am. Well, I will be if you agree to help me.'

Zac's eyes narrowed. 'Help you how, exactly?'

Nina held his gaze. 'I need you to keep watch. And, if necessary, I need you to get me out of his apartment.'

* * *

Zac didn't like any of this.

And he was wishing he had called Dexter, because then he wouldn't be alone in knowing about Nina's crazy-arsed plan.

Not that she would have listened to her brother.

She had already made her mind up that Julian was guilty and she had decided that it was her job to expose him. She had told Zac that she was going to do this with or without his help and he couldn't keep an eye on her unless he went along with her hare-brained scheme.

So he had watched Scott Thomas's video with her. It was amateurish and, for the most part, Scott was an over-the-top conspiracy theorist, reading far too much into situations and blowing them out of proportion with outlandish explanations. But there were four missing women – Zac had checked – and the first one, Maria Adams, had vanished not long after Julian had returned from the US.

The police had found nothing to link them and there was no evidence to suggest anything sinister had happened, but still, a small part of him worried in case Nina was right.

With Dexter away, it was down to Zac to look out for her.

Not that he would ever tell her that, aware she would scoff and no doubt roll her eyes, telling him that she didn't need a bodyguard.

And yes, this was Nina, and she was smart and capable, but she could also be stubborn and a little reckless at times.

Besides, if things were reversed and he had a sister, he knew Dexter would be the same.

Zac focused on the responsibility, all the while ignoring that this whole Julian situation was also bothering him on a more personal level.

It wasn't something he was ready to address.

Not that there was time to anyway, given Nina's impetuous timeframe.

'So when is this date with Julian?' he had asked her after reluctantly agreeing to help her, trying his best to keep his tone neutral.

Her answer had given him palpitations.

'Tomorrow night.'

What? So soon?

'Don't you think you should wait a bit until we have a plan?'

'I have one,' she had told him, sounding annoyed. 'If you will just listen, I will tell you what I need you to do.'

So he had listened and she had explained, and it was why he was now up far too early on Saturday morning, sipping coffee out on the balcony as the sun burned through the mist, promising another scorching hot day.

Not that Zac could enjoy it. He knew he was going to spend all day fretting about what could go wrong tonight.

Nina's plan was foolish and potentially dangerous, and it left too much room for error.

And while he might have his doubts about what she had seen, she wasn't wavering.

'Why, if you believe Julian did something to Peyton, are you so determined to put yourself in harm's way?' he had asked in a last-ditch attempt to stop her. 'You don't even know her.'

As he'd suspected, Nina didn't have an answer for that, but he could tell from the stubborn glare she gave him that it wasn't going to stop her.

He had toyed again with calling Dexter, but if he did that, chances were that Nina would shut him out completely, and then he would lose what little control he had over the situation.

That was why he raised Mark's binoculars now, aiming them at Julian's apartment, then across Jarrold Bridge and the car park behind the law courts, wanting to assure himself that he would have a clear view of what was going on tonight.

Nina had agreed to go for a drink with Julian in the Adam and Eve pub.

In a way, that was good. The pub was a two-minute walk from the apartment complex, which meant they would be close. Zac didn't like that it involved going over Jarrold Bridge, but then he guessed wherever they went in the city would involve crossing the river.

The police suspected Maria Adams and Peyton Landis were in the water. Had Julian put them there?

At least the bridge was close to River Heights and Zac intended to be watching like a hawk.

Nina's plan then hinged on getting an invite up to the penthouse apartment.

That was the bit he really didn't like.

If she was correct and Peyton had been with Julian the night she had gone missing, exactly what had happened behind closed doors?

'It will be fine. I'll make sure he knows I've told you I'm with him,' she had assured Zac. 'And you will be watching for my signal to get me out of there as soon as I'm ready.'

She seemed to think she would be able to snoop while she was there, find this pendant she claimed to have seen, which was just ridiculous, because if the woman had been there, then Julian was likely to have wiped all trace.

Even worse, if Nina did find it and Julian caught on to why she was really there...

No, it didn't bear thinking about.

He reminded himself that at least she hadn't followed Leonard's lead and tried to break in. Zac didn't trust the old man at all, and he was angry that Leonard had put new ideas in Nina's head.

Would she have agreed to this date if she hadn't spoken to Leonard?

The meddlesome fool had a lot to answer for.

There were so many things that could potentially go wrong tonight.

Best-case scenario: Nina ended up looking like a dick, and had to admit she had been wrong about Julian.

But worst case? She could end up dead.

28

Julian Wiseman had asked Nina Fairchild out on a whim.

The very first time he had seen her was when they had passed on the bridge, and he had been aware that she was staring at him, checking him out. He had thought enough of the brief encounter at the time to wonder if she lived at River Heights, and had he not been in such a foul mood, he might have stopped and spoken to her.

She wasn't his usual type, but he had thought she was pretty enough, in a girl-next-door way, and it fed his ego that she was interested in him. Perhaps, he decided, she was worth keeping on the back burner.

Though, if she was a neighbour, he would have to be careful. He didn't like to play too close to home.

The second time he had run into her she had been with Zac Green and initially Julian had assumed she must be Zac's girlfriend. Not that Zac had introduced her as such, but then he hadn't actually introduced her at all. Julian had sensed tension between them, as if they had been fighting. Was it a lovers' tiff or did they just not like each other?

Although he was curious about their set-up, he backed right off the idea of getting to know Nina better. She had a connection to Zac, and just the fact they knew each other would make it messy.

A shame, because during that second encounter he had picked up on new details about her, like the colour of her eyes. They were almost golden in shade, but surrounded by a darker rim that made them pop. They reminded him of staring into a glass of whisky.

And there was an appealing clean, fresh scent about her that he'd picked up on straight away. No cheap soap or stale cigarette odour clinging to this one. But it was her determination to be involved in the conversation that had really piqued his interest.

She hadn't been impressed when Zac had ignored her, those fascinating eyes heating in annoyance, the jut of her chin and the pout of her mouth telling Julian that she had a stubbornness and a temper, and she wouldn't accept being ignored.

Spirit was the quality he appreciated most in a woman, and once he was back in his apartment and had managed to get rid of Tabitha, he had googled Nina, curious to find out more about her.

But then the whole sorry mess with Peyton Landis had distracted him from any further thoughts of her, and Julian was still determined to find out who had reported him to the police.

His money was still on Leonard Pickles and he was a little surprised the old busybody hadn't already confessed, knowing he was the sort of person who would enjoy telling Julian what he had done.

At some point, he would get to the truth and when he did, he would get his revenge, whether it be Leonard or someone else.

Thank God he had managed to persuade Tabitha to give him an alibi or he could be in prison right now. The crush she had on him was annoying, but he had to admit it had its uses too. The stupid woman would do anything to help him.

It was the second time she had covered for him, first with Katy, then with Peyton, and all he'd had to do was turn on the tears – okay, admittedly, they had been genuine, but he had been in one hell of a panic – then let her lie to the police.

Belatedly, he remembered her parents' anniversary party, cursing when he realised he had double-booked.

Well, he couldn't go now. He would be letting Nina down. And if he was honest, he really didn't want to mingle with his and Tabitha's friends and family anyway.

She would be annoyed with him, but she'd eventually get over it.

At least he hoped she would, recalling her recent threats.

Six years ago, with Katy, he had been certain Tabitha would never tell anyone she had given him a false alibi, but it seemed that over the time he was away she had grown in confidence and also in her own self-importance. Julian didn't appreciate being told he 'owed' her and having the favour she had done him lauded over him.

By helping him, she had implicated herself, and he had assumed that was enough of an incentive for her to stay quiet, but had he underestimated her?

She would be in trouble if the truth ever came out that she had covered for him, but not as much trouble as he would be in. The mere thought of the police knocking at his door again was enough to make him break out in a cold sweat.

No, she wouldn't do that to him. She was in love with him and her foolish belief that one day he would reciprocate her feelings kept her loyal.

He hoped.

Still, her threats bothered him and he decided he would

have to keep an eye on her. If she started to become a real problem, then he would figure out a way to deal with her.

For now, he turned his attention back to Nina, watching her exit her building and approach the bench in the courtyard gardens where he was waiting for her.

She wore her dark hair loose and the early-evening sun picked out shades of mahogany in the rich brown colour, while her bold dress that he couldn't quite decide if it was red or orange subtly skimmed her curves and was complemented by her tan.

Yes, he had definitely made the right choice, picking his date with Nina over Giles and Diane Percy's anniversary party, and he was glad he had seen Nina in the supermarket car park.

His imagination was already working overtime thinking about all the things he would like to do to her.

Not that he could let himself get carried away like he had done with Peyton, as they would no doubt have to go back to his place and he couldn't take those risks again. But still, they could have fun. He would just have to be careful to show some control.

It was almost a shame they had to go through with the pretence of a drink first.

Still, he understood the game, and if he wanted to get Nina naked, he needed to apply some charm and plenty of alcohol first.

'I love the dress,' he told her, getting to his feet. Already, he was imagining himself unzipping it later tonight.

She gave a self-conscious little shrug, but smiled and thanked him. 'Probably a little OTT for the pub, but it's one of my favourites.'

And she had worn it for him. She was certainly eager.

The annoying interruption of his mobile phone buzzing in his pocket distracted him and, frowning, he reached for the handset, wishing he hadn't bothered when he saw Tabitha's name flash up on the screen.

'Is everything okay?' Nina asked.

'Yes, yes. Fine.' He rejected the call, irritated that Tabitha dare spoil this moment, and ignoring the irony that she was no doubt calling because he had just ruined her night. The party for her parents would be in full swing by now and instead of focusing on them, Tabitha would likely be wondering where in the hell he was.

Well, tough.

He smoothed his expression, forcing a smile for Nina as he slipped the phone back in his pocket. 'Right, where were we?'

He had allowed her to choose the pub, amused when she picked the Adam and Eve, which was literally just across the bridge from where they lived.

It would be stumbling distance back to his place, though, and perhaps that was why she had picked it.

Keen to get this charade out of the way, he gestured towards the path, every inch the gentleman, at least for now.

'Right. Shall we?'

29

Tabitha had called Julian six times now, each one going to his voicemail, and her mind was in overdrive imagining all kinds of terrible scenarios.

He had promised her he would be here tonight and she had believed him, so something must have happened. Had there been an accident or was he was in some kind of trouble?

She longed to leave the party; to go and find him, needing reassurance that he was okay, but tonight was about her parents and there was no way Kevin and Jemima were going to let her skip out early. They had already been kind enough to host. At the very least, they expected her to be here.

Perhaps later she would wonder why they were so unbothered about Julian's whereabouts. He was their flesh and blood, but it seemed Tabitha was the only one who cared where he was.

Jemima seemed more concerned that Tabitha was okay and that her parents were having a good time, while Kevin was working the room. Ever the host, he had pasted on his social face and was keeping his guests entertained.

'You need to stop worrying about that boy of mine,' Jemima said eventually. She had followed Tabitha upstairs and out onto the terrace that led off from the first-floor landing, overlooking the extensive and well-manicured gardens to the west of the house. 'You only get one life, Tabitha. Don't waste it waiting for someone who is always going to let you down. Go downstairs and enjoy yourself.'

Annoyed at the advice, Tabitha took a moment to answer. Down below them, there was music and chatter as the guests mingled, the sun now low in the sky as the warm evening crept towards dusk. Soon, the solar lanterns that hung from the trees and the strings of fairy lights that zigzagged overhead the partygoers would start to glow, turning the garden into an enchanted wonderland.

Giles and Diane Percy had been delighted when their meal out with friends had turned into something bigger, the party catching them both completely off guard, and Tabitha had to hand it to Jemima – the woman certainly knew how to throw a party.

The team of caterers she used were consummate professionals, discreetly moving between guests topping up glasses and serving canapés, and they had prepared a mouth-watering buffet, which would be unveiled shortly.

Earlier, Tabitha had marvelled at it, but now she was sure she couldn't eat a thing. It was making her sick to her stomach that Julian wasn't here. After everything she had done for him, it was the one thing she had asked in return.

There had to be a genuine reason why he wasn't here. There simply had to be.

'He promised he would come,' she told Jemima now, close to tears.

She had gone to so much effort for him, sorting her hair and nails, wearing her new outfit, the one that Jemima had helped her to pick that made her feel special. The one she had planned to knock Julian dead in.

Now it had all gone to waste.

'He does this, Tabitha. You should know him by now.' Jemima offered her a handkerchief. 'I love Julian. Of course I do. But he is a selfish man. Lord knows Kevin and I have tried our best with him, but none of us are ever going to change him.'

She paused while Tabitha blew her nose, gulping down a sob.

Her make-up that she had been so careful to apply would be ruined.

'You are a smart, kind and capable woman,' Jemima continued, 'But I worry you're throwing your life away waiting for something that is never going to happen. You deserve a good man who can give you everything and love you back.'

If only it were that easy to move on.

Did Jemima not understand anything about the depth of Tabitha's feelings towards Julian? This wasn't just a childish crush. She'd had one of those on him when they had been teenagers, but over the years it had deepened into love. And she knew Julian felt the same way, even if he only showed it on the occasions he was vulnerable, because that was the true him. It was the version that most people never got to see.

When he dropped his guard, when he needed help, he knew Tabitha was the only one who was really there for him. He had told her so. She just had to be patient and not give up on him like everyone else had.

Of course she didn't say any of this now, thanking Jemima and promising her she would be okay. She was glad when the woman relented, giving her a reassuring squeeze on her arm before leaving, saying she would see Tabitha downstairs.

Was it really as simple as Jemima seemed to think? Had Julian really let her down again or had something happened to him? Right now Tabitha wasn't sure which scenario she would find more upsetting.

She watched the friends and acquaintances of her parents as they mingled, laughing and chatting, not a care in the world, then pulled out her phone and tried to call him again.

Still no answer, and she paced the terrace like a caged animal, desperate for answers.

She checked his WhatsApp, saw he had last been online about an hour ago. There were no clues on his social media to help her, and he wasn't active on Messenger.

What if Jemima was wrong? What if something bad had happened?

Tabitha's mind crept to a dark place. The thought of a world without Julian caused palpitations and the beginning of a panic attack.

Gasping for air, she dived into the nearest bathroom, splashing cold water onto her face, then gripping both sides of the sink as she attempted to steady her breathing, trying her best not to be sick as black dots swam into her vision.

After the worst of the attack had subsided and she started to feel strong enough, she spent time touching up her make-up, then smoothing nervous hands over her hair, which still looked model glamorous.

To anyone meeting her for the first time, she looked like a woman who was comfortable in her own skin, but, truthfully, deep down she felt like a fraud, the earlier sliver of confidence she had gained seeing herself in her new dress brutally crushed away.

Still, she put on her game face and headed downstairs to rejoin the guests, painting on a smile when Jemima caught sight of her, ushering Tabitha over so she could introduce her to the son of one of her friends.

Tabitha made an effort to chat, feigning interest in what the man was saying, even though she had failed to listen when she had been told what his name was.

He was good-looking, in an inoffensive way – all floppy blond hair and even teeth, and he didn't seem to take himself too seriously, but he was no Julian.

No one was.

Eventually, she broke away, excusing herself. She checked on her parents, glad that they at least were having a lovely evening, and she thanked the caterers for the wonderful job they were doing. When Jemima caught her eye, mouthing to ask if she was okay, Tabitha was sure to flash her a bright smile.

Every so often, Kevin would pull her into a conversation, usually involving work. This might be a party, but it was also an opportunity to network. Each time, he heaped praise on Tabitha, telling people that as his personal assistant she was the lynchpin in his company, and how without her the place would fall apart.

He was over-exaggerating, but at least this was a role which she knew she deserved. She worked hard and was good at her job, and in these conversations she felt like she was making a relevant contribution and had earned the praise.

Whenever she was able to escape, she snuck away to a quiet corner and checked her phone, willing it to ring as Julian realised he had missed calls and messages. Each time, though, the weight of disappointment crushed her, and her anxiety levels shot through the roof when she saw there was nothing from him.

She held out until 10 p.m., the party now in full swing, confident her parents, as well as Kevin and Jemima, had drunk enough that they wouldn't notice she had gone.

Just a quick drive over to River Heights to check Julian was okay. She could be back again before anyone realised she was missing.

30

Zac hadn't planned on spending all of his Saturday night spying for Nina. She had told him she would message him when she and Julian were about to leave the pub and head back to River Heights, and asked that he keep an eye on Julian's apartment so he could give her an excuse to leave when she was ready.

Her plan for extraction was simple. She would walk out onto the balcony and signal him an okay hand gesture. Zac was then to call, citing some kind of made-up emergency that she needed to leave immediately for.

It all sounded easy enough. What could possibly go wrong?

Zac dreaded to think.

He had just ordered his kebab when Nina had walked into the living room, all dressed up and ready to go out, the deep orangey-coloured dress she wore which hugged curves he hadn't before noticed, immediately drawing his attention.

Usually she was fresh-faced and dressed casually, but tonight her legs were elongated by gold heeled sandals, her hair sleek around her shoulders, and her make-up, although subtle, accentuated all of her best features. Especially the smoky colours she had painted around her eyes, which made her golden irises glow.

'Wow.'

The word wasn't meant to be spoken aloud, but it was too late to take it back.

He had expected her to laugh at his reaction, and he was ready to start backpedalling, but then she spoke, seeming genuinely surprised by his compliment.

'Really?'

Her vulnerability had caught him off guard, so he'd decided to own it.

'Yes, really. You look gorgeous, Nina. You're gonna knock him dead.'

As he spoke those last words, there was an unfamiliar stirring of jealousy in his gut, and although he tried to ignore it, he knew deep down it was because he didn't like that it was Julian Wiseman who she had made this effort for.

It's not real, he reminded himself.

This was all to try to prove that Julian had lied about being with Peyton Landis.

Still, Zac didn't like it, and the possibility that Julian could be involved in the woman's disappearance bothered him. He didn't want Nina putting herself in any kind of danger.

With that thought in mind, he had found it impossible to settle, watching from the balcony as she greeted Julian down in the courtyard, seeing – then inwardly seething over – the man's more than appreciative reaction to her appearance, and not liking it one bit as they left the complex, heading along by the river and over Jarrold Bridge.

As they crossed the car park at the back of the law courts, he lost sight of them behind the trees, but that didn't stop him taking his kebab outside, all thoughts of watching a movie gone, as he positioned himself on the balcony, the binoculars and his phone on the table beside him, ready and alert for if Nina needed him.

She wouldn't be difficult to spot in that dress.

31

Julian Wiseman wasn't terrible company, but Nina learnt early on in the evening that he was a guarded man when it came to revealing things about himself. He tended to deflect if she asked him a question, firing one back rather than answering her, which made her feel a little like she was being interviewed.

Whether that was because he felt his life was none of her business, she wasn't sure, but it certainly came across that way. He was polite, though, and he seemed genuinely interested in finding out about her, listening intently as she answered his questions, and he was generous too, insisting on paying for all of the drinks, even though she had tried to get her purse out on more than one occasion.

Being in his debt made her a little uncomfortable and she hoped he didn't consider this as payment for later favours. She wanted information, but she wouldn't sleep with him to get it.

Remembering back to the night she had watched him on his balcony with Peyton Landis, he hadn't wasted any time removing the woman's clothes. Nina would have to make sure she kept her wits about her when they eventually went back to

River Heights, especially if she managed to get herself an invite up to his penthouse apartment.

For now, she wasn't at risk of being pawed at and he was keeping his hands to himself as they sat at one of the benches outside the pub, enjoying the warmth of the evening sun before it disappeared.

She had always liked the Adam and Eve. It was the oldest pub in Norwich and had a charm and solitude about it, tucked away from the hustle and bustle of the city, but on a popular route that led to the river and close to the pay-and-display car park, so there were always people about. It was a location where she felt safe, but it was also quiet enough that they could talk.

Despite Julian's good manners, she did sense an air of entitlement about him, and while he was on his best behaviour trying to impress her, she noticed that courtesy didn't extend to others. He had been a little rude with the bartender when they had first arrived, his disapproval evident when they hadn't stocked the whisky he had wanted, and he had also been dismissive to an older couple walking by when the woman stopped to compliment Nina on her dress. While Nina had been flattered, thanking her, Julian had looked annoyed at the interruption, turning his back on the woman when she was still talking to them.

Nina had bristled at his reaction, but tried to shake it off, reminding herself why she was here. This wasn't a real date. She didn't have to like him.

He also didn't seem to have much sense of humour, or at least if he did, it wasn't one that he shared with Nina. There were a few times she made a joke and it either went completely over his head or he barely cracked a smile. His seriousness was a little bit dull and she couldn't help but think about how different Zac's reaction would have been.

That was the one thing Zac was good at. When he wasn't annoying the shit out of her, he knew exactly how to make her laugh.

She thought back to his reaction earlier when he had seen her dressed up and ready to leave the apartment. His 'wow' had caught her off guard as she hadn't expected that kind of response from him at all, and the way he had looked at her in that moment had made her skin sizzle and her stomach churn. It had left her feeling very confused as she headed down to meet Julian.

Thinking of Zac now, she was struck by the realisation of how much more fun she would be having if it was him sat opposite her instead of Julian.

Again, she reminded herself this wasn't real. She was here tonight for an entirely different reason.

So far, she had steered clear of any mention of Peyton Landis, but the second glass of wine she was sipping was boldening her confidence, so when Julian commented about how he liked living centrally in the city, where everything was in walking distance, she couldn't resist the opportunity.

'It's great during the day,' she agreed, 'but I'm always a little wary after dark, especially with the women who have gone missing recently.'

She thought she had overegged it, because his expression immediately turned cagey and he stared at her for the longest moment. Had she just roused his suspicion?

'Missing women?' he asked eventually, his tone giving nothing away, and now it was Nina's turn to fall silent.

He was seriously going to pretend he didn't know?

Deciding it was too dangerous to suggest something sinister might have happened to them, Nina tried to play it safe. 'You must have seen it in the news. The police think they might have fallen in the river.'

Julian studied her face as if looking for any trace of a lie.

'I don't really take much notice of the news,' he told her. 'Too gloomy and depressing. Besides, why would that put you off walking through the city after dark? Just stay away from the river if you're worried, or be careful you don't fall in.'

He followed his dismissive comment with a wolfish smile and Nina couldn't decide if his intention was to try to intimidate her or if he had been trying to make a joke.

If so, it wasn't funny.

Their conversation was a little stilted after that. One of the bar staff came over to check for empty glasses and Nina used the excuse to nip to the loo.

As she sat in the stall and fished in her bag for her phone, she remembered that the pub was supposed to be haunted. Not the toilets, she hoped. Though what was waiting for her outside scared her more than any ghosts.

Zac had already WhatsApped her. A simple 'How's it going?'

'He's not giving much away, but the night is young and I'm hopeful he will invite me up to his apartment,' she replied, not wanting Zac to know she was a little bit spooked.

'Just be careful,' his message came back.

She would, though this whole date night would be a complete waste of time if she didn't get the chance to look for the pendant.

Before she left the toilets, she slipped her phone back into her bag, conscious that when they got to Julian's, she would need it out so she could hear Zac's call when it came.

Even before they had arrived at the pub, Julian's phone had kept vibrating, something he'd become increasingly annoyed about each time he glanced at the screen. When it continued to interrupt their conversation after they had sat down with their drinks, he had eventually snatched the phone up from the table, switching it off completely and slipping it in his pocket, before pressuring Nina to put her handset away too.

'We're on a date,' he'd said, 'we should be focusing on each other.'

If it was a real date, then Nina would have been inclined to agree, but for her it wasn't and she needed to be able to get in touch with Zac.

Maybe she could discreetly get her phone out and leave it sitting on the counter if they went back to Julian's apartment. Either that or she would have to turn the volume up. She couldn't risk missing Zac's 'get me out of here' call.

For now, she returned to the table, taken aback when she saw Julian had been back up to the bar, a fresh glass of wine sitting next to the one she had been nursing.

Nina politely thanked him, keeping quiet that she hadn't planned on having another drink. The wine she had drunk had already gone to her head and she was conscious she needed to be thinking clearly and have her wits about her if she did go home with him.

The sun had set completely now, night settling in, and it also made her a little uncomfortable that they would be walking back in darkness. It was only across the car park, along the river and over the bridge. Just a few minutes' walk. But Julian's comment about being careful not to fall in had unnerved her.

Luckily, he seemed to have glossed over that earlier moment of awkwardness when she had mentioned the missing women, going for a complete subject change.

'So, tell me about your work, Nina.'

Not the most exciting topic, but she would roll with it, and she spent the next few minutes trying to make copyediting sound as interesting as possible. Truthfully, she loved her job. It just wasn't the most interesting thing to explain to someone.

'Do you work for your dad's business then?' she asked as soon as there was a lull in the conversation.

So far, she hadn't been able to establish exactly what it was Julian did for work. He had mentioned helping his uncle with his nightclubs in the US – one of the few bits of personal information she had managed to pry out of him – but nothing of what he had been doing since he returned to the UK in the last year.

'I suppose you heard about my own venture,' he told her, already seeming bored.

That was the other thing about him. There was an arrogance, where he seemed to assume Nina knew things about him. At least about things that were readily available in the public domain. As if he was important enough that she would have automatically spent her time reading up whatever newspaper articles she could find on him.

Which she had, though not for the reasons he assumed.

And perhaps that would explain why he was a little guarded about his personal life. Did he just assume everyone was familiar with his attachment to the Katy Spencer murder?

Nina decided to play dumb. 'No, what was that?'

'I tried to start up a nightclub back here.'

She managed to inject a note of wow into her tone, wanting him to think she was impressed. 'Really? Which one is yours?'

He gave her a vaguely irritated look. 'It never happened. There was a whole debacle with the council. Noise pollution issues. It's all on the EDP website,' he told her dismissively, referring to the local newspaper and seeming to intimate that if she wanted to read about it she could do so online. 'Do you like clubbing?' he asked.

Honestly, no. Back in her early twenties, it had been okay, but Nina was thirty-five now and the idea of spending her night in a hot, loud, sweaty room held no appeal whatsoever.

'I haven't been inside a nightclub in several years,' she told him, not wanting to come across as too unenthusiastic.

'So tell me what you do like to do.'

'You mean as in hobbies?'

He nodded. 'Yes. What makes your brain tick?'

A loaded question. How did she summarise her interests into a brief answer and what exactly were they? She had always thought of herself as having a fairly active social life. She had plenty of friends and enjoyed meals out and coffee dates. And when she had been with Michael, most weekends had been spent with their core group either at the pub or round each other's houses. But thinking through what hobbies she did have – cooking, reading, gardening – except she no longer had a garden to look after – it all seemed rather dull.

She told him those three anyway, adding on swimming – because she had used the complex pool – and kayaking. Going out once with Dexter a couple of years ago counted, right?

Belatedly, she realised Julian had neatly sidestepped her question too, putting the pressure back on her, and she still had no idea what he did for a living, if anything at all.

He looked as bored as she expected with her answer, so she quickly threw it back.

'What about you. What do you like to do for fun?'

He didn't reply immediately, but considered the question much as she had.

'What do I like to do for fun?' he repeated, musing over the words before answering. 'I guess we're going to have to get to know each other better before I decide whether I can trust you with my deepest and darkest secrets.' The hint of a smile on his lips spread and there was a carnal look in his eyes as he stared at her, gauging her reaction. 'You can be assured, though, that I definitely know how to have fun.'

Nina's heart started thumping. He had just turned the subject sexual and the air was charged with tension. But the way he was studying her made her feel like a trapped subject in a laboratory. If he was going for seductive, it wasn't working on her, and she was more than a little creeped out.

For the first time, she began to wonder if she was out of her depth.

Whether he picked up on that fact or the alcohol was loosening his tongue, now he had made that comment he seemed to be settling into his theme, and although the subject changed, moving back into safer areas, she sensed he was testing her boundaries, dropping sexual innuendoes into their conversation to see if she bit.

Nina ignored them all, but it was making her uncomfortable. From some of the comments he was making, she suspected he had deviant tendencies and a party table of drugs in his home. Meanwhile, she had never had a one-night stand, had been sick when she tried weed, and the most adventurous her sex life had ever been was when she and Michael had done it in a tent at Glastonbury.

Not that she was going to have sex with Julian, but he was clearly more experienced and she had seen how he was with Peyton. Going into his apartment with him would be like walking into the lion's den. What if he tried to force her to do drugs or wouldn't let her leave?

Maybe she should call this off. She would suggest they head back and thank him for a pleasant evening, and if he said anything about going upstairs with him to his apartment, she would politely decline. She could even message Zac again and ask him to come get her.

Or you can pull up your big-girl knickers and see this through.

Was she really going to wimp out now? If she did then she would never get any answers. She would have to accept the lie that he and Tabitha had told the police, and she wasn't sure she could do that.

Nina thought of Tabitha now. Unsure how she fitted into this situation. Was she involved in Peyton Landis's disappearance too?

The question popped into her head for the first time and immediately she wondered why she hadn't asked it before. She had always known Tabitha was covering for Julian, so why had she not considered that she might be involved?

It was her appearance. Middle-class, inoffensive, professional. She worked for Kevin Wiseman, and although there was an air of authority about her, it was different to Julian. She didn't have that edge about her that he did. Tabitha was more like one of those rich pony club girls or the head prefect in school, while Julian had a snaky charm, but seemed the type who would sell you out or double-cross you at the first opportunity.

They were chalk and cheese and it made no sense that they were friends.

Or was their connection deeper than that?

Tabitha had seemed gooey-eyed over him.

Were they lovers?

Julian had introduced her as his father's assistant, which, thinking about it, was odd, because why would Tabitha be hanging out with him on a Sunday afternoon if she was simply an employee? And Nina had seen her about, heading into his building on more than one occasion.

It was also Tabitha who had called him tonight. Nina had

seen her name flash up on the screen before Julian had switched his phone off.

The call had irritated him.

Perhaps they were lovers who had fallen out.

Were they on a break?

Or did Tabitha know he was here on a date with Nina? Just as she had known he was with Peyton? Perhaps she was waiting for them back in his apartment.

Were they some kind of double act like Ian Brady and Myra Hindley or Fred and Rose West?

Nina's blood chilled.

Rose West had looked perfectly normal before the truth came out about her.

Annoyed that her imagination was going into overdrive, she told herself to get a grip. She was being ridiculous. Tabitha hadn't been in Julian's apartment that night. It had just been him and Peyton.

As far as she was aware.

Unless Tabitha had been hiding.

Stop it, Nina.

It was the wine, she decided. The third glass was going to her head.

Deciding to tackle the subject, she pushed her glass to one side and looked at Julian.

'Tell me about Tabitha?' she asked boldly.

He didn't react quite as she was expecting, looking surprised, then sneering his nose slightly as if Nina had mentioned something distasteful. 'What about her?' he asked, watching and waiting, as if to see where this was going.

'She's your friend, right?'

'Why do you ask?'

'Just curious. I've seen her about a few times, usually

heading up to see you.' Nina forced herself to smile flirtatiously. 'I don't want to tread on any toes.'

Julian's pallor turned grey, as if he might be ill. 'You're not.'

He wasn't giving anything away about their relationship, and Nina's probing had apparently pushed him to a decision.

'Are you going to finish that?' he asked, pointing to her half glass of wine. 'It's nearly last orders.'

Was it really that time?

When she shook her head, he looked a little irritated, before picking up her glass and downing the contents.

'Let's get out of here,' he told her, sounding impatient and starting to get up from the table. There was a sudden vibe about him, an aggressive restlessness, and it made Nina nervous.

'Just a second. I need the loo,' she told him, not missing his eyeroll as she dashed into the pub.

Aware she didn't have much time, she fumbled through her bag for her phone, calling Zac instead of messaging.

The fact he answered immediately settled the queasiness in her stomach a little.

'Is everything okay?' he demanded, sounding worried.

'Yes. It's fine.' Already, Nina was starting to feel stupid. She was overreacting to her situation. Nothing bad was going to happen to her. She just needed to go prudish on him if he thought they were going to have sex. He wouldn't like it, but that was tough. It wasn't as if she wanted to see him again.

'So, are you going back to his?'

Was it her imagination or did Zac sound a little bit annoyed about the idea?

He had always known this was the plan.

'I don't know yet. It hasn't been discussed. But if you can keep a lookout, I'd appreciate it. We'll be walking back in a few minutes.'

'Got it,' he said tightly.

'Okay, thanks. Well, I guess I'll see you in a bit.'

There was a pause.

'Nina, you don't have to go through with this. I can come and get you if you want.'

Knowing he would do that for her warmed her heart, but it also bolstered her confidence.

'Thank you, but I'm good,' she told him. 'Wish me luck.'

32

Julian had played nice, but now he was tiring of the charade.

Nina Fairchild had been pleasant enough company, if a little dull, but perhaps that was on him. It had been difficult to focus on the mundane topics of conversation they spoke about when that orange dress she wore moulded around her breasts, completely distracting him, and he'd had far more whisky than he had planned to while listening to her wittering on.

By the time he insisted they leave, his head was buzzing and he was more than a little drunk, and he was getting irritated that so far she had completely ignored every hint he had dropped about sex.

It annoyed him, as he couldn't get the measure of her or figure out how far he could push her boundaries. And now, heading back to River Heights, she seemed eager to get over the bridge, picking up speed as she crossed it and putting distance between them.

Just what kind of game was she playing?

She had better not be one of these prudish prick-teasers who had let him pay for her drinks all night and now thought she was going to head home without him.

Julian had suffered the torment of that dress all night and now he was desperate to see what was underneath.

He caught up with her at the entrance to the complex when she finally came to a halt, glancing briefly up at her apartment, before turning to face him. The night was still incredibly warm, humidity clinging to the air, and the heat, together with the exertion of hurrying after her and the alcohol firing his blood, had resulted in a light sheen of sweat that coated his skin beneath his linen shirt. He was desperate to shed his clothes.

The path Nina stood on was an equal distance between the two blocks. Which way was she planning to go?

'Thank you for a lovely evening.'

That sounded final, and a slow rage coiled in Julian's gut.

'The night's still young if you fancy a nightcap,' he suggested, managing to keep his tone pleasant.

He was certain she was going to say no, but after a moment of hesitation, she surprised him, a slow smile spreading across her face.

'I have to confess I've been dying to see inside your apartment.'

Well, that was a turn-up for the books.

'I'll give you the special tour,' he offered, winking.

'Sounds great.'

Despite saying the right things, she still sounded a little hesitant, and not wanting her to change her mind, he quickly slipped his arm around her waist, anchoring her to him. A move that seemed to catch her off guard, judging from the breathy little gasp she released.

'This way,' he said, manoeuvring her in the direction of his block, her lovely, clean scent filling his senses.

He was already having thoughts about getting Nina's dress off before they reached his apartment, but she was still a little skittish and he was aware of how tense she was pinned against his side. He didn't want her to bolt and impatience thrummed through him as they waited for the lift to descend.

He would get her upstairs and fix her another drink, he decided. The more intoxicated she was, the more compliant she would likely be and the more he could get away with doing. He could force himself to wait a little bit longer now he knew she was pretty much a sure thing.

The dirty thoughts were making him hard, but then the lift pinged, the doors sliding open, and his mood immediately soured, seeing the smug face of Leonard Pickles staring back at him.

Bloody typical. This nosy old fool was the last person he wanted to bump into.

Leonard looked at Julian and then at Nina, and Julian was suddenly aware of resistance as she tried to pull herself free of his arm.

Did she have a problem with them being seen together?

Annoyed, he tightened his grip.

'Well, this is unexpected,' Leonard said, making no attempt to get out of the lift. 'Mr Wiseman and Miss Fairchild. I never expected to bump into you two together.'

So he knew who Nina was then. Julian supposed he shouldn't be surprised; Leonard poked into everyone's business.

Nina said nothing, but her body was stiff with tension and she didn't look happy.

'Are you going to get out?' Julian snapped. This interruption was irritating.

Leonard shook his head. 'I just remembered I forgot something. I'll have to ride back up with you.'

Of course he bloody had. Julian knew from the growing smirk on the old man's face that he was full of shit.

He was tempted to wait, but that might look suspicious, especially as Leonard was now stepping back to make room for them.

'Are you getting in?' he asked pointedly.

Scowling, Julian walked them into the carriage.

None of them said a word as the lift ascended and the silence that hung between them was uncomfortable with tension. Leonard stared at both of them for the duration of the short journey, while Julian sulked and Nina paid particular attention to her shoes.

When the lift stopped on the fifth floor, Leonard bade them both a goodnight. 'I'll leave you kids to it,' he said. 'I expect you both have plenty to talk about. I'll be seeing you, Nosy Nina.'

Nosy Nina?

Julian was about to ask him what he meant by that, but Leonard was already out of the lift, the doors closing behind him as he headed over to his apartment.

'Why did he call you that?' he asked.

Nina shrugged, but didn't make eye contact. 'I have no idea. I don't even know who he is.'

Julian wasn't sure if he believed her, but he wasn't about to get into a discussion about it.

He gestured for her to go first when the doors opened on the sixth floor, thoughts of Leonard Pickles already slipping from his mind as he stared at Nina's shapely rear.

Unlocking his front door, he stepped back to gesture her inside.

'Welcome to my den.'

* * *

Tabitha was crossing the courtyard, heading towards Julian's building when she saw the couple on the footbridge, her breath catching as she recognised Julian's tall figure illuminated in the glow of the lit bridge steps. There was a woman with him and although she walked slightly ahead, her bold figure-hugging dress standing out, the way Julian's focus was on her, it was clear they were together.

The slice of betrayal that cut into Tabitha's chest was sharp and sudden, and unsure how to react, knowing only in that moment that she didn't want them to see her, she changed her path, heading instead to the maintenance room, her hand shaking as she fumbled with her key card. Inside, it was blessedly empty, and pressing her face to the crack of the door, she waited in the darkness for their approach.

As the woman stepped into the grounds of the complex, she turned to say something to Julian, her familiar face caught in the brightness of a street lamp.

It took a few seconds to register how she knew her, though, but then Tabitha remembered the encounter with Zac Green and a frisson of relief eased the tension in her shoulders.

Nora... no, Nina. That was her name.

She was Zac's girlfriend, wasn't she?

Why was Julian with her when he was supposed to be at the anniversary party?

It made no sense.

But then Julian snaked his arm around Nina's waist, pulling her close in a move that definitely didn't look platonic, and Tabitha's world turned on its head.

She double blinked, shock making everything numb.

It took a moment for her to register the betrayal, watching them turn to walk towards Julian's apartment block, and then the sharp sting of bitter disappointment hit.

She had called Julian a dozen times, but he hadn't answered, and leaving her parents' anniversary party, she had driven over here beside herself with worry, terrified something had happened to him, only to find out he was with another woman.

Tabitha never asked anything of him. Just this one favour. But in true Julian Wiseman stye, he had let her down.

For a moment, she struggled to breathe, panicking as her heart rate accelerated, and she didn't realise she was crying until her tears started dripping off her chin into her cleavage. Glancing down, she saw the wetness had stained the top of her pretty, new dress.

All this effort she had gone to for him and he had ruined everything.

Wracking sobs shuddered through her body as Julian and Nina disappeared inside his building and she gasped for air, hyperventilating as her tears fell harder.

How could Julian do this to her, after everything she had done for him?

Even his own mother had tried to warn her, but Tabitha had been too stubborn to listen. She had put her life on hold for Julian, believing that one day he would see her worth, that he would finally understand she was the one. He was her everything.

He knew full well the sacrifice she had made, lying to the police to give him yet another alibi.

Tabitha wasn't a fool. She knew Julian slept with other women. But tonight he had promised he would be there for her. It stung, realising that a date with a woman he barely knew was more important to him than being with Tabitha on her parents' special night.

How dare he?

Perhaps she should threaten to go to the police and tell them she had lied.

She wouldn't, of course. If the truth came out that she had given Julian a false alibi, then she could go to prison. She had never been in trouble with the law before and she would probably lose her job and everything. Her parents and the Wisemans would never forgive her if they discovered what she had done.

Though, did it even matter?

Julian was all she cared about and he was probably laughing at how foolish and trusting she was, swallowing every line of bullshit he had ever thrown her.

Fresh tears leaked at the humiliation and she reached into her handbag for a tissue, wiping at her tears, then blowing her nose.

She still loved him.

Perhaps she should go up to his apartment and confront him. Let him know that he had been seen and tell Nina exactly what kind of man she was about to climb into bed with.

That would ruin his plans.

It was tempting, but then Tabitha opened up the compact mirror she kept in her purse, and horror had her recoiling. Her eyes were swollen and her skin blotchy, mascara trailing down her cheeks. She couldn't let Julian see her like this or let him know he had destroyed her evening. And she couldn't bear the thought of pretty, perfect Nina getting to witness her in this state either. Not while she was such a mess.

Instead, she blew her nose again and patted her eyes, unable to resist pulling up the camera footage for the hallway on the sixth floor. Julian's door was shut and there was no sign of him or Nina. They were no doubt inside, ripping each other's clothes off.

Tormenting herself, she rewound the feed, finding the

moment of them stepping out of the lift. Julian still had his arm around Nina, releasing her only to open the door to his apartment. Then they were walking through the door and it closed behind them.

Unless Tabitha was going to confront them, there was no point in her being here, but the thought of returning to her parents' party alone and looking such a mess filled her with dread. She really wasn't in the mood for answering questions or making any more small talk.

And she realised, going through to the small washroom, that the state of her face was not fixable. The crying had left her skin too red and puffy. Everyone would know she had been crying.

Damn Julian for doing this to her. She would find a way to get him back.

33

Nosy Nina.

For a moment there, Nina had been convinced that Leonard was going to expose her.

He had looked shocked and then angry when he had first seen her with Julian, but then that annoying smirk had crept back on to his face.

No doubt he was wondering what the hell she was playing at.

When he had insisted on riding back upstairs with them, she had readied herself for the worst, certain he was about to tell Julian everything, and relieved as hell when he did actually keep his mouth shut. His snide little parting comment was annoying, as it had made Julian curious, but it could have been so much worse.

At least he was gone now and Nina found herself at the entrance to Julian's penthouse apartment wondering if she was about to make a huge mistake.

She had felt claustrophobic the moment he had put his arm around her when they were outside, his furnace of a body pressed against hers on a night that was already too warm, and she had been far too aware that he was going to expect sex when they got upstairs. That she was going to have to find a way to discourage him.

Plus, she wanted to be able to snoop, to try to find the pendant. How the hell was she going to do that if he immediately started pawing at her?

Not liking that her legs were trembling, she stepped into the apartment, recognising some of the furniture from the night she had been spying through the binoculars.

The room seemed bigger now she was actually inside it and everything looked sleeker and more expensive. There were no personal touches anywhere, the leather sofas lacking cushions, and there were no photos adorning the shelves. It was a masculine space and had an imposing aura that actually felt quite intimidating.

And the dip in temperature was a shock to Nina's system as well. After the heat outside, it was like a freezer in this apartment. Much cooler than it ever got in her brother's place.

All of the surfaces were empty and glossy clean, and the hard floor beneath her heels echoed loudly. She slipped off her shoes, bare soles now pressed against the cold tiles as she stepped further into the room, conscious that if the chance to snoop arose, she would now be able to sneak around quietly.

Behind her, the door clicked shut and she glanced over her shoulder. Seeing Julian twist the key in the lock did nothing to settle her nerves.

'Wow, your balcony is huge,' she said, hoping to distract him as he moved towards her. 'Can we go out there?'

He simply nodded, but didn't move from where he was standing, so Nina went ahead and unlocked the patio doors, stepping outside, grateful to be back out in the warm night air.

Although it was only one storey further up than Zac's place, it was weird being on the top of the building and seeing the view from a different angle. Immediately, she glanced towards the other block, looking for his apartment, relieved when she spotted a figure sat at the patio table.

Zac was doing exactly as she had asked and was ready and waiting her instruction.

If things started to get uncomfortable, she would give him the signal and he would help her get the hell out of here.

Julian hadn't joined her outside and, glancing back into the apartment, she saw he was busy at the kitchen counter fixing drinks.

Giving Zac a quick thumbs up to let him know she was okay, she searched the area where Peyton had been standing, looking for the pendant. It wasn't there. Had Julian found it first?

'Nina?'

She jumped, hearing him call her name, quickly heading back inside to join him and forcing a smile as he handed her a glass.

Not wine, though, and she frowned at the contents. 'What's this?'

'Whisky.'

Yuck. She wasn't a fan of the spirit, but before she could turn it down, he was clinking glasses with her.

'To new beginnings,' he toasted, taking a generous mouthful. 'Come on,' he urged. 'Drink up.'

Nina made a show of putting the glass to her lips, but faked taking a sip. 'Cheers,' she told him, aware he was watching her.

'Did I tell you how pretty you are and how gorgeous that dress is on you?'

He had, at the start of the night, but he had obviously forgotten that.

Not liking that he was still staring at her, as if contemplating making a move on her, she moved out of his line of vision, making a show of looking at various things.

'You promised me the grand tour, remember?' she reminded him, setting her glass down on the kitchen counter when he wasn't looking, along with her bag. At some point, she was going to have to figure out a way to get her phone out so she could hear it when Zac called.

'You can see most of it from where you're standing,' he told her, sounding a little amused, and she could hear the slur in his voice. 'But come on.'

She feigned interest as he pointed things out, then took her through into the inner hallway, showing her the two spare bedrooms, one of which was set up as an office, the main bathroom, then opening the door to his bedroom. He gestured for her to follow him inside the room, but Nina lingered in the doorway.

From where she stood, she had a clear enough view of the grey panelled wall and the large bed with its brown leather headboard, flanked by two minimalist bedside tables on which sat industrial-style bare bulb lamps. To the far side of the bed, an open door led into the en suite and in the corner of the room was an accent chair, fashioned in the same brown leather as the headboard.

It was all very masculine, but also looked so ordinary, and it was hard to believe anything had happened to Peyton Landis here.

Julian moved to the foot of the bed, sitting down on the edge of the mattress so he was facing her, and she wondered if he was waiting for her to join him.

'You're an intriguing woman, Nina Fairchild,' he said when it was clear she wasn't going to. 'I'm still trying to work out what makes you tick.'

This was beginning to sound a little like dangerous ground.

'Wine,' Nina told him brightly. 'Wine makes me tick. Do you have any?'

She didn't wait for him to answer, heading back down the hallway and into the living area. Behind her came footsteps and what sounded like an impatient sigh, and her heart sank.

How was she supposed to snoop when he was clearly on a mission to get her out of her clothes?

You always knew it would be like this. How did you think it was going to go?

Foolishly, she had pictured a carry-on from the pub. The two of them sitting out on Julian's huge balcony and Nina excusing herself to use the loo, perhaps taking a brief detour into the other rooms.

What an idiot she was. She had seen how he had been with Peyton Landis. She had been forewarned.

'Did you drink your whisky?' he asked, looking around for her glass.

'No,' she admitted, retrieving her still full glass from behind her bag and handing it to him. 'I don't really like it.'

She watched as he downed the rest of his own glass, before finishing hers.

Dumping both empty glasses on the counter, he met her gaze.

'I have wine, but it comes with conditions.'

Uh-oh.

'What kind of conditions?' Nina asked, dreading what the answer was going to be.

'Red or white?' Julian asked, ignoring her question.

'Um, red please.'

She watched him select a bottle of expensive-looking Rioja from his wine rack and uncork it, then fetch two glasses from the kitchen cupboard.

'Come on,' he told her, heading out onto the balcony.

To her relief, he took a seat on one of the sofas, setting down the bottle and glasses on the coffee table.

'Sit,' he told her, and it sounded like an order, not an invitation.

Nina glanced towards her apartment, relieved that Zac was still on the balcony.

This far away she had no idea if he was watching them through the binoculars. Feeling a little self-conscious, she perched herself on the edge of the opposite sofa and reached out to take the glass of wine Julian had just poured her.

He pulled back his hand at the last moment, leaving her snatching at thin air.

'Conditions first,' he reminded her.

When she stayed silent, worried he was going to say she had to sleep with him, he continued.

'We're going to play a game of truth or dare.'

That wasn't what she had been expecting and her first reaction was to say a firm no, but then she hesitated.

Julian was clearly planning to use this to his advantage and Nina had no doubts that he would turn the questions sexual. But could she work this to her advantage too if she could find the right probing questions to ask? Nothing obvious, of course, because he was hardly going to confess to murdering Peyton Landis or having sex with her on his balcony – but it was a way to find out more about him.

She nodded. 'Okay, let's play.'

He seemed pleased with her answer, handing her the wine,

and she took a generous sip, hoping she wasn't about to make a huge mistake.

'Right. My turn,' he told her and Nina frowned.

'Hold on. What happened to ladies first?'

He didn't like that, but she pushed ahead anyway.

'Truth or dare?' she asked him.

'Dare,' came his immediate response.

Not the answer she was expecting or wanted to hear and she scrambled for something suitable for him to do, her gaze landing on the wine bottle. If she got him really drunk, hopefully he might let something slip.

Picking it up, she poured the Rioja into his glass, filling it to the brim. They were generous-sized glasses and there wasn't much left in the bottle when she was done.

'Drink up,' she challenged, fully expecting him to refuse.

He hesitated, looking amused, but then picked up the glass and slowly drank from it, all the time holding her gaze, and not stopping until the glass was empty.

Putting it back down on the table, he told her, 'My turn.'

Nina steadied herself, ready for the question.

'Truth or dare?' Julian asked.

There was only one option for her as dare would offer up too many potentially dangerous possibilities.

'Truth,' she answered, suddenly conscious she might be walking into a trap.

She waited, her heart thumping, as he took his time considering what question to ask. Although she was tempted to pick up her own wine glass and take a steadying sip, something to keep her fidgeting hands from fretting, she was conscious she needed a relatively clear head.

'Why did you agree to go out with me tonight?'

Nina's eyes widened, surprised by what he had asked. She

had been expecting something a little more blunt, like 'Are you going to have sex with me tonight?'

She had asked for a truth, but she couldn't give him an entirely honest answer, not without confessing why she was really here, so she improvised.

'Because I find you interesting,' she told him.

It wasn't exactly a lie. She was interested in him. She was interested in why he had lied about Peyton Landis and what he had to hide about the night she had gone missing.

Of course, she couldn't tell him that.

He seemed pleased with her answer and looked like he was about to elaborate on it, so Nina quickly pushed on.

'Truth or dare?'

'Truth,' Julian answered immediately.

'When was the last time you brought a woman up here?'

The question was out before she could really consider the implications, and from the way Julian was staring at her, he was wondering why she had asked it.

Stupid Nina.

But then she realised he wasn't in deep thought. The alcohol was slowing his reactions. He had been drinking doubles in the pub, then he had finished both of the generous measures he had poured them when they came up to his apartment, followed by the wine she had challenged him with.

'My mother popped in yesterday,' he told her, smirking.

'That's not what I meant.'

'Then you should have thought about phrasing your question better.'

When Nina pouted, annoyed with herself, he added, 'You don't strike me as the jealous type.'

'I'm not.'

'You don't have to deny it. I think it's cute.'

Laughing to himself, Julian picked up the wine bottle, pouring the rest in his glass. He didn't top up Nina's glass or offer her more, though she had barely had any of her wine anyway.

'Okay, truth or dare?' he asked, taking a sip.

'Truth.'

Julian considered her for a moment, swaying slightly on the sofa, his pale grey eyes heavy and unfocused. He was definitely drunk. He managed to pull her back into his line of vision, though his words were slurred when he spoke. 'Tell me one of your darkest secrets.'

Nina furrowed her brow. Did she actually have any? She was annoyingly squeaky clean and tended to mostly wear her heart on her sleeve. This whole sneaking around thing, trying to find dirt on Julian, was probably the most underhand thing she had done, but even that was with the best of intentions.

'Well?' Julian pushed.

'Hang on, I'm thinking.'

No, not completely squeaky clean. There was one bad thing she had done, that she had never confessed to, and her cheeks burned as she remembered deceiving Michael.

'My ex-boyfriend has a signed book by Stephen Fry. It was a birthday gift that he really wanted.' Nina paused, checking Julian was paying attention.

'Go on,' he encouraged.

'So I might have accidentally missed the signing and decided to improvise. I bought a copy of the book from Amazon, then copied Stephen Fry's signature from a sample I found online.'

'You devil.' Julian was smirking again and his tone was sarcastic, and Nina had the impression this wasn't the type of secret he was looking for. 'My turn again,' he said, 'and I'll go truth as well.' He put his empty glass down with a thud on the coffee table and looked expectantly at her. 'So what will it be? Do you want to know a really dark secret, Nina?'

He wanted her to ask him.

Was he that drunk that he was about to confess his lie about Peyton Landis?

Why else would he have brought the subject of secrets up, and be prompting her what to ask?

Unless this was some kind of trap.

Nina's palms were damp and there was a gnawing niggle in the pit of her stomach. Apprehension mingled with anticipation.

'Go on then, tell me one of your dark secrets,' she said, aware of the tremor of nerves in her voice.

She held her breath and waited, as Julian's smile grew, then dropped from his face.

He looked deadly serious when he spoke.

'I want to use my knives on you.'

34

Dylan Hargreaves had been on the Saturday early shift, so he didn't want anyone realising he was still at River Heights when it was close to midnight.

Still, spotting the door to the maintenance room was ajar was bothering him. Whoever was on lates would have finished at 10 p.m., with any calls then going through to the emergency mobile number. They must have forgotten to lock up.

Eventually, he decided he would head down and take care of it. As it was late, there were hopefully few people about and no one would see him.

Big mistake.

As he went to pull the door shut, a noise at the back of the room made him jump, and his eyes widened as a door swung open and a shadowy figure stepped into focus.

A switch flipped, light flooding the room, and realising it was Tabitha Percy, his heart sank.

For a moment, she seemed so distracted she didn't even seem to notice him. She looked completely different to normal, her hair in a fancy updo and she was wearing a blue party dress.

Normally, she favoured neutral-coloured suits and it was a surprise to see her in something colourful.

'What are you doing here?' she asked, finally registering his presence, and as she stepped closer, Dylan noticed that her face was puffy. Had she been crying? If so, she seemed okay now, her frown melting into concern. 'Is everything okay?'

'The door was open,' he told her. 'I thought you might be a burglar.'

To his surprise, she laughed.

'No, I'm definitely not one of those. You're here late tonight,' she commented. 'Shouldn't you have left over an hour ago?'

'Uh, yeah. I forgot something and had to come back.' Dylan's gaze swept over the main desk before he snatched up a Norwich City Football Club mug. 'Coffee doesn't taste the same in another cup,' he grinned, realising how pathetic he sounded.

If she knew he was lying, she didn't say and keen for the encounter to be over, he offered to lock up.

She studied him for a moment, her lips pursed as if she wanted to say something. Eventually, she smiled. 'No, it's okay. I'm leaving now. I'll do it. You get going. You're back on shift in the morning.'

Nodding, Dylan thanked her, though cursed under his breath.

She had no idea how he was spending his free time.

35

Zac almost missed the moment things changed.

He had watched Nina and Julian return to River Heights, Nina leading the way back across the bridge in her vivid orange dress, and then the way Julian had possessively put his arm around her, holding her close.

He hadn't liked that, annoyance burning in his gut.

It was because he was worried about her and she was his best friend's sister, he told himself, ignoring that the fire was fuelled by jealousy.

Then they disappeared inside Julian's block and he was left to wonder, and to seethe over, what might be happening inside the lift. It seemed like ages before the lights went on in the penthouse apartment.

Zac was already there with the binoculars, relieved at the clear view he had, especially of Nina's dress. He wouldn't lose sight of her in that.

And then she was out on the balcony and giving him a signal to let him know all was okay.

It was annoying that he couldn't hear what they were talking about, but at least he could see them. Well, apart from the brief period when they disappeared back inside and he started to worry that they were in the bedroom.

Nina wasn't into Julian that way. She thought the guy was a potential murderer.

What if he had her trapped and wouldn't let her go?

Zac tried to call Nina's phone, but it went to voicemail, and he was about to grab his keys and head over there, when suddenly they reappeared.

They had been out on the balcony since, Julian appearing to get hammered, especially after drinking the full glass of red wine that Nina had poured him, and growing a little bored waiting for her to give him another signal, Zac had dropped the binoculars briefly to reply to a couple of WhatsApp messages.

When he raised them again, Nina was on her feet and backing away into the apartment, and she looked freaked out, shaking her head and holding her hands up, as if warning Julian to stay away. Julian was talking and gesturing, but whatever he was saying wasn't calming her down. The only saving grace was that when he tried to get up to follow her, he appeared to be so drunk that he wobbled on his feet before falling flat on his face on the decking.

He didn't look to be a threat, but Zac wasn't taking any chances. This was Nina.

Grabbing his keys and his phone, he hurried out of the apartment.

She answered the second time he called her. He had just stepped in the arriving lift carriage and hadn't even had a chance to press the button to take him to the ground floor.

'Hello.' She sounded a little breathless.

'What the fuck is going on, Nina? What did he just say to you?'

Instead of telling him, she said, 'It's okay. I'm okay.'

'You didn't look okay. Tell me what happened. I'm coming over.'

'No, you don't need to do that. Zac, listen. I'm fine. He's passed out drunk and snoring his head off out on the balcony.'

That was hardly reassuring.

'If that's supposed to make me feel better, it really doesn't.'

'Look, I get you're worried, but I'm not ready to leave yet.'

There was a long pause.

'Nina?'

'I can't talk right now, but we have him, Zac. He did this. He killed Peyton Landis.'

What the fuck? What the hell had Julian said to her exactly? Had he confessed?

More importantly, why was she sounding excited about it, as if being in the home of a killer was normal?

'Nina, I want you out of there now!'

'I can't leave, not yet. He's out cold. I'm fine. I need to find Peyton's necklace. If not, it's just his word against mine.'

'What did he say to you?'

'We'll talk when I get back.'

'Nina?'

It was too late; she had already ended the call, but to hell with it if she thought she could just expect him to sit in the apartment and wait. She'd just told him Julian Wiseman had murdered someone.

Zac was going over there, whether she liked it or not.

* * *

When Julian had first spoken the words, shock had Nina freezing to the spot, and despite the warmth of the night, her skin had covered in goosebumps.

He had said he wanted to use his knives on her.

And her response?

'What?' she had asked, dumbstruck, as everything went numb.

It took a few seconds of staring at him and wondering if she had misheard – not quite the way she had expected to react in this situation – and Julian repeating the words, before her brain had actually registered danger, and her body scrambled into action.

She was up from the sofa, everything trembling, knowing there was no time to waste calling Zac. She had to get the hell out of Julian's apartment. And now.

Her response had him backtracking at a hundred miles an hour, despite his alcohol-slowed reactions.

'I was joking. Of course I didn't mean it. But your face was a picture.'

Each word was more slurred than the last and it seemed his brain was thinking ahead, but his body couldn't keep up.

Nina had already been backing into the apartment, hands up in warning, ordering him not to follow her, relieved when he suddenly tripped over his own feet, falling face down on the decking.

He had hit the ground with an almighty crash, a dead weight falling, and when he didn't get up again, for a moment she had panicked that he was dead.

Yes, he might have just intimated that he wanted to kill her, but dead was not good. Julian was the son of one of the richest men in the county. What if his family tried to blame her?

She hadn't want to go over and check for a pulse in case she was wrong and he grabbed hold of her, but she supposed she should call an ambulance.

From outside. Get out of his apartment first.

Ignoring the nagging voice in her head, she had instead shut and locked the balcony door. It wasn't ideal and if he woke up suddenly he could break the glass, but at least it was a safety buffer that would buy her time if needed.

Grabbing her bag from the kitchen counter, she had started to reach inside for her phone, interrupted by what sounded like a low rumble of thunder.

Her head had shot around, realising it was coming from the balcony and half expecting to see Julian pressed against the glass. Instead, he was where she had left him and it took her a second to realise he was snoring.

Nina had released a long, shuddering sigh of relief.

Okay, he wasn't dead. That was good, but it did mean he could wake up at any moment, and her primary instinct was still to run, to put as much distance between them as humanly possible. But even as she'd headed to the door, she'd realised she had been handed an opportunity. The pendant hadn't been outside on the balcony, but while Julian was enjoying a drunken sleep and currently stuck outside, she could snoop through his things to try to find it.

She needed to do this, at least for her own peace of mind.

Julian might have said he was joking and tried to laugh his comment off, but Nina had seen the heated look in his eyes before he admitted to his secret and she knew that he had meant what he'd said about his knives.

What would have happened if he hadn't tripped? Would he be cutting her up right now?

Was that what he had done to Peyton Landis?

Nina knew the woman had been here and she owed it to her to look around and see if she could find something to prove it.

That was when Zac had called and while she wasted precious time speaking to him, she kept an eye on the balcony, hoping like hell that Julian stayed where he was. After reassuring Zac that she was okay, she ended the call.

This was her one opportunity.

She wouldn't be foolish though – safety first – and before doing anything else, she went to the front door, relieved Julian had left the key in the lock, unlocking it and pushing it open, putting the key in the other side of the lock. She left it ajar as she went back into the apartment, confident she could make a speedy getaway, leaving Julian locked inside if things went south.

He no doubt had a spare key, but it would slow him down.

Despite her eagerness to look around, she was aware she was trembling. She was in the home of a murderer and the pressure of the moment, of ensuring she stayed safe, was causing her quite an adrenaline rush.

She had to find the pendant or something else incriminating or tonight would be wasted. She wouldn't ever get another chance.

After a quick glance to check on Julian, she began in the living room and kitchen, places where she had a view and could keep reassuring herself he was still out for the count.

She hunted through cupboards and drawers, searching for anything that would back up what she had learnt about him tonight.

He wanted to use his knives on her.

She kept coming back to that, aware that she hadn't given him the chance to elaborate how. And try as she might to focus on the task at hand, her imagination was running wild.

Stop thinking about it, Nina.

She opened the fridge door, half expecting to find it full of bottles or vials of red liquid. Finding instead mundane items such as cheese, milk and lager did nothing to settle the ball of stress growing in her gut.

What had he done with his victims' bodies?

And how many other women had he hurt?

It occurred to Nina that if he had killed Maria, Tammy and Julie as well, that made him a serial killer.

Rule of three, right?

Dear God. And here she was in his home.

She had to expose him, but she was conscious she didn't want to end up dead herself.

It was in the bedroom that she found the first potential clue.

In the first of the two bedside table drawers was a jewellery box containing cufflinks.

Nina almost missed it, her trembling fingers pulling out other items, but then she backtracked, honing in on the word Nix. It looked familiar and it only took her a second or two to make the connection. Nix was the name of the jewellery store where Maria Adams had worked.

Perhaps it was a minor connection, but Nix jewellers was a small independent shop and Julian owned cufflinks from there.

Had he purchased them himself or had they been a gift?

Nina took a quick photo of the box before putting it back in the drawer. Nothing else stood out as extraordinary and, making sure everything was how she had found it, she moved round to the other side of the bed, pulling open the drawer to the other unit, her eyes widening at the pair of handcuffs casually laying on top of a Terry Pratchett novel.

Had he used these to incapacitate Peyton Landis before killing her?

She took another photo, closing the drawer, then went back through to the living room to check on Julian, gasping in horror, every muscle in her body tightening, when she realised the spot where he had been lying was empty.

Where the hell was he?

The door was still closed. And locked, she hoped, though, she had no intention of getting close enough to find out. It didn't matter that she hadn't finished searching. She was getting the hell out of here.

Slowly she backed up, keeping her movements as quiet as possible, just in case he was inside the apartment. She kept her eyes trained on the balcony doors, fighting every instinct to run. She was almost at the living-room door.

This had been a stupid idea. She should have left the moment he'd passed out and not looked back. But no, she had to be one of those idiots she screamed at in horror movies for doing the wrong thing. What the hell had she been thinking?

Another step back. Into the hall now.

Why hadn't she listened to Zac?

Her body collided with something and there was a crash as she almost lost her footing.

Spinning round, her eyes wide, she stared at the offending item as her heart threatened to beat out of her chest.

A coat stand.

It's just a bloody coat stand.

And by bashing into it she had made enough noise to wake the dead, she realised, hearing a banging noise coming from the living room.

She didn't wait to find out if it was Julian, her survival instincts kicking in as she turned and bolted out of the front door, pushing it shut and locking him inside. She left the key in the lock, hoping it would jam any spare he might have.

Her plan was to take the stairs, figuring that she could probably get down those before the lift had even arrived, but then she heard the familiar ping and realised it was already on the top floor.

In her panicked state, she didn't think to question why anyone would be on their way up to the top floor, even though Julian had mentioned over the course of the evening that he had the floor to himself and that the other penthouse apartment stood empty.

As the doors opened, she went to step inside the lift, screaming when she realised it was already occupied.

She was so worked up, it took her a few seconds before she realised it was Zac.

Who, to be fair, looked as shaken as her.

He caught hold of her by the elbows, tugging her into the carriage.

'What the hell's going on?' he demanded.

There wasn't time to explain now. Zac was going to have to be patient for a short while longer.

'We need to go.'

He wasn't listening to her 'Where is he?' he asked. 'What did he do to you?'

'Not now, Zac. We have to go!'

To Nina's relief, he hit the button for ground level and she drew in a shaky breath as the doors closed.

'You hung up on me,' Zac grumbled. 'That was never part of the plan. How the hell am I supposed to keep you safe when you cut me out of the loop?'

'I'll explain everything once we're out of here. I promise.'

And then she would call the police.

They would have to act now, wouldn't they?

She had the photos of the jewellery box and also the handcuffs. Plus she could tell them what Julian had said to her. That he wanted to use his knives on her.

They should have believed her when she had reported him the first time, instead of buying into his phony alibi.

Well, now she had proof for them and hopefully if they searched his apartment they would be able to find out what had really happened to Peyton Landis.

36

I had been hiding in the stairwell nursing a throbbing headache when Nina let herself out of the penthouse apartment, locking the door behind her.

Not that it was going to help her when the danger she feared was already outside and waiting for her. I had anticipated her taking the stairs, not wanting to wait for the lift, but then Zac Green had appeared, ruining my plan to surprise her.

It was a frustrating setback, but I will find a way to get her.

It's her fault for teasing and taunting in her siren dress. I tried my best to ignore it, telling myself I could let this one walk away, but, as always, my frustrations grew, the red mist clouding my judgement. She has made me look like a fool and she needs to be taught a lesson. She needs to be punished.

But for now I am distracted by another problem.

Leonard Pickles has been a pain since the day we first met, but although I thoroughly dislike the man, I have always taken him to be a harmless busybody. His recent behaviour, though, has my guard up, which is why I am now standing in his apartment intoxicated with anger and frustration at having missed out on my chance with Nina.

Leonard is asleep and I can hear him snoring, his bedroom door closed. Still, I will have to be quiet. Using the torch on my phone, I go from room to room curious to see if he has any secrets of his own. Anything I can perhaps use as leverage against him.

Unfortunately, he is a disappointment. The place is sparsely furnished and has zero personality. There are no personal knick-knacks, other than a photo frame by the mantlepiece – a picture of a woman I assume is his late wife – and if he wasn't such an irritant, I might feel sorry for his sad, pathetic excuse for a life.

But then I see the spare bedroom, a space which he has converted into an office. It is packed with surveillance equipment and set up like one of those police investigation rooms you see on the television.

It's the whiteboard that draws my attention, and a ball of rage grows in the pit of my stomach as I read the questions he has written.

Who does this man think he is, bloody Columbo?

Leonard Pickles is more than an interfering busybody, I realise. Just how much does he know?

The sound of a door opening draws my attention.

I've been so caught up in what I found, I hadn't noticed that the snoring has stopped, and now it's too late for me to leave.

Turning off my torch, I wait in the dark.

Hopefully he is just using the toilet and will go straight back to bed.

Tension thrums through my body and I clench my fists together, part with nerves, part with anticipation, unsure how the next few minutes are going to play out.

37

'*This* is your evidence?'

Zac looked at Nina so incredulously, she faltered a little, before becoming defensive.

'Yes!' she snapped. 'What's wrong with it?'

'It's a jewellery box and a pair of handcuffs, Nina.'

'Proof that Julian has been in the shop where Maria Adams worked,' she huffed, not liking that she still didn't have him on side.

He had been concerned when he had showed up outside Julian's apartment. Almost overly so, worried that she was okay, and although he was still angry with her for going silent on him, Nina thought he finally believed her.

Back in his apartment, he had insisted she sit down while he checked her over for any sign of physical injury, even though she assured him she was fine, then he'd ordered her to drink a can of Coke to help calm down the shaking from her adrenaline spike. Afterwards, he had gently persuaded her to tell him what had happened.

Julian's comment about using his knives on her had rattled him, Nina could see that, but it was her claim that she now had enough evidence to call the police that changed things, and right now she was reminded of everything that wound her up about Zac Green.

He shook his head, looking again at the two photos she had taken. 'So let's say I go into Next and buy a T-shirt. If one of the sales assistants goes missing over the next few months, does that make me a prime suspect?'

Nina snatched her phone back, setting it down on the coffee table. 'Next isn't a little independent shop. It's not the same.'

'Okay, well swap it for one,' he challenged. 'It's still a stretch.'

He might be mad at her for hanging up on him and cutting him out of the loop; she got that, but it didn't give him the right to discredit what she had found, and it irritated her that she was now starting to doubt herself.

'Explain the handcuffs then,' she demanded.

'Really?' The smug smirk on Zac's face had her seething, especially when he added, 'I'm guessing you and Michael didn't own any of those.'

Nina glared at him. 'I'm glad you think this is funny. I was laughing my head off when Julian said he wanted to use his knives on me.'

The smile disappeared and she could tell she had hit a nerve.

'I never said I found any of this funny, but you told me you had evidence he had killed Peyton Landis. This isn't it, Nina.'

He surprised her by reaching for her hands, his warm fingers wrapping around hers and squeezing gently when she tried to pull away.

'Look. I'm as freaked out as you about what he said to you and I agree it's not normal, but you know as well as I do that he will lie if you call the police. It will be your word against his.' Zac held her gaze. 'I will back you all the way if you do report it, but you need to know they won't take the jewellery box or the handcuffs seriously. They prove nothing.'

Nina's shoulders sagged, annoyed that everything he had just said made perfect sense. In the heat of the moment, she had believed she was gathering evidence, everything feeling connected to the comment Julian had made, but now she took a step back, she could see that Zac was right.

That meant she was back to square one. But, even worse, she had no idea how things stood with Julian.

She had left him locked out on his balcony and when he sobered up he was going to remember that he had revealed his true self to her. Did that put her in danger or would he try to pass it off as a joke when he saw her, as he had done so initially?

She had gone out tonight hoping to find answers, but instead it felt like she had opened a can of worms. And Zac might not believe what Leonard Pickles claimed to have overheard, but Nina couldn't help but wonder now if perhaps she should have listened to him. After all, Leonard was the only one who seemed to believe her.

'I just want to do the right thing by Peyton Landis,' she told Zac now. 'She's disappeared without a trace and I know Julian is involved.'

'I understand,' he told her, his tone sober. 'Look, why don't you sleep on it and if you still want to, we'll go to the police station together tomorrow?'

Nina nodded, appreciative of the offer. This was the Zac she had grown fond of over the last couple of weeks. 'Thank you.'

He gave her hands another gentle squeeze before letting go and Nina immediately found herself missing the contact. It was probably a comfort thing after the scare she'd had, she told herself, refusing to believe it could be anything else.

Getting up from the sofa, she walked out onto the balcony. The binoculars were still on the patio table where Zac had left them and she picked them up, looking through them at the penthouse apartment. There was no sign of Julian, though the lights were all still on, and she wondered if he was still locked outside.

She doubted it, as she would surely see sign of him, but if he was still out on the balcony, she refused to feel guilty about it. It wasn't cold out. In fact, far from it. If he couldn't get back indoors, he would have to yell down to one of his neighbours.

Nina's lips twitched, remembering that Leonard lived just beneath him.

That could be interesting.

'Can you see him?' Zac asked, joining her.

Nina lowered the binoculars, shaking her head. 'I assume he's managed to get back inside.'

If he had, that didn't sit comfortably either.

Would he try to contact her?

He had her number, though she hadn't heard anything from him since she had left.

What if he tried to come after her?

He knew where she lived.

No, he wouldn't be stupid enough to do that.

Besides, she had Zac here with her.

An unwelcome thought crept into her consciousness. Waking up in the dark to find Julian looming over her, a knife held to her throat. Zac in the other bedroom, fast asleep and unaware of the danger she was in.

She must have looked rattled because he touched her arm, frowning. 'You okay?'

Nina nodded vigorously to try to convince him, but the truth was, now the drama of the evening had passed and she had actually had time to think about what had happened, she wasn't sure she could face being alone tonight. She knew she would have to keep the light on and that she wouldn't sleep a wink, fearing every tiny noise.

Zac would probably laugh at her if she told him, so she didn't. Instead she asked, 'Do you fancy watching a movie?'

He seemed surprised at her suggestion. 'Now? It's almost midnight.'

Nina shrugged. 'So? It's the weekend and no work tomorrow, and I need to chill and switch off before bed. But it's fine. If you're not up for it, I can just watch something by myself.'

His expression was unreadable as he studied her, and she squirmed a little, certain he could read her thoughts. 'I didn't say I wasn't up for it,' he said after a moment. 'Do you have anything in mind you want to watch?'

Relieved, she said, 'Anything light-hearted, I think. Something funny.'

'*Monty Python*?' Zac suggested.

'I was thinking about something a little more up to date.'

'*Monty Python* doesn't gets old, and it'll make you laugh.'

It usually did, but Nina wasn't in the mood for it. After debating a few more titles, they settled on *Hot Fuzz*. Although both of them had seen it before, they agreed it had plenty of laugh-out-loud moments, and for a while the film did the trick, distracting Nina from everything that had happened. Zac, in an old T-shirt and joggers, sprawled out the length of one sofa, while Nina, who had changed into her PJ shorts, shared the other one with Hannibal. Still, as the end of the movie neared, she kept glancing towards the hallway, paranoid that they had forgotten to lock the front door. She would have to check it before they went to bed. Or perhaps she would wait until Zac was asleep, then come back through to the living room and watch some more TV.

Zac picked up the remote to turn off the screen as the credits rolled and an uncomfortable ball of dread tightened in the pit of Nina's stomach. She used the bathroom first, then discreetly checked the front door while Zac brushed his teeth.

Satisfied it was definitely locked, she went over to make sure the balcony door was too. Not that Julian would gain access via a fifth-floor balcony – unless he was Spider-Man.

'Are you okay?'

Zac's voice behind her made her jump.

It was a question he had asked her a lot this evening.

'Yeah,' she said, giving him the same answer again.

He hesitated. 'Julian's not going to be stupid enough to try to get in here, Nina.'

There he was again, reading her mind, and her cheeks burned as she turned to face him.

'I know he won't,' she agreed, keeping her tone breezy.

Despite the hour, he looked alert, though his hair was a scruffy mess from where he'd been resting his head back against the cushions and the navy *Sloth loves Chunk* T-shirt he wore – that he had owned for years and she knew was a homage to one of his favourite films, *The Goonies* – was creased.

He was familiar and safe and sometimes irritated the crap out of her, but there was also a newness about him, or perhaps it was a side that had always been there but she was only just discovering, and she was still navigating the pull it had on her, not yet ready to admit she was attracted to him.

Sometime over the past couple of weeks what he thought about things had started to matter to her, though. And, more specifically, what he thought of her.

She wondered if he realised it because the way he was studying her, like he wanted to say something but couldn't quite formulate the words, made her suspect he did.

His reaction tonight when she had come through into the living room ready for her date had surprised and flattered her, warming something deep inside, and she had smiled to herself in the lift going down to meet Julian that she had just managed to stun Zac Green into saying 'wow'.

It was why she was putting on a brave face now. He had always thought of her as Dexter's little sister, despite their closeness in age, and she knew he was being protective of her because her brother wasn't here. She didn't need him thinking she was a fool for worrying. Although she was, she could take care of herself.

'Goodnight,' she told him, wishing he would offer to stay up until dawn with her and watch movies. She wouldn't ask him to, though. Instead, she headed to her bedroom.

'I'll be right next door,' Zac reminded, following after her.

And you'll be asleep, she thought, but didn't say it.

'I know,' she repeated.

Stepping into the bedroom, she closed the door, leaning up against it, aware her heart was thumping. Understandable due to nerves, but deep down she knew it was something else as well.

Realising she had forgotten Hannibal, who would be having a shit fit in the middle of the night when he realised Nina had locked him out of the room, she opened the door again, surprised to find Zac standing the other side.

His hand was raised, as if he had been about to knock, and he too looked caught off guard, though he recovered quickly.

'What are you—' Nina spluttered, but she didn't get to finish the question, as Zac stepped into her personal space, taking her face in his hands and lowering his mouth to hers.

Initially, she didn't react, her feet glued to the spot and stunned by what was happening, his lips warm and gentle against hers, but then his fingers were threading back into her hair sending tingles to every one of her nerve endings, as he possessively deepened the kiss.

The kiss.

Oh God. Zac Green was kissing her.

A warmth spread in her belly, the need to have more finally kick-starting her brain, but as she started to react, moving into him as she kissed him back, he pulled away.

Nina's legs were trembling, threatening to buckle under her, and she was suddenly a hot sticky mess despite the air-con.

'What was that?' she managed, surprised she was even able to speak.

Zac's sea-green eyes were heavy with lust, but it was the cheeky lopsided grin breaking out across his face, dimpling his cheeks, that almost undid her.

'Something to think about,' he teased.

And then the bastard was turning away, heading towards his bedroom as if he hadn't just given her the best kiss of her life.

Nina saw red. He did not get to do that.

His door had already closed and she wasn't polite enough to knock, storming into his room.

'You do not get to start something like that without finishing it,' she fumed as his eyes widened, this time taking charge and hooking her arms around his neck, not giving him time to react as she greedily kissed him again.

He didn't need much encouragement, lifting Nina, her legs hooking around his waist before they tumbled onto his bed, and he did a fine job of keeping her distracted, thoughts of Julian no longer on her mind as they explored and teased and satisfied, discovering new sensations and pleasures as they became familiar with each other on the most intimate of levels.

As night gave way to dawn, they finally fell asleep, an exhausted mess of tangled limbs, but in the quietness of the morning, as sun streamed through the window, Nina found herself awake again, and she couldn't help but worry about what this new day might bring.

38

The storms that had been threatening for weeks were forecast to finally hit Norfolk on Sunday and although the day started off with deep blue cloudless skies and sunshine, there was a stillness and a stifling mugginess clinging to the air, thanks to the high levels of humidity.

The oppressive heat didn't help Julian's mood and he was tired and agitated, having been awake much of the night, and now desperately craving the fix he had been denied last night.

He had been a fool to drink so much, knowing his control tended to slip when he was inebriated. Alcohol had caused his shitty decisions with Peyton Landis, and now again with Nina Fairchild. If he had stayed sober, he wouldn't have revealed his true self to Nina last night, but the whisky had lit a fire in his belly, setting him on the same path of self-destruction that had got him into trouble before.

Despite some patchy moments, he remembered her reaction clearly. Although he had laughed away the comment about using his knives, pretending it was a joke, she had reacted badly and the last thing he needed was for the police to show up at his door again.

As she had gone to leave, he had tried to stop her.

After that was blackness, though mercifully for only a brief time. When he had awoke, his face hurt from where he had face-planted the decking and he quickly realised he had been locked out.

That was when he had spotted Nina still inside his apartment, and he had watched through the window, as she riffled through his drawers and cupboards, her actions concerning enough to sober him up fast.

What the fuck was the nosy bitch doing?

When he had failed to get her attention, he had headed downstairs using the fire escape stairs, grateful they could be accessed via his balcony. By the time he was back upstairs, she had gone, though luckily she had left his key in the front door.

Julian needed to head out and take care of his craving, aware it would help to clear his head and help him think straight.

He just hoped Nina didn't cause him any problems, by blabbing his secret to anyone.

Showered and dressed, he felt a little fresher, while two cups of strong coffee helped to kick-start his brain and soothe the edges of his hangover.

Still, urgency licked a fire in his belly.

He needed a fix and now.

Unlocking the safe that he kept hidden behind a painting in the hallway, he reached inside for his precious leather-bound case, his blood heating in anticipation as he opened it, revealing the set of sharp silver knives.

It was time to go play.

39

Peyton Landis was still the headline news story on the local radio station playing in the gym, as Conrad Mackenzie worked out.

Eventually, she would slip down the priority list when there were no fresh leads and after a while she wouldn't get mentioned at all. It was always the way. People were fickle like that. Other stories came along and they lost interest. Still, for Conrad, that day couldn't come soon enough.

That nosy old Leonard Pickles had spooked him with his claim about Peyton being at River Heights.

Knowing someone had seen her that night made him prickly under the collar. Because if they had knew Peyton had been on the complex, then what else might they have witnessed?

* * *

When Dylan Hargreaves realised Tabitha Percy had been in the maintenance room last night, for a moment he had honestly thought it was game over.

Usually, the woman intimidated him a little, but last night she had seemed distracted and her face was puffy, like she had been crying. Still, running into her had been dangerous and it could cost him his job.

At least he had been smart enough not to ask why she was upset, just as he didn't show any curiosity as to why she was working late while all dressed up, like she was off to a party. He had just wanted to get out of there with as few questions asked as possible.

For now he was safe, but it was a lesson that he needed to be more careful.

He was a man who had secrets and he couldn't risk anyone exposing them.

40

One thing Tabitha had always been good at was compartmentalising, so looking back at her meltdown on Saturday night she was embarrassed and annoyed with herself.

Julian had been her focus for so long and the way he had callously let her down when she finally thought they were connecting had tipped her over the edge. The anger was always there at the futility of her situation, but she had learnt to control it and to cover it up.

Last night, she had dropped her guard.

She wasn't stupid. She realised there were other women. But she had always dealt with that knowledge in her own way, reminding herself that ultimately they meant nothing to Julian. That one day he would come to his senses and see her waiting in the wings. Behind closed doors, she might get upset, sobbing for the man she loved, but publicly she was a true professional.

Until last night.

She had let her parents down and the Wisemans too. But worse than that, she had also let herself down, and if there was a way to dial back the clock and rewrite the last twenty-four hours, she would.

Usually, she was so in control of her emotions. The fact they had boiled over left her feeling foolish and scared.

She hated Julian for ruining her evening, almost as much as she despised herself, but after having a few moments of despairing self-pity when she first awoke, certain she wouldn't be able to face the day, she knew she had no choice but to pull herself together.

That was who she was: Tabitha the trooper.

She was a person who pulled herself together with a typically British stiff upper lip, and today she promised herself she would be focused.

Still, her stomach dropped when she saw the missed call from her mother. There was a WhatsApp message from Jemima too, asking if she was okay. Nothing from Julian, though, she noted bitterly.

Scared her parents might decide to swing by, she called them first, shutting down her emotions and going into robot mode as she apologised to her mother for ducking out of the party early, making up an excuse that she had started to feel unwell and didn't want to pass anything on in case she had a bug. Luckily, Diana Percy was more interested in sharing gossip from the party, only briefly enquiring how she was feeling today, and Tabitha listened numbly as her mother chattered away, using the time productively to message Jemima back with the same story.

The response she received, *Take care of yourself, Tabitha. X*, was ambiguous.

Did Jemima mean because she thought Tabitha was unwell or had she seen through her and was referring to their conversation last night?

A little unsettled, Tabitha tried to push it to the back of her mind, aware she needed to be focused for when she confronted Julian.

Returning home to her little house last night, she had realised that things were reaching boiling point. She couldn't continue down this path. It was destructive and unhealthy, and eventually she was going to implode with the pressure of everything.

She still loved him, but she needed him to realise how badly he had hurt her this time, and she also had to get it through to him just how much he truly meant to her. That no other woman would ever be there for him the way she was.

Tabitha was more than familiar with the phrase 'cruel to be kind', and it was time she applied it to Julian.

There would be no more subtle reminders of everything she had done for him. This time she was going to spell it out that she held the power to upend his life.

Her hope was that this would force him to realise his true feelings for her.

It was a low move, blackmail even, holding the threat over his head that she would retract her alibis unless he gave her what she wanted. And there was a risk attached to her bluff – because, of course, she really had no intention of going to the police and telling them she had lied – but she was desperate.

Her hands shook as she applied careful make-up, trying her best to disguise the fact she had spent much of the night crying, and she fumbled with the zipper on her grey dress. It was one of the few outfits she owned that she felt comfortable in, and, okay, it didn't scream look at me, like Nina's orange dress had, but it was demure and expensive.

If she was giving Julian an ultimatum, then she wanted to be looking her best, and reminding him that she moved in the same privileged circles as him. With that in mind, she pushed Tiffany stud earrings through her lobes and fastened on the gold tennis bracelet her parents had given her for her fortieth birthday, before appraising her reflection in the mirror.

She wasn't a fool and knew she wasn't physically in the same league as the women Julian tended to go after, but she had other qualities she believed set her apart. Loyalty, breeding and substance. Women like Nina Fairchild might be fine for a cheap one-night hook-up, Tabitha thought unkindly, but they weren't marriage material.

As she drove into the city, parking in her usual spot at River Heights, she told herself that deep down Julian knew that. He wasn't a stupid man. These women meant nothing to him, surely.

She drew in a steadying breath as she stepped into the lift, aware of the pounding of her heart and not liking the fact her legs were trembling. As the carriage rose, she considered the consequences of Julian's actions, and sickness churned in her stomach.

Her steadfast belief in him had never wavered, but for the first time she worried about the pedestal she had always put him on. What if she was wrong? What if the worthy man she had convinced herself was hidden deep inside him didn't exist?

She had always been so sure of him, but did he deserve her devotion?

The lift pinged for the sixth floor and she pushed the sudden doubts away. She wouldn't falter now. He had been her everything for too long.

The key to his apartment was still in her purse, but she knew he would be angry if she used it. Instead, she rang the bell and waited, aware this was her do-or-die moment.

Julian had to agree to her terms. He simply had to. There could be no other choice.

He kept her waiting and she stubbornly knocked and rang the bell repeatedly, knowing he must be home as his Porsche was in the car park and she was familiar enough with his routine to know he wouldn't be using the leisure facilities or have headed out on foot on a Sunday morning.

It was only as she heard the click of the lock that it occurred to her he might have company.

What if Nina Fairchild had stayed over?

It wasn't Julian's style to let a woman spend the night, but perhaps Tabitha was wrong.

What if this one was different?

She almost turned and fled, but the door was already opening, Julian scowling at her, and she was relieved to see he was up and dressed, all of the blinds open in the apartment.

'I'm going out,' he told her dismissively.

No apology that he had let her down last night. Did he even remember he was supposed to have gone to her parents' anniversary party?

Tabitha adopted her no-nonsense, assertive approach, the one she used at work and in situations where her confidence was shaken.

'We need to talk,' she told him, pushing her way past him into the apartment.

It was probably paranoia, but she was certain she could smell the subtle scent of perfume clinging to the air. Was Nina still here?

No, she couldn't be. Julian said he was on his way out. He valued his privacy too much and wouldn't leave Nina alone here.

Julian huffed theatrically, but at least he closed the door, following her into the living area. 'I don't have time to play these games, Tabitha. I have somewhere to be.'

'You had somewhere to be last night, too, but I guess my parents' anniversary party was too far down your list of priorities.'

She saw the twitch in his cheek. The telltale sign that he knew he was in the wrong, despite the furrowed brow and the hand that went to his head, as if he was only just remembering.

'Oh, that. I'm sorry. Something came up.'

'Something or someone?' she asked, her tone tight with stress.

His bloodshot eyes glared at her. 'What's that supposed to mean?'

This was her moment, Tabitha realised. Her time to challenge him. Something she had never been brave enough to do before. Not when it came to his women.

'I saw you with her last night. That Nina woman.'

For a moment, Julian wavered and she watched his expression go from wary to contrite and then swing to anger. 'So?' was the only response he gave her, and she could hear the thunder in that one word. He was warning her not to push it.

'So, being with her was more important to you than the party?' she pushed.

'Were you spying on us?'

Julian asked the question in such a mocking way, as if he was thoroughly disgusted with her behaviour, that Tabitha's cheeks flamed.

'No!' Her protest was automatic, not wanting him to think the worst of her. 'Of course not. I was worried about you when you didn't show up at the party. I was scared something had happened to you. I tried to call you.'

'My phone was off.'

It hadn't been initially. Had he switched it off to avoid her? Tears threatened as her resolve weakened. How was he managing to switch this around to make her look the bad person?

'I was worried about you,' she repeated. 'You promised you wouldn't let me down.'

'Well, boo hoo, Tabitha. I did.'

* * *

Julian knew he should dial it back, but Tabitha had picked the wrong moment to confront him. As annoying as the woman was, she had her uses and was handy to keep on side. Mostly, he tolerated her, but the frustration and need for release was making him mean.

Right now, she was standing in the way of his fix and he needed her to go.

She was making no attempt to move, though, despite him brutally destroying her confidence in the space of a couple of minutes, and he could see she was on the verge of tears.

Hell, no. He didn't have time for this drama.

He started to speak, to tell her she needed to leave, one hand already on her arm and prepared to throw her out if necessary. When she angrily shook him off, her eyes flashing with temper, it caught him a little off guard.

'You have no idea of the things I do for you,' she snapped. 'I always have your back and you know I drop everything to help you. Name me one other person who would give you an alibi and save your neck as I have done?'

Julian rolled his eyes and sneered. 'Oh, so you're going down this route again, are you?'

Yes, she was right. She was probably the only person who

would give him alibis. Two of them, in fact. The only person stupid enough to. It was the reason he kept her around. She was handy at cleaning up his mess.

'It's time you started appreciating me, Julian. You know we're good together. We work. Women like Nina Fairchild and Peyton Landis, they would never look after you the way I do.'

Wait. Was she trying to gain leverage so she could date him?

He knew she liked him, but was this what she was really after? A relationship or, God help him, a ring on her finger?

It was time he put her straight. Yes, he might be taking his frustration out on her now and later he would apologise and win her back. But this thing between them, it was a friendship of sorts. It was nothing deeper.

'What exactly do you think is happening between us, Tabitha?' he asked, trying his damnedest to keep the edge of irritation out of his voice.

She reddened, her bottom lip wobbling, but didn't answer.

'We're not in a relationship. That means I can date whomever I like,' he continued. 'And, truthfully, we're never going to be in a relationship. I'm sorry, but I'm not attracted to you.'

There. Band-Aid ripped off and he hadn't been a dick about it.

Not that it stopped the tears. Big, fat, ugly ones were dripping down her cheeks and making her face blotchy.

'But you said...' She trailed off, gulping for air.

'I said what?' he asked impatiently. He was going to explode if he didn't get his release soon.

'You said I'm the only one who understands you.'

Julian stared at her blankly, wondering what the hell she meant, but then the penny dropped. It was a line he had fed her on a couple of occasions.

Was that how she had interpreted it?

'You told me these other women meant nothing. They were something you just had to get out of your system.'

Yes, he had once told her that too when she was being a little testy and disapproving about his string of one-night stands. And it wasn't necessarily untrue. The women he slept were meaningless. He couldn't even remember most of their names.

But Tabitha had managed to create her own narrative. At no point had he ever led her to believe that one day he would be done sleeping around, at which point he would settle down with her.

Was she insane?

'I'm not in love with you. I'm sorry, but you've managed to twist everything I've ever said to you. I'll be clear now, though. We're never going to be together. I'm never going to date you, certainly never marry you. And I'm never going to have sex with you...' He forced himself to add, 'Again,' because, idiot that he was, when he was younger he had foolishly gone there.

He could see this was breaking her, but it was necessary. She had accused him of leading her on and he wanted to be certain she understood how things were between them.

'I'm sorry,' he repeated, shrugging. 'But it's just the way it is.'

Tabitha was sobbing so hard now she couldn't speak, tears choking her each time she tried, and Julian waited impatiently, wanting her to leave.

Realising he was going to struggle to get her out of the door, he made a decision.

'Look. I need to go. Lock up and let yourself out when you're done.'

He didn't like leaving people in his apartment, but she had already helped herself to a key that he would bet money on she hadn't returned, and it wasn't as if he left anything incriminating out that she could find if she snooped.

Remembering how he had watched Nina Fairchild going through his things last night, his irritation cranked up a notch.

He clutched his knife case tighter and backed away from Tabitha, eager to leave, and he had almost made it out of the door when she spoke.

'Don't you dare walk out on me, Julian.'

She had finally found her voice, and although it was shaking, there was a determination behind her words.

Annoyed, he turned to face her. 'I'm late!' he snapped.

'You don't get to treat me this way. Not after everything I have done for you. It's time you repay the favour.'

Julian's lip curled. 'What the hell are you talking about now?'

'If you don't give me what I want, I'll go to the police and retract my alibi.'

She would do what?

He stared at her now. At the spite in her wet eyes and the jut of her defiant chin.

She was trying to blackmail him, to scare him into submission.

Raw rage shook through him, quelling his initial burst of fear. How fucking dare she?

'You know giving a fake alibi is a criminal offence,' he reminded her, surprised at how he managed to keep his voice calm.

He watched her waver and knew immediately that he had her. She was trying to call his bluff.

'I'll still do it,' she said, but he knew she was lying.

Walking up to her, he pushed his face into hers, wanting to intimidate her and was pleased when she backed up.

'If I go down, I promise I am dragging you with me,' he warned.

Silly bitch. She didn't get to threaten him like this.

'I want you gone when I get back. And I think it's best if we don't see each other for a while.'

Tabitha gasped, seeming shocked.

Had she honestly expected him to bow to her command?

He shook his head, disgusted. 'Don't you ever dare threaten me like that again.'

This time when he walked to the door, she didn't try to stop him. Slamming it shut behind him, he marched over to the lift. Fury was pumping through his veins and he needed to rid himself of his aggression before he exploded.

Tabitha had picked the wrong fight.

She was going to regret ever messing with him.

41

Zac Green had some moves that Nina hadn't been expecting and she rolled over to his side of the bed, where a path of sunlight streamed through the window, pressing her face into his pillow where the scent of him still lingered.

Her body ached, but in the most satisfying way. No wonder, given they had been up much of the night. Thank God it was Sunday and she had no plans. She was going to be good for nothing all day.

Belatedly, she remembered Zac's suggestion that he would go to the police with her if she wanted. He had told her to sleep on it, but her mind had been otherwise occupied. Now she considered what Julian had said to her and the things she had found, wondering what she should do.

In the cold light of day, she realised Zac was right and the photos she had taken proved nothing, but still that creepy fucker had said he wanted to use his knives on her.

Definitely not normal and Nina was right to be freaked out.

It was her word against his, though. Would the police even be able to do anything?

Annoyed that she was having to consider the problem when she would much rather be thinking about Zac, she flopped over on her back and pulled the duvet over her head.

He had woken her this morning by trailing deliciously tingly kisses down her spine, which, of course, had led to other things, and she just wanted to bask in the afterglow for a little bit longer.

Unlike Zac, who had headed out for a run.

He had promised he would pick up a late breakfast on his way back, cheekily telling her he would be more than happy to find her still in his bed when he returned, and the fact this wasn't over for him had Nina smiling to herself.

She had woken briefly as dawn started to break, wondering if this was a one-off thing.

Zac had kissed her first, but she had been the one to initiate sex, and she had no idea what he was looking for or if he wanted anything at all. After last night, this morning could have been weird and perhaps uncomfortable, but instead it had actually felt natural.

Now she was being honest with herself, the chemistry had been brewing between them ever since Zac's return. Nina didn't want to get ahead of herself, but she liked the idea of exploring this – whatever it was – further.

She had fully intended to take up Zac's suggestion and stay in bed, but now she had remembered Julian, he kept creeping back into her thoughts. There were no missed calls or messages from him, which surprised her, and groaning to herself, she threw back the duvet and went to get in the shower, passing Hannibal who was curled up just outside the door and gave her a judgy look that seemed to intimate, 'I know what you've been up to all night.'

Guiltily remembering she was here because she was

supposed to be looking after him, she detoured into the kitchen, Hannibal hot on her heels and chirping away to remind her that his breakfast was late. Luckily, she spotted Zac's note before the Ragdoll conned her into opening a pouch of food, smiling as she read it.

Hannibal's been fed. Don't let him convince you otherwise.
Z x

To placate the cat, she gave him a cuddle and a handful of treats before heading into the bathroom.

Fifteen minutes later, she was dried and dressed, and trying to make herself feel human again as she sat out on the balcony with her first cup of coffee.

Raising the binoculars again, she scanned the penthouse balcony. There was no sign of Julian. Was he still locked outside? She swept the perimeter again, this time careful to take in every detail, for the first time spotting the fire escape to the side of his apartment. Had he used that to get down? There was no sign of any smashed windows. It felt almost surreal remembering she had been up there last night while Zac had watched them from where she sat now.

Dropping her gaze, she focused on Leonard's apartment. The curtains were drawn at his balcony doors, which was odd as it was already ten-thirty. Was he still asleep?

He had been shocked when he saw Nina and Julian in the lift last night, and it had been the perfect opportunity for him to tell Julian the truth about how she had called the police. But he hadn't.

Although she was wary of him, she wondered now if perhaps he had been on the level with her when he had told her what he had overheard.

Zac said he didn't believe him, but Nina was wavering. Maybe Leonard had been telling her the truth and he had overheard Julian talking with his friend, Tabitha.

It was hearsay, but surely the police would take their concerns more seriously if there were two witness accounts?

Should she try to speak to Leonard?

She would have to wait for him to appear because there was no way she was going into Julian's block of apartments and risking bumping into him.

She decided that she would wait to speak to Leonard when she next saw him. It was definitely the right course of action and it meant she could focus her day on Zac.

Nina dropped the binoculars down to ground level now, wondering if there was any sign of him. There wasn't and she guessed it was wishful thinking. He had only left for his run half an hour ago.

Another figure caught her attention, though, and focusing through the lenses, Nina's heartbeat quickened, realising it was Julian.

He was walking briskly, a scowl on his face and something – it looked like a leather pouch or case – under his arm.

So he had definitely managed to get back inside.

Briefly she dropped the binoculars, worried he might look up, though it was unlikely he would see anything, but he didn't even spare her apartment a glance, heading straight to the car park and over to where his Porsche was parked.

Nina watched him get in the vehicle, speeding off out of the car park, her mouth dry.

Was he going to be gone long? Would she have time to go and speak to Leonard?

It was risky, but she could keep an eye out for Julian's car. If she saw him returning, she would have to get the hell out. And it would be better if she could speak with Leonard sooner rather than later, as the police might wonder why it had taken her so long to report what Julian had said to her.

Mind made up, she scribbled a quick note for Zac, letting him know where she had gone in case he came back in the interim, then let herself out of the apartment.

She just hoped Leonard was still prepared to talk to her.

42

'Hold the lift.'

The door had started to close when a beefy hand halted it and Conrad stepped into the carriage, his face lighting up when he realised it was Nina.

'You're in the wrong block,' he joked as he pressed the button for his floor. 'Unless of course you were coming up to see me.'

Nina resisted rolling her eyes. This man had all the lines. Did he hit on every woman he came into contact with? It wouldn't surprise her.

'Sorry, but I'm visiting someone else,' she told him, biting down on her smile.

Conrad needed no encouragement.

'Who's that then?' he winked. 'Your new boyfriend, Julian Wiseman?' He leaned in conspiratorially and she got an unwelcome whiff of post-workout body odour. 'You should watch yourself around that one. I've heard plenty of stories about him.'

He had?

Nina was tempted to ask what kind of stories, but she didn't have time. She needed to speak to Leonard before Julian returned.

'It's not Julian and he's not my boyfriend,' she said instead. 'If you must know, I need a word with Leonard Pickles.'

There, that would give him something to ponder over.

Was it her imagination or did Conrad seem annoyed? 'You're going to see Leonard? What do you need with that nosy old man?'

'That's for me to know and you to wonder about,' she teased.

'I doubt he's in. Knowing Leonard, he'll be busy poking his nose into someone else's business.' Conrad sounded flustered. He hesitated, as if he wanted to say something else but wasn't sure if it was a good idea. 'The man's crazy anyway,' he said after a moment. 'Has he told you that he thinks that missing woman, Peyton, was here the night she disappeared?'

Nina's heartbeat quickened. 'He does?' she managed, hoping she managed to sound surprised, though her face heated. She prayed it didn't give her away. 'Why would he think that?'

What else had Leonard told Conrad?

'I would stay away from him if I was you,' Conrad advised, now apparently the authority on whose company she should be keeping.

Before Nina could ask why, the lift pinged, arriving on the fourth floor.

'Catch you later,' Conrad said, seeming distracted as he stepped out, and as the doors closed again, Nina wondered why he had seemed so rattled.

Hopefully he was wrong and Leonard would be home. Right now, he was her only hope of proving to the police that Julian was involved in Peyton Landis's disappearance.

* * *

Dylan was about to leave the apartment when Leonard's doorbell rang.

Cursing under his breath, he peered through the security peephole.

For a moment, he could only see long, dark hair, but then the visitor turned, giving him a clear view of her profile.

Nina Fairchild.

What was she doing here on Leonard's doorstep?

He watched her pace out of view, then back again, impatiently ringing the bell a second time when she didn't get an answer.

Just go away, he muttered to himself.

This wasn't good. Dylan's shift started soon and he couldn't leave while Nina was outside.

Instead of giving up, she tried knocking.

Still nothing.

Leonard's not home. Go away, he willed, his eyes widening when he realised she had hold of the door handle, pushing it down as she tried to enter Leonard's apartment.

What the hell did she think she was doing?

Luckily it didn't budge.

Understanding she was wasting her time, she shrugged and went to wait for the lift.

Dylan waited until he saw her outside the building before leaving the apartment.

Deciding to take the stairs, not wanting any of the other residents to know where he had been, he headed down to the ground floor.

Once he was in the lobby, he felt safe.

Nobody was going to question why he was down here. He was often about, addressing various issues.

In the maintenance room, he switched the cameras back on for the fifth floor. Easily done and it was unlikely anyone would have noticed the streaming was down before he arrived.

Dylan had to be careful, very careful, no one else on the complex found out where he had been.

43

If Leonard was home, he wasn't answering and, frustrated, Nina turned to leave.

She stepped over to the window first, checking the car park and wanting to be sure Julian hadn't returned, relieved to see the space where he parked his Porsche was still empty.

As she waited for the lift, she wondered if Zac was back yet.

She would tell him about her plan to speak with Leonard before going to the police.

At least that was if Leonard agreed to talk to her after their previous exchange.

Perhaps he was in his apartment and just avoiding her. The doors all had those little peepholes. Had he been spying on her?

No, she was being paranoid. He simply wasn't home. And he might be an awkward old man, but Nina believed he still had a moral compass. Besides, he was as intrigued with what was going on as she was.

She was so caught up with thoughts of Leonard, it took her a second to realise the lift was coming down instead of up.

There was only one floor above.

Julian's.

Shit.

She had taken his lack of car as certainty he wasn't home and although her instinct was to run for the stairwell, the ping announcing the lift's arrival told her she was too late. It didn't stop her backing away, though, and as the doors slid open, she saw it was occupied.

But not by Julian.

Nina recognised the woman inside. It was his friend, Tabitha, and she looked like hell, her face puffed and blotchy like she had cried a river.

Okay, so this was a little uncomfortable.

At least it wasn't Julian.

Nina got into the lift, in part glad that Tabitha didn't acknowledge or talk to her. The woman seemed almost out of it.

It didn't stop her feeling mean, though. What if something bad had happened? She was really upset and Nina couldn't just ignore her.

'Are you okay?' Nina asked tentatively.

For a moment, she didn't think Tabitha had heard her, but then she seemed to gather herself, her eyes still raw from crying, but managing a quick smile.

'Yes, I'm fine, thank you,' she replied a little stiffly.

Nina pressed the button for the ground floor and the pair of them stood in uncomfortable silence as the lift began to descend.

'He's not a good person,' Tabitha announced, somewhat abruptly, as they passed the third floor.

Was she talking to herself or to Nina? And who was she referring to?

She had been coming down from Julian's apartment. Had he been the one to upset her?

'I'm sorry?' Nina reacted, keeping it vague. She had no idea if Tabitha knew about their date last night.

At first, she didn't think she was going to get an answer; the woman still looked completely preoccupied, but then she turned to Nina and seemed to really notice her for the first time, the redness around her eyes making her blue irises appear brighter as she stared at her.

'Julian,' she elaborated. 'He uses people.'

Nina's heart thumped. Was Tabitha about to admit she had given him a fake alibi? It certainly seemed like the pair of them had fallen out.

She was debating how to respond when the ping of the lift announced they were on the ground floor. As the doors opened, Tabitha appeared to check herself on what she had said. Shaking her head and muttering under her breath, she stepped out of the lift.

No. Nina couldn't let her leave without trying to get to the truth.

'Wait.' She caught up with her on the path outside. 'What do you mean Julian uses people? Has he done something to you?'

Tabitha's eyes widened. 'Can you keep your voice down, please?' she hissed, glancing around as if to check no one was eavesdropping. Although it was just the two of them, she seemed reluctant to expand on what she had said in the lift. 'Look, please just forget what I said,' she said, walking away towards the car park.

Not possible and Nina was now like a dog with a bone as she hurried after the woman, struggling to keep up with her long-legged strides.

As Tabitha approached a black Range Rover, she glanced back in irritation.

'Why are you following me?' she asked, sounding frustrated. 'What do you want?'

Was she covering for Julian or simply scared?

Nina was reminded that she had only heard Julian's version of their relationship history. He had been dismissive of Tabitha when Nina had asked him about her, insisting she was just a friend, but they were clearly close enough for Tabitha to lie for him. She had wondered last night if they were lovers who had fallen out. The fact that Tabitha had just left his apartment looking upset added weight to that theory.

In the lift, she had shown a moment of vulnerability, but now the shutters were down and she had her professional face on.

Could she be persuaded to drop it again?

Nina softened her tone. 'Has he used you?'

Tabitha hesitated as she studied Nina, a telltale twitch under her eye suggesting she wasn't as confident as she tried to appear.

'It's Nina, right?' she asked. When Nina nodded, she added, 'I saw you with Julian last night.'

Oh, shit. Had she?

'It was just a drink. He said the two of you are only friends. I don't want to tread on anyone's toes.'

Tabitha gave a weary sigh, and for a moment Nina thought she was going to say otherwise, but then she shook her head. 'You're not, but I do think if you're considering dating him that there are some things you need to know about him first.'

'There are?' Nina tried not to sound too enthusiastic. She had no intention of seeing Julian Wiseman again full stop, but Tabitha didn't need to know that. Especially not if she was about to spill the dirt on Julian. 'What things?'

Again there was a hesitation. Why was Tabitha so reluctant to reveal the truth?

'I'm not comfortable talking about this here,' she said, and Nina could feel her pulling away again.

'We could go up to my apartment if you like,' she offered.

Tabitha shook her head. 'No, I mean here on the complex.'

Jesus, was she worried the place might be bugged? Nina's imagination was running away with her. 'Okay, where?'

'Can we go for a drive?' Tabitha clicked her fob at the car. 'I think clearer behind the wheel. I'll tell you everything and then you can decide if you want to see him again.'

Nina didn't need to be asked twice, climbing into the passenger seat.

As Tabitha reversed out of her parking space, then pulled out onto the ring road, neither of them were aware they were being watched.

44

Zac had hoped to find Nina still in his bed when he returned to the apartment, keen to spend more time with her. Last night had been both unexpected and the perfect culmination to two weeks of building sexual tension.

He had never set out to try to seduce her, and before he returned to the UK, he could honestly hand on heart say he had never entertained sexual thoughts about her. Those had kicked in after that first night back when he had found her half naked in his bed, and they had been growing ever since.

She had always been Dexter's younger sister and although Zac enjoyed annoying her, he was protective of her too. That's why he quashed down his annoyance when he read her note saying that she had gone to visit Leonard and he hoped she wasn't going to be disappointed.

He had warned her what the old man was like and suspected he was playing games with her for nothing more than his own amusement, but she hadn't listened, and much as her stubborn-headedness infuriated him at times, her enthusiasm and willingness to always believe the best in people were qualities he loved about her.

Well, except for Julian Wiseman. She had doubted him from the start and Zac had spent much of his time in the gym wondering if perhaps he should trust her instincts where Julian was concerned.

Initially, he had been swayed by his and Julian's childhood connection via their parents, but, truthfully, he barely knew the man. Nina had never veered from her belief that Peyton Landis had been in Julian's apartment. Perhaps Zac needed to be more supportive.

Hungry from his run and justifying his huge appetite by telling himself that he didn't know what Nina would fancy so it was best to get a selection of food, he set it all out on the table. Snagging a Danish pastry off one of the plates, he sat down to wait for her.

* * *

Conrad had watched Tabitha Percy emerge from his building with Nina hot on her tail, panic coiling in his stomach.

When he had left Nina, she had been going up to see Leonard, despite Conrad's best attempts to deter her. He hadn't missed her blush either when he'd mentioned Peyton Landis's name.

She had seemed a little bit flustered, as if she had already known the woman was at River Heights that night, and Conrad was now wondering if Nina and Leonard were in cahoots.

Especially when he then saw Nina talking to Tabitha. Tabitha's expression had gone from guarded to annoyed as the two of them spoke and that was enough to send fresh paranoia skittering through Conrad's veins.

He thought back to the night Peyton Landis had disappeared, recalling his encounter with her clearly.

Had Leonard sought him out to tell him on purpose?

Had the old man or Nina seen them together?

Conrad had been jittery ever since.

Now Nina was telling Tabitha, who Conrad knew worked for Wiseman Homes.

As they headed towards Tabitha's car, he panicked that this was about him. Were they going to go to the police?

This was bad. He could be in big trouble.

Yes, sometimes he joked around with women, but it was only banter. What had happened that night was an accident. He hadn't meant to do it.

Needing to know where Nina and Tabitha were off to, he grabbed his keys and hurried downstairs after them.

45

'I lied to the police.'

Tabitha hadn't given up her confession easily, aimlessly driving around the outskirts of the city as she spoke about Julian and how much of her life she had dedicated to loving him. She told Nina about the mean way he had spoken to her this morning, ripping her heart into shreds, and her realisation that he had been using her.

At times, she had sounded bitter and angry, the speedometer creeping higher as she subconsciously applied pressure to the accelerator, and Nina was on the verge of saying something when Tabitha seemed to check herself, slowing back down. And when she wasn't mad at her situation, tears of frustration and hurt leaked from her eyes. At one point, she was sobbing so hard she had to pull over to blow her nose.

Nina's heart squeezed for her and she couldn't help but compare their situations. After two weeks of living together, she and Zac had finally confronted their feelings, and while whatever was happening between them was too new to put any kind of label on, both of them seemed to be on the same page. Meanwhile, poor Tabitha had seen her world fall apart, the man she was in love with rejecting her, and cruelly too.

There was no need to mention any of this. They were here to talk about Julian's lies. Tabitha didn't need to hear about Zac and Nina saw no relevance in telling her she wasn't dating Julian either. She didn't want to give the woman any kind of false hope.

Tabitha was best to be as far away from Julian Wiseman as possible.

And although Nina was sympathetic, they had been driving for fifteen minutes before they even touched on the subject of Peyton Landis. She was conscious that Zac was probably back from his run and he would be wondering why she was still over at Leonard's apartment. Plus he was bringing food.

She hadn't eaten anything and her stomach kept growling.

She wanted to check her phone. See if Zac had been in touch and to let him know she would be back soon, but Tabitha seemed so skittish and fragile, Nina didn't want to do anything that might spook her. Not until she had told the truth about Julian.

Her patience eventually paid off.

Finally, when she managed to guide the subject round to the missing woman, Tabitha didn't even try to hide what she had done.

'I lied to the police,' she repeated, sounding almost relieved to unburden herself of the secret.

'It wasn't you on the balcony with Julian that night,' Nina said quietly.

Tabitha fell quiet, then, for the first time in a while, she glanced over at Nina, her eyebrows knotting. 'It was you who reported Julian then.' It was a statement, not a question.

Shit. Nina hadn't meant to reveal what she had seen.

Though, did it really matter now?

'I saw them together. Julian and Peyton,' she admitted.

'It was wrong of me, pretending I was with him,' Tabitha admitted, her focus once again on the road. 'But at the time Julian was in a panic. He was so scared and seemed really vulnerable. Instinct kicked in and I reacted without thinking.'

Scared and vulnerable? Nina bit down on her anger. What about poor Peyton, she wanted to ask. How must she have been feeling?

'You need to report this. Call the police,' she urged. Tabitha couldn't stay silent about what she had done. 'I know you lied, but they will go easier on you if you come forward of your own accord.'

Please let her agree.

They drove in silence for a few moments, fresh tears leaking down Tabitha's face as she gripped the steering wheel tightly. Eventually, she nodded, glancing over at Nina.

'I know I do,' she said. 'But I'm scared and I would rather do it in person. Will you come with me?'

* * *

Conrad was getting frustrated as he trailed Tabitha's Range Rover. The two women seemed to be driving around with no destination in mind, which surprised him, as he had been certain they would go straight to the police station. Instead, though, he felt like he was on a tour of the city's outer ring road and he was watching the needle of his fuel gauge creep lower. It was almost on the red and he would have to stop for petrol soon.

If they did go to the police, then he would keep driving, he decided, head down to his friend's place in North London and try to come up with a plan. He had been the last person to see

Peyton Landis alive and he hadn't come forward. There would be consequences for that.

It was driving him crazy wondering what they were discussing inside the car, and although there were a couple of moments where he doubted himself, questioning if perhaps he had got this wrong, that he wasn't the topic of their conversation, he didn't dare take the risk of leaving them and going back home.

For his own peace of mind, he had to know where they were going.

When the Range Rover eventually indicated, to his relief turning into the petrol station in Cringleford, he pulled off the road behind it, managing to get to a pump at the other end of the forecourt. There was a van parked between them, but still he waited, watching, letting Tabitha fill her car and go into the shop to pay, before getting out of his Mondeo and sticking a tenner in his tank that he paid for at the pump.

He was confident that Nina hadn't seen him, and he was back in his car before the van between them pulled away. Driving over to the side of the forecourt, he waited for Tabitha to return.

She came out of the shop moments later, two cups of Costa coffee in her hands.

They seemed to take forever to leave, doing the same as Conrad and pulling over to the side of the forecourt, and he tapped his knuckles against the steering wheel in frustration.

What the hell were these two up to?

* * *

'Here, I got you a coffee,' Tabitha said, handing Nina one of the two Costa cups. 'Flat white. Hope that's okay.'

'Thanks.' Nina took her coffee black, but she didn't say so. It was a kind gesture and she was sure she could manage to drink it.

She understood that the coffee was a delay tactic, as was, she suspected, stopping for petrol.

Tabitha was anxious about going to the police and admitting what she had done and although she had resigned herself to the fact she had to confess the truth, she was dragging her heels.

Nina could be patient just a little bit longer.

She had checked her phone while Tabitha was in the shop paying, replying to messages from Rachel and Tori, then smiling as one pinged up on her phone from Zac.

> Hurry up back. I'm hungry.

The winking emoji he had added suggested his appetite wasn't just for food.

Nina had sent him a brief reply.

> Me too. I'll be back soon. xx

She didn't elaborate. It would take too long to explain where she was and she couldn't risk spooking Tabitha. She would update him once they got to the police station and she had a better idea of how long they were likely to be. If Tabitha was arrested or taken through for questioning – Nina had no idea how these things worked – Zac would have to come and pick her up.

'Thank you for doing this with me.' Tabitha managed a watery smile as she sipped at her coffee. 'I'm not sure I would be brave enough to do it by myself.'

And that was exactly why Nina was here. She didn't want the woman backing out.

Once the police knew that Julian had been with Peyton Landis, hopefully they would be able to locate where she was.

Sadly, after all this time, it was unlikely she was still alive.

Still, her family needed closure and Peyton deserved justice.

'It's no bother. I'm glad you've decided to do the right thing.'

Nina took a sip of her coffee, wincing at the taste. She really didn't like milky drinks. Gamely she took a couple of bigger sips, backhanding froth from her mouth.

Yuck!

'The thing that bothers me the most is what my parents are going to think of me,' Tabitha said, her hand shaking on the cup. 'How disappointed they will be.'

'They might be a little shocked at first, but I'm sure they will support you,' Nina was quick to assure her.

She wondered how her own parents would react if she had lied as Tabitha had. Her mother would be furious and her father quietly disappointed, but they would ultimately stand by her, she was sure. Tabitha's parents would do the same, wouldn't they?

Sensing how nervous the woman was, but knowing they couldn't sit on the forecourt forever, Nina spent a few more minutes trying to reassure her, before more firmly insisting they really needed to go to the station.

Letting out a shaky sigh, Tabitha reluctantly put her cup in the central console and started the engine. Nina had only managed half of hers so kept her drink on her lap. Perhaps when they reached the police station she could discreetly dispose of the rest.

As Tabitha drove, she fell quiet. Nina assumed she was thinking about what she would say when they arrived, but when she glanced over, she saw the woman kept looking in the rear-view mirror and she seemed a little agitated.

'Is everything okay?'

She nodded brusquely. 'Yes. Well, I think so.'

She was silent for a moment.

'Someone might be following us. There's a dark blue Mondeo a couple of cars back. I'm sure it was behind us earlier before we stopped for petrol.'

Was she just being paranoid?

Nina glanced in the wing mirror. There was going to be more than one blue Mondeo on the road. 'Well, good job we're going to the police station if there is,' she said lightly.

Tabitha's smile was tight as she agreed.

'Just humour me, okay, I'm going to take a couple of turns to see if I'm right.'

Nina resisted rolling her eyes, recognising another delay tactic, but saying nothing as she leant back against the headrest.

Tiredness from being awake most of the night had her yawning and she was eager to get back to Zac. Tabitha didn't have the air-con on and despite the front windows being cranked open a notch, it was hot in the car. The warmth was making her sleepy.

She dozed off momentarily as Tabitha took the Range Rover down a few side streets, and when her eyes opened again, they were back on the main road.

'Did he follow us?' she asked, remembering.

'No, it was a false alarm.'

Nina nodded, unsurprised. 'We should really go to the police station now.'

'We are. I promise.' Tabitha's kept her focus on the road ahead. 'I just want this over with.'

Satisfied, Nina let her eyes drop shut again.

The next time she opened them, she glanced in the side mirror again, surprised to see the blue Mondeo was still on their tail.

46

Nina had been gone over an hour now and, while Zac didn't want to act like he was breathing down her neck, he was starting to get a little bit worried. Especially when he tried to call her and it eventually went to voicemail. The WhatsApp message he followed it up with was still unread.

She had told him in her last message that she would be back soon and that was almost forty-five minutes ago.

Annoyed with himself for acting like a stalker, he stepped out onto the balcony, using the binoculars to check out Leonard's apartment. All of the curtains were drawn, despite it being almost midday. Why would he and Nina be sitting in the dark?

Perhaps he should keep his nose out, but something didn't feel right about this.

Grabbing his keys, he headed over to find out what was going on.

* * *

Julian knew he should have called first instead of just showing up at the house. Rage, both at himself for being presumptuous as well as at the woman who wasn't home, burned through his veins.

His craving was almost unbearable and he was struggling to think straight. He needed to use his knives, to make those sweet cuts and taste the hot blood as it pumped from her body.

So where the fuck was she?

* * *

Leonard wasn't answering his door and Zac had given him plenty of opportunity, repeatedly ringing the bell and then knocking.

Nina had said this was where she was going, so why did neither of them appear to be here?

Irritated, he checked his phone again. He hadn't heard from her and the WhatsApp message was still unread. He tried calling again, hoping he might hear her phone ringing inside the apartment, but, as before, it cut straight to voicemail.

Determined to find out where Nina was, he bent down so he was close to the keyhole.

'Nina? Are you in there?' he called.

He waited a few seconds, but there was no response.

He called again. This time, louder. 'Nina!'

A few seconds passed before he heard what he thought was a grunt.

Not Nina and whoever it was sounded in pain.

Leonard?

'It's Zac Green. Is that you, Mr Pickles?'

He waited a beat before a frail voice broke through the silence.

'Help me.'

Definitely Leonard.

Zac tried the door handle. No surprise that it was locked.

Had the old man had some kind of accident? And why wasn't Nina with him?

'Hang tight,' he yelled through the door. 'I'll be right back.'

* * *

Dylan was in the maintenance room when Zac Green found him; the usually laid-back owner of 5A appearing agitated.

'I need you to let me into Leonard Pickles' apartment,' he demanded, and Dylan's eyes widened.

'Why?' he asked.

It wasn't protocol to comply with what Zac was asking. The team needed good reason to enter anyone's apartment without permission and they couldn't let other residents inside.

'Something's up with Leonard. I think he's had an accident.'

Zac explained hearing the frail cry for help coming from inside the apartment and Dylan realised he had no choice but to go and check it out.

Up on the fifth floor, the spare key to Leonard's apartment pressed into his clammy palm, he listened as Zac called through the keyhole.

At first, there was no response and Dylan was certain Zac was either mistaken or this had been some kind of ruse to try to get inside, but then came a croaky splutter, followed by one word.

'Please.'

Zac looked at Dylan, as if to say I told you so. 'You heard that, right?'

He nodded and put the key into the lock, sparing a glance at the apartment of Leonard's neighbour, Becky Johnson, before pushing open the door, not liking how close for comfort this all was.

Was today the day he was going to get caught out?

While he hovered cautiously in the doorway, Zac wasn't waiting around, pushing past him and disappearing through into Leonard's living room.

That was where they found him. He was lying on his back in front of the sofa, bathed in a pool of blood, his face grey and a knife protruding from his chest.

Judging from the mess the room was in, with furniture upended and cushions on the floor, whoever had attacked the old man had been in a raging fit of anger.

Now it made sense, the noises Dylan had heard in the middle of the night.

At the time, he'd had no idea what the hell Leonard was up to and knowing he couldn't risk going and checking, aware he had already almost landed himself in trouble, he'd plugged his earphones in and drowned out the sound, trying to get back to sleep.

All he had been worried about at the time was getting caught in Becky's apartment. She was away on holiday and Dylan was watering her plants.

That had changed when he'd arrived home from work one night to find his fiancée, Rose, in bed with his best friend.

Dylan had fled the flat they shared, refusing Rose's requests to go home and talk, and with nowhere else to crash – he had no family or other friends locally – he had set up camp at Becky's place.

He meant no harm. It was just temporary and he would make sure everything was back in place with no sign that he had crashed there by the time Becky flew home on Wednesday, but aware he would lose his job if he was found out, he had kept it very quiet.

Leonard Pickles was the only neighbour who might twig what he was up to, but Dylan had been careful, managing to fly under the radar.

Now, here he was worrying about sleeping in a resident's apartment, meanwhile Leonard had almost been murdered. 'We need to call an ambulance,' he spluttered, taking a moment to realise Zac already had his phone out.

'Police and ambulance,' he said. 'Someone has been stabbed.'

As Zac patiently gave the address, Dylan looked down at Leonard.

'Who did this to you, Mr Pickles?' he asked, but when the old man tried to take a gasping breath, he started to splutter.

'Was it Julian?' Zac followed up sharply. A simpler question that required a nod or shake of the head, though Leonard was struggling to do either despite his best efforts.

Dylan's eyes widened. 'You think Julian Wiseman stabbed Leonard?'

Zac ignored the question, his face pale with worry, his phone still to his ear. 'Nina came over here to see Leonard earlier this morning.'

'Yes, I saw her knock on his door.'

'You did?'

Dylan realised he had blurted the words without thinking. It was the stress of the situation. He had never had to deal with anything like this before.

Still, Zac seemed too preoccupied to question where he had been at the time to see her. 'I can't get hold of her. Her phone's switched off,' he said instead.

Now that was something Dylan could help with.

'She was with Tabitha Percy earlier,' he said, recalling how he had watched the two women from Becky's window. 'They were heading over to the car park when I last saw them.' Belatedly, he remembered seeing Conrad Mackenzie heading out of the building in a rush just after. 'He looked like he was on his way over to join them,' he said, mentioning Conrad's name now.

On the floor, Leonard started spluttering and choking.

'Take it easy, Leonard,' Zac tried to calm him 'The ambulance is on its way.'

Ignoring Zac's words, the old man continued trying to talk. 'Dit... Did't... He'd it.'

Dylan mouthed to himself what Leonard was trying to say, but it still made no sense. Was he trying to tell them who had attacked him?

Finally, Leonard managed to spit out the words he wanted to say.

'He did it.'

47

I had never gone to Katy Spencer's wedding planning to kill her, but then I discovered she had a secret, one that devastated my world, and what I can only describe as a red mist took over.

It wasn't me there that day. When I look back at the events as they unfolded, I do so as if I am in another body watching down. My body was a vessel acting of its own accord and it wasn't aware of the consequences.

How fortunate I was that I was never even considered a suspect. I literally got away with murder, and thanks to Julian Wiseman I had the perfect alibi, ready to defend me if anyone ever looked my way.

It wasn't something I felt good about, though.

I mean, I was glad Katy was dead. Good riddance and all that. I just wish I hadn't been the one to kill her. It didn't sit comfortably taking another life.

For a long time after, I tried to walk the righteous path, to atone for what I did, but this last year has been difficult. The anger inside me has required an outlet, and there have been women I have had no choice but to punish.

But things have been different this time. I have managed to harness my rage and I have learnt I can inflict pain, but I don't have to kill.

Well, until last night.

It's a shame I had to kill Leonard, but he didn't really leave me a choice.

With these women, it is different. I might inflict pain, but I don't take their lives. If they wish to die, then it's on them completely. I let their bodies shut down, but I don't do anything to assist the process.

My conscience is clear.

48

Julian shielded his eyes from the sun as the car door opened. Grace O'Connell lifted a questioning eyebrow when she saw him waiting for her.

'Juju.' She purred her special nickname for him affectionately. 'What are you doing here?'

Despite the stifling heat, she was dressed in a high-necked black jumper dress and wore thick tights, yet he knew her skin would be cool to touch.

'I need to see you,' he told her, trying and failing to keep the desperation out of his voice. 'Where were you?'

Her blood red lips curved. 'You know I go to church on a Sunday.'

He had forgotten, but now, as he spotted the silver crucifix around her neck, he remembered.

Oh the irony. His mother's best friend. The divorcee who had seduced him on his seventeenth birthday and who had introduced him to blood play. What would the vicar say if he knew the truth about her? What would his parents say?

No one except her lovers knew that Grace kept her body

covered to hide the knife scars of her fetish. Julian's mother had extended holiday invitations to Grace on many occasions, always disappointed when they were turned down. Only Julian knew the true reason why. It would be harder to hide her scars in a sunnier climate.

When Grace had first asked Julian to cut her, he had been appalled, disgusted. Now it was a craving he couldn't give up.

But Grace wasn't his exclusively and he had to wait his turn to play. The giddy need to slice skin had him frantically searching for new partners and taking risks as he revealed his required tastes.

Never Tabitha. God no.

Julian knew she would let him, but his fetish was his secret and he couldn't risk cutting her. If his family saw the scars, if they learnt the truth, they would never forgive him.

Katy Spencer was the only woman who had totally consumed him, where he hadn't felt the need to cut her, but she was dead, and every female body since was a canvas he wished to paint red on.

Peyton had let him cut her arm, but then she had freaked out, fleeing his apartment. And with Nina he hadn't even got that far.

Grace glanced now at the leather case under his arm and arched a dark eyebrow.

'I guess you'd better come inside.'

49

When Nina awoke again, she was still in the passenger seat of Tabitha's car, but they had stopped, the engine off and the driver's seat was empty. Blinking heavy-lidded eyes, she realised they definitely weren't at the police station. Instead, they were in the driveway of a house, high hedgerows preventing her from seeing if there were any neighbouring properties, and the sun no longer out. Instead, heavy, dark clouds hung overhead as the sky rumbled ominously.

Remembering the blue Mondeo, Nina glanced towards the wing mirror, surprised when she realised the car was parked behind them.

She couldn't see a driver and there was no sign of Tabitha either.

What the hell was going on?

Fumbling with her seat belt, she managed to click the lock open, then reached for the door handle. Her head was still groggy with sleep and her fingers clumsy as she tried and failed to open the passenger door.

Just how long had she been out of it?

Voices came from ahead, distracting her, and she glanced up. Her eyelids were heavy, threatening to drop shut again.

Standing in the open doorway to a garage, she spotted Tabitha. She looked panicked, gesturing a lot with her hands and pacing about in front of a man who seemed to be blocking her path back to the car.

Wait, was that Conrad? Why was he here?

Nina had to get out of the car and find out what was going on.

She tried again to open the door, this time succeeding, but as she started to get out, her limbs were floppy and unresponsive, and she lurched forward, landing on the gravel driveway on her hands and knees, managing an inelegant grunt. She was aware of the sharp stones digging into her palms and her shins, though strangely it didn't hurt as much as she imagined it would. It was as if there was a numbness dulling her senses.

The commotion was enough to attract attention and as she tried to get up, Conrad moved towards her, a scowl on his face. As he neared, fat spits of rain hit the ground, the heavens finally opening.

Nina tried to speak, but her tongue was big and useless in her mouth.

Why are you here, she wanted to ask, and what the hell was he playing at following them?

She had questions for Tabitha too, the most pertinent one was why weren't they at the police station?

Had Tabitha changed her mind?

Nina was angry and frustrated, but also so tired, and the fog in her brain was confusing her. Why the hell did she feel so bad? Was she coming down with some kind of bug?

And Conrad was swimming in and out of focus. She could

hear him and he sounded annoyed, the tone of his voice matching the thunder in the sky.

He was moving into her personal space now and she tried her hardest to roll away on the wet ground, but then she saw Tabitha in her periphery, and the woman was charging out of the garage with a shovel in her hand and a determined look on her face.

Shit.

Nina heard the thud as it hit the back of Conrad's skull, his expression going from angry to stunned, his mouth dropping open and his eyes widening, then he was stumbling forward, almost kicking her in the face, and she watched in horror as he collapsed to the ground.

What had just happened?

Was Tabitha defending them?

She watched as the woman raised the shovel, hitting him a second and a third time.

What was she doing? Conrad was angry, but he hadn't actually attacked them. Or was Nina missing something?

What exactly had happened while she had been asleep?

Tabitha's focus had shifted now to Nina and as she helped her to her feet, bearing the brunt of Nina's weight, Nina tried to speak.

Why was her speech so slurred?

'Shush, you're not making any sense,' Tabitha told her, helping her to walk towards the house. 'Let's get inside and out of the rain, make you comfortable before the rest of the drug wears off.'

Drug? What drug?

Had Conrad done something to her?

She had been sleepy in Tabitha's car, struggling to keep her eyes open before finally dozing off. That was before they had even spotted Conrad.

The Costa coffee that Tabitha had given her – had she laced it with something?

No, she had this all wrong. Tabitha had bought the coffees in the garage. Either there was something wrong with their machine or Nina really was coming down with a bug.

Why hadn't they gone to the police station, though?

And how did Conrad fit into all of this?

Was he dead?

She tried to ask the questions, but Tabitha was ignoring her.

Was this her house? Why were they in her house?

There were cream panelled walls and a console table with a powder-blue vase filled with daisies. Next to the table was an umbrella stand in the shape of a duck and a pair of wellington boots. It was all very country living and twee.

They were heading upstairs now, the edge of each wooden step bashing against Nina's ankles as her feet struggled to keep purchase. If Tabitha let go of her at this point, she was fearful she would tumble back to the bottom.

The other woman was puffing out big breaths, the exertion of supporting another body taking its toll, but she didn't slow or loosen her grip, appearing determined on getting Nina to the top of the stairs. As they reached the landing, she produced a key, pushing it into the lock of the one closed door. Then she was opening the door and forcing Nina inside, shoving her face down on the floor.

Why was Tabitha suddenly being so rough with her?

Trying to push herself up, her limbs starting to comply, but still too unsteady to fully support her, Nina collapsed again.

'What… are we… doing… here?' she managed.

'This is your new home,' Tabitha said, finally deciding to

answer her. 'We're going to get you settled and then we can have a nice little chat about how you shouldn't take things that don't belong to you.'

What the hell was she talking about? The woman wasn't making any sense.

Nina tried again to get up, her hair falling in wet strings around her face. This time, she focused on where she was: a yellow room with white shutters.

'He isn't yours.' Tabitha's tone was sharp, different to before. 'You don't get to have him.'

Who? Was she referring to Julian?

As Tabitha pulled her into a sitting position, Nina could see more of the room. There was a daybed in front of the window with pretty cushions and a teddy bear, and shelves neat with books and ornaments.

Those weren't what drew her attention, though, and her focus was on the hardback chair in the centre of the room, the legs bolted to the floor and ropes winding around the wooden spindles and chair legs. Plastic sheeting lay beneath it and the cream seat cushion was stained in red.

Suddenly, Nina realised she was in a whole lot of trouble.

* * *

Leonard was growing agitated as he kept trying and failing to talk, and Zac had been doing his best to calm him down. The sirens were getting closer and the ambulance was just minutes away.

He was still on the call to the emergency responder, listening to the woman's instructions, knowing he couldn't leave until the police and paramedics had arrived, and it was worrying the hell out of him where Nina was, especially after Dylan said he had seen Conrad Mackenzie following her and Tabitha to the car park.

'It's okay, Mr Pickles,' Dylan said earnestly.

'He!' Leonard managed to rasp.

'Yes, you said it was a he. We'll be sure to tell the police.'

Leonard was shaking his head, struggling to formulate the words he wanted to say. He seemed to be having particular difficulty with his 's' as he tried to explain what had happened.

'S... ss... sss...'

He beckoned Zac, who leaned in closer.

'S... ss... she.'

Zac frowned at Dylan, not sure what he meant, but then Leonard found a burst of energy, the words spilling out.

'Not he. *She* did it.'

50

It was Nina's fault she was here.

Last night, Tabitha had waited for her in the stairwell of Julian's apartment block, fully intending to try to lure the woman into accompanying her down to her car.

It was easier when you were female. There were plenty of hooks you could use, from offering a lift – as she had done with Peyton Landis – or asking for help with something. Women tended to trust other women and she gave off none of the danger vibes that would automatically be there if she was a man.

After Zac had showed up, Tabitha knew she had missed her opportunity. Instead, she had turned her attention to Leonard Pickles.

The old man had already been bothering her, poking around and talking to his neighbours about Peyton Landis, but then last night after tormenting herself, watching the camera footage of Julian and Nina outside Julian's apartment again, she had rewound too far and seen Leonard loitering on the penthouse landing.

Just what was he up to?

Knowing he was still out on his walk, she had let herself into his apartment wanting to snoop, but then she had discovered his whiteboard and realised some of the questions he was asking were hitting too close to home.

She hadn't intended to kill him, but his return had caught her off guard. When he'd realised she was there, Leonard hadn't reacted well and she had been forced to deal with him. Figuring she would have to come back and deal with his body later, she had headed home to prepare her spare bedroom so it was ready for another guest.

Julian had really hurt her last night, blowing off her parents' anniversary party to be with Nina, and she was still working out what to do about him, but in the meantime, Nina needed to be punished.

These women with their pretty doll outfits and perfect hair and skin, they had no idea what it was like to live in the real world. Everything came so easily to them and they were thoughtless when it came to caring about other people.

This morning, she had awoken focused and ready to tackle all of her problems. She would talk to Julian and make it clear that he knew how she felt, then, when the opportunity rose, she would lure Nina away from the complex.

The ketamine she kept in her car had been obtained using a bogus prescription she had written for herself using her father's prescription pad. It was weaker than what she could purchase from the dark web, but a double dosage was generally enough to keep Julian's sluts under control.

What she hadn't counted on was Julian's brutal rejection.

Before, she had always had hope, and a belief that these women were something he had to work out of his system. That when he was done, he would settle down with Tabitha.

Learning the truth and how he really felt had broken her.

The chance encounter in the lift with Nina offered the perfect opportunity for Tabitha to lure the woman to her car, but Julian's spiteful words were still playing on a loop in her head and she was so distraught, her focus was gone.

If Nina hadn't pushed, if she hadn't insisted on poking her nose in, Tabitha would have let her walk away. Instead, she had hovered like an annoying fly and eventually Tabitha's control had snapped.

These women, they wouldn't have given her the time of day if they hadn't wanted something from her. One unintended comment spoken aloud and Nina wouldn't let it drop, trying to persuade Tabitha to rat on the man she had loved for almost all of her life.

None of the bitches understood Julian the way she did. And that included Katy Spencer, who Julian had actually claimed to be in love with.

Not that Tabitha had realised that when she had agreed to accompany Julian to Katy's lavish weekend wedding in the Lake District, where he was best man to her husband-to-be, Hugh.

At the time, Tabitha had been flattered and hopeful when Julian had asked her to be his plus-one. They had slept together a handful of times over the years, but this was a big deal. A weekend away to a wedding was more of a commitment.

Rosewood Manor was located just outside of Hawkshead; a gorgeous butter-yellow building with a thatched roof and trailing roses, set in several acres of beautifully tended gardens and woodland. The manor house itself only had a handful of guest bedrooms, which were reserved for the bride and groom's immediate families, and all of the other guests were in luxury lodges scattered throughout the grounds.

Tabitha's enthusiasm had dampened slightly when she'd realised Julian had booked them separate lodges on the estate, but still she was swept up in the fairytale of the weekend. It was not until later that she learnt he had only invited her to be his cover, as he didn't want to rouse suspicion. No one at the wedding – including his best friend, the groom, Hugh – realised that Julian had been having an affair with Katy for the last four months and that he was trying to persuade Katy to call off her wedding.

Tabitha had only realised this when she went to Julian's lodge on the eve of the wedding, and the ugly memory of what she had witnessed that night was still etched clearly in her mind.

* * *

Most of the wedding party were still in the manor, where a respectful evening meal had gradually become a bawdy pre-wedding booze up. Some of the guests had slipped away after dinner, including the bride and also Julian, who had told Tabitha he wanted to go over his speech, but Hugh and his friends were propping up the bar and buying in rounds of shots.

Tabitha watched, amused, but when they tried persuading her to join in, she took it as her cue to leave. She didn't mind the occasional glass of wine or fizz, but she wasn't a big drinker.

Cutting down the lantern-lit path that led to her accommodation, the scent of jasmine clinging to the warm night air, she spotted a light on in Julian's lodge and decided to stop by and see how he was getting on with the speech.

Perhaps he could read it to her or they could share a nightcap together. It might lead to something more.

The door was ajar, but she knocked out of politeness before easing it open, surprised when she heard music. Some R&B track, though Tabitha wasn't familiar with the artist.

'Julian?'

She stepped into the lounge area, eyes on the bedroom door, when she heard a grunting sound.

Had he fallen asleep?

Instead of calling him again, she crossed the room, pressing her face to the crack in the door, double blinking when she realised Julian wasn't in the room alone.

A woman was sat astride him on the bed, and she was naked.

Tabitha's breath caught and for a moment she stood frozen in place as betrayal threatened to choke her.

He had brought her here as his date, but he was having sex with someone else.

Initially, she didn't realise who the woman was, but then Julian spoke her name.

'God, yes, Katy. I love you.'

That was the push Tabitha needed. Completely distraught, she fled back to her own lodge, heading straight into the bathroom and raising the toilet seat. As she threw up, she was certain she would never recover from this.

The next morning, she told Julian she felt unwell and would have to skip the ceremony and her plan was to spend the rest of the weekend alone in bed until she could finally leave the godforsaken place, but then, half an hour before the wedding, she heard a noise outside and saw Katy from her window, the bride looking stunning in her gown as she knocked frantically on the door to Julian's lodge.

Julian wasn't there and Katy appeared desperate to find him.

Tabitha should mind her own business and go back to bed. But irritation that Katy should even be here when she was supposed to be getting married, burned in her gut, and after splashing water on her tired face and smoothing her fingers over her hair, she headed outside to confront the woman.

She intended to tell her to get to the ceremony, that she had a man waiting for her who loved her, but instead she found herself confessing that she knew about the affair, pretending Julian had confided in her. 'He hoped you would come,' she lied, when Katy admitted she couldn't go through with the wedding.

'I'm in love with him,' Katy declared, her wide blue eyes filling with tears. 'There, I said it. I love Julian. And I know he loves me too.'

The words were a vice tightening in Tabitha's stomach and she thought she was going to be sick again. This woman with her perfect hair and make-up, standing here in her expensive dress, she already had everything. Why did she have to be greedy and take the one man Tabitha loved?

At first, Tabitha wasn't sure if she trusted herself to speak, wanting to throttle Katy on the spot, to squeeze the life out of the Barbie doll of a woman, so when her lies came tumbling out, the words so smooth she almost believed them herself, it was like she was watching from the outside in.

'It's going to be okay,' she promised. 'He already told me he can't watch you get married. He hoped you would feel the same. That's why he made a plan. He wants me to take you to him.'

Tabitha had never considered herself to be an actress, but she had put on one hell of a convincing performance and had Katy so pathetically grateful for her help, willingly getting into her car.

'I don't have my phone,' Katy realised, as Tabitha started the engine. 'I left it in my bag back in my room.'

'You can't go back for it now. Not without causing a big scene. Let me take you to Julian. You just have to trust him. He has it all figured out.'

This woman didn't deserve Julian and Tabitha was going to

make damn sure she never got her claws into him again, her confidence growing as rage at Katy smouldered in her gut.

There was an abandoned barn that she had come across on her walk the previous day and pulling her car off the narrow lane, she smiled reassuringly at Katy.

* * *

'It's just a few minutes' walk through the woods,' Tabitha said, leading the way.

'Is that where he is?' Katy asked hopefully, spotting the building through the trees, as she struggled to keep up with Tabitha's fast pace.

Now they were almost here, she wanted this over, already picturing the rusty shovel with the broken handle that she had found in the barn the previous day, her fingers tightening around it and raising it in the air, ready to strike.

'In here,' she gestured as they reached the open door.

Katy stepped inside the shadowy barn, standing in the path of light that came through the open door looking so damned pretty in her dress, as she looked around for Julian.

'He's not here. Are you sure—'

She never got to finish the sentence, the first smack of the shovel cracking against the back of her skull and sending her sprawling to the ground.

The blow wasn't enough to kill her, but Tabitha showed no remorse, even as Katy screamed and begged her to stop. There would be no mercy. Last night, this woman had been responsible for every ounce of Tabitha's pain. She deserved everything that was happening to her.

It was only after Katy was dead that the magnitude of what she had done hit home.

How the hell was she going to get away with this?

There was blood on her clothes and she had to get back to the car, then into her lodge once she arrived back at the venue.

It was pure good fortune that she made it back without being seen, and that she had a supply of plastic carrier bags she had collected over the years for shopping, that she kept in the boot of her car.

She parked as close to her lodge as possible, grateful that Rosewood Manor was quiet. The guests must still all be at the ceremony, wondering where Katy was. If anyone was out looking for her, Tabitha was fortunate not to encounter them.

Unsure what to do with the shovel, she panicked, trying the doors of a few of the other cars and dumping the weapon in the boot of an unlocked Volvo.

Back in her chalet, she stripped and wrapped her bloody clothes in more plastic bags, hiding them in the back of the wardrobe under a pile of spare pillows and blankets, before getting in the shower and scrubbing her skin raw, trying to remove the stains, both physical and psychological, of what she had done.

Afterwards, still feeling tarnished, she ran a bath, and she was still sitting in the tub, the water having long run cold, when Julian came to tell her that Katy had vanished.

It turned out that he hadn't actually gone to the ceremony, unable to watch Katy going through with the wedding, but people were now looking all over the estate for her.

Initially, he was hopeful and excited that she was perhaps hiding somewhere, waiting for things to quieten down before she made contact, but then, when she failed to get in touch, he – like the other guests – began to grow fearful. How ironic that he would be the one to stumble across the barn and find his beloved's body?

The ensuing mess almost broke Julian, and Tabitha was beside herself when he was suspected of killing Katy.

What had she done?

Ultimately, it was her alibi that saved him. And while it had freed Julian and she was relieved to have been able to help, she quietly noted that by saying she had been with him that day, she had also protected herself from any suspicion.

Kevin Wiseman was furious when the family name was in the press for all the wrong reasons, and even though Julian was released without charge – the groundsman, Eric Grogan, who owned the Volvo and who had been working alone that day, taking the hit for Katy's murder – Julian wasn't the same man.

Even though he was innocent of Katy's murder, there was still the fallout that he had been having an affair with her, Katy's phone revealing the many messages she and Julian had exchanged.

Hugh was heartbroken and furious, blaming Julian indirectly for Katy's death, claiming that if Julian hadn't tried to persuade her to break things off she would never have left the venue the day of her murder.

Several of their mutual friends sided with Hugh, and Julian found himself to be something of a social pariah. Between that and the headlines, eventually it was agreed he would go and live abroad with his uncle, at least until things had calmed down.

Tabitha had been heartbroken all over again, wanting to go over to the US with him, but he didn't want her there. It had been a hard lesson to learn. She had killed for Julian and then lost him. It had been a reckless and foolish mistake and this was how karma had repaid her.

While he was away, she had initially tried to date, but no one she met measured up to Julian, so instead she focused on her work.

When eventually he had returned to the UK just before Christmas, she had honestly believed she was over him. It had been more than five years.

But then he had walked into the reception of his father's office and smiled at her.

'Tabitha, how are you?'

He looked so handsome and he seemed pleased to see her, scooping her up in a hug, the scent of his aftershave clinging to her clothes all afternoon.

She fell even harder the second time, and initially it seemed there were no obstacles in the way, nothing to stop them being together.

Except Julian wasn't wired that way. He told Tabitha that she was the only one who had ever really understood him and was there for him, but his head was still easily turned by other women.

Tabitha tried her best to ignore it, but slowly it was grinding her down and Maria Adams was her breaking point.

Julian had first encountered Maria on a Christmas shopping trip with Tabitha, just a few weeks after returning from the US.

The day out had been Tabitha's idea. She would help him buy gifts for his parents and brother, she told him, knowing she had a better idea of what they would like, and after trying to persuade her to go alone and do the shopping for him, to which she of course refused, Julian had agreed to tag along.

Tabitha had seen a bag she thought Jemima would like in one of the city-centre boutiques, but Julian had been distracted by the perky sales assistant who was manning the counter at Nix, the small independent jewellers next door.

Jemima had ended up with a bracelet that Tabitha wasn't sure would be to her taste, while Julian had treated himself to a pair of cufflinks and Maria's telephone number, after Tabitha had been forced to watch them flirt for close to half an hour.

That night, she had found Maria on the store's website, then obsessively stalked her on social media.

A few nights later, she was out with some of the Wiseman Homes employees for a pre-Christmas drink in one of the city bars when she saw the woman again.

Normally, Tabitha wouldn't have gone. Bars and clubs weren't her kind of thing and she would have much rather been at home. But Julian had shown up at the office that afternoon, summoned for a meeting with his father, and a few of the guys at work had persuaded him to go out.

Keen for any opportunity to hang out with him, Tabitha had tagged along too.

The evening had started so well, but then Julian had wandered off from the rest of the group. Tabitha had found him in an alleyway with his tongue down Maria's throat.

They would have probably gone home together that night, but Julian had been drinking heavily and ended up passing out drunk.

A couple of the guys helped to get him into the back seat of Tabitha's Range Rover and it was as she was driving him home that she spotted Maria walking along by the river.

Julian was still out cold and Tabitha had pulled her car off the road, not sure what her true intentions were at the time. All she was thinking was that the river was freezing cold and there was no one about. If an inebriated woman got too close to the water, an accident could easily happen.

Except it didn't quite play out that way, as Maria heard her approaching. Recognising Tabitha from earlier, she greeted her with a warm smile, at which point Tabitha panicked, unsure if she could go through with it.

Not again.

Instead, she ended up offering the woman a ride home.

And that would have been the end of it, except Maria – seeing Julian asleep in the back – cheekily told Tabitha to drop her off at his place instead. That she would spend the night with him.

As rage built, Tabitha instead drove them out to Newton Flotman and her little house on the edge of the village, figuring Maria had no idea it wasn't Julian's place.

Leaving him sleeping in the car, she followed Maria inside and used one of her heavy ornaments to bash her over the head.

After finding some rope in the garage and tying the woman up, she drove Julian back into the city, staying with him long enough to help him into bed and make sure he had water and paracetamol close by, before returning home.

Three days after she had tied Maria to the chair in her pretty spare room, torturing her both mentally and physically, the woman begged to die. They had reached a stalemate of sorts, both of them realising that Tabitha had gone too far and would be in a huge amount of trouble if she ever let Maria go.

The problem was, Tabitha couldn't bring herself to kill her, not after what had happened with Katy. So instead, she left Maria alone. She simply locked the door and stayed away from the room.

When she eventually dared enter ten days later, it was over. And she felt a surprising lack of remorse.

Maria's body had shut down by itself. Yes, Tabitha had prevented her from leaving, but technically she hadn't killed her.

Finally, she had found a guilt-free way to cope with Julian's indiscretions.

Of course, she didn't know about all of them. She couldn't

keep her eye on him twenty-four-seven, but the ones which took place under her nose, those she took care of.

Like Tammy Helgens, who was working at Dunston Hall, where James Wiseman had celebrated his fortieth birthday, and had spent more of her evening flirting with Julian than serving drinks, and Julie Rodriguez, who, years ago, had worked at Wiseman Homes and who bumped into them in the city one lunchtime. She had blatantly ignored Tabitha, but was all over Julian, making unfunny little comments about how their names went together.

Tabitha discovered that drugs slipped into a cup of coffee or a glass of wine were easier and less problematic than blunt objects. And she learnt the art of lying persuasively. She pretended she was Julian's best friend, he had asked her to check up on them or take them out to lunch, offer them a lift or drop off a gift to them.

It became easier to get creative with her stories.

And she was never caught out because one of Julian's greatest faults worked to her advantage. Aside from Peyton Landis, who had been a spur-of-the-moment attack – Tabitha witnessing the pair going up to his apartment when she was on site, dealing with the aftermath of the power cut – he didn't even realise the women he had used and discarded were missing. He was so wrapped up in himself and never even bothered to learn their names in some cases.

Had he even known Nina's? He had met her briefly when she was with Zac, but that had been two weeks ago.

Tabitha looked at the woman now. She was semi-conscious, but still very confused.

Time to tie her to the chair before the drugs wore off.

She was about to take care of that when a loud crash below

made her jump. Not thunder, and startled she crossed to the window, her heart thumping in panic when she realised that Conrad Mackenzie was no longer outside where she had left him.

Where the hell was he?

She glanced down at Nina, confident she wouldn't be going anywhere and deciding finding Conrad was the greater urgency.

The damn man had been a thorn in her side ever since he had moved in at River Heights. He was always late paying his maintenance charges and there had been reports of his causing trouble with some of the other residents and sneaking into the women's changing rooms in the leisure club.

Tabitha perhaps should have realised he was a bad omen when she saw him talking to Peyton Landis. A warning that she should stay away from this one.

She hadn't listened, though, already in a mood after dealing with the blackout, and seeing Peyton following after Julian had triggered her.

What she should have done was gone home, but instead she had lingered, foolishly letting herself into the empty penthouse apartment next door, where, with the balcony door ajar, she could hear every disgusting grunt and sex noise Peyton was making as she and Julian fucked.

When the woman had left, Tabitha had followed.

She wasn't prepared and knew nothing about this one, but in that moment she hadn't cared.

By the time she exited the building, intending to approach the woman, she saw she was too late, and she had watched in the shadows as a drunken Conrad Mackenzie had tried to chat Peyton up, following after her when she walked away.

He was persistent, trying to grab hold of her arm, and Peyton had lashed out at him, slapping him hard across the face before fleeing.

Tabitha should have stayed away, but Conrad was too drunk to give chase, managing to stagger a few steps before giving up and heading into his apartment block. Seeing Peyton over by the car park, fumbling for her phone in her bag, Tabitha had swooped in to help.

The woman didn't know her, but Conrad had freaked her out – the man was harmless, but Tabitha guessed in the middle of the night and when he was inebriated, he had probably come across as scary. Then, Tabitha noticed Peyton's arm was bleeding too.

Had Conrad done that to her? It looked like a knife wound.

Very out of character for him to actually hurt someone.

Peyton had sobbed with relief when Tabitha offered her a ride back to Attleborough. Luckily, she wasn't interested in going to the police about what had just happened and wanted to go home.

Sadly for her, she never made it.

It was strange how some missing people cases managed to pick up more media attention than others. Peyton's disappearance had garnered far more attention than the other women Tabitha had punished and perhaps that was why Conrad had become so paranoid.

He had never reported his encounter with Peyton to the police and seemed to have it in his head that Tabitha and Nina knew about it and were intending to report him. Hence why he had followed them this morning.

And now he was a big problem because he knew Nina was here.

After Katy Spencer, Tabitha had promised herself she would

never violently kill again, but she had failed last night, stabbing nosy Leonard Pickles, and now she was going to have to take care of Conrad too.

She couldn't risk him leaving here alive.

51

Tabitha had disappeared from the bedroom and realising that this was her one chance to escape, Nina tried to push herself up onto her hands and knees.

She still wasn't entirely sure why the woman had brought her here or why she had tried to drug her, but she was beginning to suspect this was to do with Julian.

He isn't yours. You don't get to have him. You shouldn't take things that don't belong to you.

Was this a jealousy thing? Tabitha had admitted to being in love with him and he had rejected her. Did she blame Nina?

It was clear from the ropes on the chair that the woman was planning to tie her up, and the plastic covering on the floor did nothing to fuel her confidence.

She understood now that this had all been a trap. Tabitha had confessed and confided in her, but she had never intended to go to the police. She had just planned to lure Nina here.

And the worrying red stains on the seat cushion suggested this wasn't the first time she had done this.

Peyton Landis, Maria Adams, Tammy Helgens and Julie Rodriguez.

Four women who had all disappeared without a trace. Were all these women intimately involved with Julian?

Nina had been convinced he was responsible for their disappearances, but Tabitha was the one waiting in the shadows, desperate for him to love her instead.

Just what lengths had she gone to to rid herself of the competition?

Oh God.

No one knew Nina was here. She hadn't explained her change of plans in her message to Zac, who thought she had gone to see Leonard. He was going to be wondering where the hell she was.

She had to help herself.

The effect of the drug was still in her system, but her mind was slowly clearing. She just needed to get her limbs working.

Was her phone still in her pocket? She tried to reach for it now, managing to flex her fingers, but couldn't feel it there.

Deflated, she realised of course not. Tabitha would have taken it. She had concocted this elaborate scheme to get Nina here. She was hardly going to leave her alone with her mobile phone.

She just hoped the closed door wasn't locked, realising it had a keyhole.

Only one way to find out.

Focusing her efforts on moving her body, Nina tried to crawl towards the door.

If she wasn't strong enough yet to fight, then she needed to find a hiding place.

But quick. Tabitha could return at any moment.

* * *

Zac had pulled out of the car park moments before the ambulance arrived.

He couldn't sit around and wait when Nina might be in trouble, instead leaving his phone with Dylan so he could stay on the line with the emergency responder.

Leonard had managed to confirm that it was Tabitha Percy who had stabbed him and he had also mentioned the name Peyton, suggesting Tabitha might have been involved in the woman's disappearance too.

'I wondered why her car was still on site when I returned from my walk,' Dylan had mused. He had Tabitha's mobile number and he had tried to call her, but like Nina's, it was going to voicemail. 'She lives in Newton Flotman. Do you think it's possible they might be at her home?' he'd asked, handing Zac a key. 'Her address will be in the files in the maintenance room. You'll need this to get in.'

It was a long shot, as they could be anywhere, but Zac had no clue where else to try.

Nina had been so certain Julian was responsible for Peyton's disappearance and that Tabitha had been lying when she claimed she had been with him that night. Was this something that she and Julian were in on together or had she acted alone?

It had never made any sense that she would give him a fake alibi.

Either way, Nina wasn't answering her calls or messages and it was as if she had dropped off the face of the planet. Zac was terrified that she could be in danger.

She was Dexter's sister. He couldn't let anything happen to her. But it was more than that. Last night, they had started something that, if he was honest, had been brewing for a while, and for the first time in a long while, things had felt really right. He couldn't lose her when they had only just begun to explore whatever was between them.

As he headed out on the Ipswich Road towards Newton Flotman, rain lashing against his windscreen, he just hoped to hell he was going to the right place.

* * *

Conrad managed to drag himself towards his car, his head throbbing like hell, still unable to believe that Tabitha Percy had just tried to kill him.

Because it had to have been her. She had been the only one behind him, his attention at the time on Nina, wondering why she was struggling to stand. Was she drunk?

Not that it was really any of his business. He should have just driven on when he saw them pull into the driveway of the house.

Perhaps he had overreacted to the whole situation.

It was Leonard Pickles who had made him paranoid, telling Conrad the police thought Peyton Landis had been at River Heights the night she disappeared.

Conrad knew the old man's reputation. He saw everything and liked to stir trouble.

If he had seen Conrad with Peyton and he told the police, what kind of trouble would Conrad be in? Would he lose his job, his apartment?

He was an idiot and should have just come forward in the first place, but Peyton's reaction when he had drunkenly touched her arm had freaked him out.

What if they thought he had killed her?

From there, everything had spiralled, which is how he had ended up here, paranoid and overreacting.

Stupid, Conrad.

And because he was curious, watching Tabitha Percy in the garage while Nina remained in the car, he had managed to get caught, Tabitha spotting him and going over to his car. She had seen him following her and suggested they have a talk.

Again, he should have driven off, but instead he had bumbled, unsure how to answer, and when she had taken an authoritative tone, he had worried she might kick him out of River Heights, so he had compliantly followed her instruction and parked on the driveway.

It had been as he was trying to reason with her, not wanting to accompany her into the house as she suggested, just wanting to be on his way, that Nina had attempted to get out of the car.

And that was when Tabitha had attacked him.

When he had woken, he was lying face down on the wet driveway, wondering what the hell was going on and feeling like he had been hit by a truck.

He was aware he was bleeding, probably from his head, as he crawled through the pouring rain, but he needed to get to his car where his phone was.

Almost there.

It took a gargantuan effort to get the door open and pull himself up onto the driver's seat and he was glad he had spent so much time in the gym building his muscles.

Reaching for his mobile, he didn't waste any time, no longer caring about being in trouble over Peyton Landis, pulling up the keypad and dialling 999 for the police.

* * *

Tabitha's heart was thumping as she headed out of the front

door, snatching up the shovel from the wet ground that she had used to hit Conrad.

The blood where he had been lying had already mostly been washed away by the rain, but there was a path carving its way through the gravel leading towards the end of the driveway, like something or someone had been dragged through it, and as she approached his Mondeo, she saw the driver's door was open.

She found Conrad slumped across the driver's seat and he appeared to have succumbed to his head injury.

Thank God for that. He had just given her quite a scare.

Snatching the phone from his hand, she slipped it in her pocket. He was a heavy man and wasn't going to be easy to move. She would get him into the boot of his car for now and stick the vehicle round the side of the house. At least he would be out of the way. Not that she had many visitors and the lane she lived down didn't have much traffic, but still it was better to be safe than sorry.

It wasn't an easy task, especially in the middle of a storm, as rain teemed down soaking her through to the skin and lightning flashed overhead. She considered herself a fairly strong woman, but Conrad was big and bulky, slippery too in the wet, and it didn't help he was literally a dead weight.

By the time she had located his key fob and moved the car, she was exhausted and sodden through, her clothes covered in dirt and blood. As she headed back into the house, she decided that once Nina was secured she would indulge in a nice long shower.

'Right, where were we,' Tabitha said, stepping into the room where she had left the woman, her eyes bulging when she saw it was empty.

* * *

There was a Range Rover in Tabitha Percy's driveway, which Zac was pretty sure belonged to her, and he pulled up behind it, hopeful that Nina was in the house. The front door, he noticed, was already ajar. Odd, given the current weather.

Before approaching the door, he wandered the perimeter of the house, just in case Nina was outside. Another car, a blue Mondeo, was parked around the side and glancing at the number plate, a personalised one that read CO14 RAD, he realised it belonged to Conrad Mackenzie.

How the hell was he involved in this? Was he helping Tabitha?

In the distance, Zac heard sirens and knew he should wait, but he was scared that every second could make a difference.

If either Tabitha or Conrad had hurt Nina, Zac was going to kill them.

* * *

Where the hell was she?

Tabitha glanced around the pretty yellow bedroom, disbelieving that Nina had got away. The drug was still in her system and her limbs had barely been functional.

She wasn't here, though, and realising she should have locked the door so she couldn't get out, Tabitha moved quickly through the other upstairs rooms, starting with her bedroom.

The window was wide open and Tabitha definitely hadn't left it like that.

Had Nina managed to climb out?

Or fallen?

The room overlooked her back garden and although it was a drop to the ground, it was possible the bushes in the borders might break any fall.

Tabitha's mouth was dry as she moved to the window to look.

She couldn't see any sign of her, but then she spotted the white trainer lying on the grass. Did it belong to Nina? Tabitha remembered she had been wearing white trainers and a khaki green dress.

Realising she had to find her before she escaped, she bolted back down the stairs.

* * *

Nina had barely dared to breathe the entire time Tabitha had been in the room, the sound of her heart thumping in her ears louder than the pouring rain outside the open window. Hearing the woman's footsteps as she descended the stairs, she realised her plan had worked.

If Tabitha hadn't taken notice of the window, if she hadn't spotted the trainer Nina had managed to throw, would she have looked under the bed?

Nina pulled herself out from beneath it now, aware her trembling limbs were regaining more manoeuvrability. The drug was gradually losing effect. Thank God.

Now she had to get the hell out of here before Tabitha returned.

* * *

The polite thing to do would be to knock, but the door was already open and did Zac really want to announce his arrival? Nudging it with his foot, he peered into the hallway.

It was deathly quiet, but then he heard what sounded like shuffling coming from upstairs.

'Nina? Are you up there?'

He was already inside now and when he heard what he was pretty certain was Nina's voice, though it sounded a little slurred, calling his name back, he took the stairs two at a time.

* * *

Zac was here. How the hell had he known where to find her?

He was touching her hair and her face, as if disbelieving it was really her, and she had never been so pleased to see him in her life.

Although they were still inside Tabitha's house, she was finally daring to believe this whole nightmare might finally be over.

'Are you okay? What the hell happened?'

'Tabitha. She drugged me. I think it was her who killed Peyton. Possibly the other women too. She's obsessed with Julian.' Nina's voice was mostly back, though her words were still a little slurred. 'We have to go before she gets back. She attacked Conrad too. I think he might be dead.'

Zac didn't need to be asked twice and ignoring Nina's instruction that she could get down the stairs if he let her lean on him, he scooped her up in his arms. 'Where is she?' he asked. 'And why do you only have one shoe on?'

'Out in the garden, I think. I threw it out of the window to try to make her believe I escaped. Hopefully she's still out there looking for me.'

'Resourceful.'

'Are those sirens for us?' Nina asked, hearing them grow closer.

'I imagine so. Let's get out of here. We can wait in the car.'

A good plan and Nina was keen to leave before Tabitha realised Zac had found her.

Unfortunately, it was never going to be as easy as that and as they reached the bottom of the stairs they found Tabitha waiting in the doorway, a large kitchen knife in her hand.

'Put her down,' she barked at Zac, her skittish gaze going backwards and forwards between them. She was soaked through to the skin, her blonde hair plastered to her head and dripping on the floor.

'It's over, Tabitha. The police will be here any moment,' he said, ignoring her request and sounding much calmer than Nina felt.

'I said, put her down,' Tabitha repeated. 'I won't ask again.'

Nina didn't like how the woman was waving the knife, looking like she might be really reckless with it. She gripped Zac's shoulder tightly, remembering what she had done to Conrad. She couldn't risk her trying to hurt Zac.

'Maybe we should do as she says,' she said in a quiet voice.

Zac's response was just one stubborn word. 'No.'

Nina sucked in a breath. This was going to end badly. How were they supposed to move past her to get out of the house?

Zac took a testing step forward and Tabitha responded by raising the knife in the air. In the next moment, there was an almighty thwack and she had a stunned look on her face, the knife dropping to the ground. She wavered for just the briefest second, then tumbled forward, face-planting the ground.

Behind her, his T-shirt covered in blood, stood Conrad, holding the shovel he had just used to hit her with.

EPILOGUE

It was as if a switch had flipped and Tabitha Percy shut down the moment she was arrested, refusing to speak a word to the police, her shocked parents, or her solicitor, as details of her heinous crimes were gradually uncovered.

At her plea and trial preparation hearing, she spoke only five words, 'Tell Julian I love him'. She refused to enter a plea and was remanded into custody.

The four bodies found in the old coal shed at the bottom of her garden, next to a large compost heap, were eventually identified as Peyton Landis, Julie Rodriguez, Tammy Helgens and Maria Adams and Nina heard via her police liaison officer that Tabitha's solicitors were trying to get the murders reduced down to manslaughter by diminished responsibility.

The case had thrust Julian back in the spotlight, especially when Tabitha's diary was discovered, revealing the extent of her obsession with him. While questions were asked of Julian as to why he had lied about being with Peyton Landis, he had been trying his best to milk money out of the Tabitha connection, painting himself as the victim in a *Fatal Attraction*-style scenario.

It backfired, though, when a journalist found out about his kink for blood play, writing an exposé in one of the tabloids. If it had been that alone, it would have blown over, but in the days that followed, past lovers started coming forward to reveal experiences with Julian's knives that hadn't been entirely consensual.

Kevin and Jemima Wiseman had been appalled. They had already distanced themselves from the Percy family, and word was, following a heated argument with them, Julian had moved in with Grace O'Connell. He was currently hiding out in her house while police investigated the claims, and shocked when the truth came out about Grace's fetish and seduction of Julian, Jemima had severed all contact with her former best friend.

The death of Katy Spencer was also being revisited and although Tabitha hadn't confessed to being responsible, Julian had admitted they hadn't been together that day. The legal team for Eric Grogan, the groundsman in prison for her murder, had issued a statement saying that they were hopeful they would get his sentence overturned.

Conrad had sheepishly confessed to the police that he had seen Peyton Landis the night of her disappearance, receiving a rap on the knuckles for not coming forward sooner. Nina was just grateful he had followed her and Tabitha that day, as things could have played out a lot more differently if he hadn't been there.

And thank God his Mondeo was equipped with an emergency boot release lever, so he had been able to free himself after Tabitha had locked him in the boot of his car.

Initially, he had milked his fifteen minutes of fame, playing the hero who brought Tabitha Percy down, and his photo was regularly in the local press with pictures of different women on his arm. But then Nina heard he had reconnected with his childhood girlfriend and he had moved out of River Heights, heading back to his home town of Great Yarmouth.

One person who had benefitted positively from the whole sorry situation was Leonard Pickles. He had been such a cantankerous old goat, always sticking his nose into other people's business, but now he was unrecognisable.

Nina had taken him flowers when he was recovering in hospital and at first she thought the grateful and friendly manner in which he greeted her was just an act, but no, it seemed almost dying had given Leonard a wake-up call. Since he had been back at River Heights, he had gone out of his way to do kind things for the other residents and he had offered Dylan Hargreaves his spare room, while Dylan got back on his feet following his relationship break-up.

For a while there, it had seemed Dylan might lose his job after his bosses found out he had been using Becky Johnson's flat while she was away, but the residents – including Becky – had all signed a petition, organised by Leonard, and Dylan had eventually been allowed to stay.

Nina hadn't been to River Heights in a couple of weeks, but Dexter had told her Leonard had put his flat on the market. Apparently he had decided he was going to stop being afraid and go on the adventures he had always planned to do in his retirement.

As autumn cooled into winter, the winds picked up, baring the trees of their leaves and covering the ground in a carpet of orange, and when Christmas arrived, Nina found herself reflecting on her eventful year.

After her brother and Mark had returned from Hong Kong, she had moved into a one-bed flat in the east suburbs of the city that was owned by Rachel's cousin, Chris. It was very different to the sleek city apartment: an older-style house that had been converted into six separate homes. Nina was in one half of the loft space and the place was tiny, but it was cosy too, with plenty of character features and a big window in the living room that overlooked the communal gardens. The rent was affordable and it felt good to be standing on her own two feet and also to have a place of her own where she could invite her friends and family round.

And Zac too, of course.

This thing between them was still too new to consider moving in together yet, but he was a regular visitor to her flat and she was the happiest she had been in a long time.

She had also reached an amicable place with Michael, who had thankfully moved on and now had a new girlfriend, Claire. He had changed his mind about keeping the house, telling Nina that he too wanted a fresh start, and they were currently waiting for the sale to go through.

Zac was also in the process of selling his apartment at River Heights to Dexter and Mark and he planned on buying a house in one of the Broadland villages. After her brother's return from Hong Kong, Zac had temporarily moved in with a friend to give Dexter and Mark their space.

At some point when he had his new house, Nina would move in with him, but for now they were both content letting their relationship grow, while maintaining their independence.

Zac had stayed over Christmas Eve and it was going to be their first Christmas Day spent together as a couple. Along with Dexter and Mark, they were going to her parents' for lunch. Her mum had soon got over her devastation at Nina's break-up with Michael when she realised her daughter was dating Zac.

He was still in the shower, as Nina pushed the diamond stud earrings through her lobes that he had bought her as a

Christmas present. After spritzing perfume, she checked her reflection, then went through to the living room to wait for him.

On the coffee table sat Zac's other gift. He had thought it hilarious to buy her a pair of toy binoculars. A cheap joke present. Despite the seriousness of the events that summer, he still liked to tease her about how her nosiness had led her into trouble.

Truthfully, after everything that had happened, Nina had no intention of ever spying on anyone ever again.

She picked them up now, intending to put them away in a cupboard.

'Are you watching the neighbours already?' Zac teased, coming into the room wearing just a towel and a sly grin on his face.

Nina went to him, not caring that he was still damp from his shower as she pressed herself up against him and smiled.

'Actually, I can think of far better things I'd rather be doing,' she told him, pushing him back towards her bedroom.

Her parents weren't serving dinner until two. It didn't matter if they were a little late.

MORE FROM KERI BEEVIS

Another gripping psychological thriller from Keri Beevis, *The Cottage by the Sea*, is available to order now here:

www.mybook.to/CottagebytheSeaBackAd

ACKNOWLEDGEMENTS

As always, I would like to start my acknowledgements by saying a huge thank you to my publisher, Boldwood Books. Caroline Ridding is a pleasure to work with and I am so grateful she is my editor. Thank you for believing in my books. To Niamh, Claire and the rest of the marketing team, for doing what they do so very well; to Wendy, who is currently holding fort for Nia and has made the transition appear seamless; to my copyeditor, Jade, my eagle-eyed proofreader, Gary, and to the rest of the team who work so hard behind the scenes, including, of course, our great leader, Amanda Ridout.

I must give a shout-out to my sister for this one, DS Holly Beevis, who patiently answered all of my police questions. I appreciate your time advising on fictional crimes when I know you are busy dealing with real-life ones.

Thank you to Maria Adams, Tammy Helgens and Julie Rodriguez for offering up their names to be murder victims, and to Claire Stannard, for suggesting the name River Heights.

To my family and friends; to the bloggers and book groups who continue to support me; to Tracy, Bev, Allison and Jo, who help run my author group; to all of my fab author pals; to Jo and Tina for beta reading for me, which is really appreciated; to my kitties, Ellie, Poppy and Finn, who were systematically destroying my house while I wrote this one. Love you, kids.

And, finally, to my fabulous readers. I have said it before and

I will say it again. I might write the stories, but you are the ones who breathe life into them. Thank you, thank you, thank you.

ABOUT THE AUTHOR

Keri Beevis is the internationally bestselling author of several psychological thrillers and romantic suspense mysteries, including the very successful *Dying to Tell*. She sets many of her books in the county of Norfolk, where she was born and still lives and which provides much of her inspiration.

Sign up to Keri Beevis' mailing list here for news, competitions and updates on future books.

Visit Keri's website: www.keribeevis.com

Follow Keri on social media here:

- facebook.com/allaboutbeev
- x.com/keribeevis
- instagram.com/keri.beevis
- bookbub.com/profile/keri-beevis
- tiktok.com/@keribeevis

ALSO BY KERI BEEVIS

The Sleepover

The Summer House

The House in the Woods

Trust No One

Every Little Breath

Nowhere to Hide

The Cottage by the Sea

The House Sitter

THE *Murder* LIST

THE MURDER LIST IS A NEWSLETTER DEDICATED TO SPINE-CHILLING FICTION AND GRIPPING PAGE-TURNERS!

SIGN UP TO MAKE SURE YOU'RE ON OUR HIT LIST FOR EXCLUSIVE DEALS, AUTHOR CONTENT, AND COMPETITIONS.

SIGN UP TO OUR NEWSLETTER

BIT.LY/THEMURDERLISTNEWS

Boldwood

Boldwood Books is an award-winning fiction publishing company seeking out the best stories from around the world.

Find out more at www.boldwoodbooks.com

Join our reader community for brilliant books, competitions and offers!

Follow us
@BoldwoodBooks
@TheBoldBookClub

Sign up to our weekly deals newsletter

https://bit.ly/BoldwoodBNewsletter

Made in United States
Cleveland, OH
21 May 2025